Lost Amongst The Stars

A Parallel Worlds Sci-Fi Adventure

Book 1

By

G J Stevens

This is a work of fiction. Names, characters, businesses, places, events, locales, and incidents are either the products of the author's imagination or used in a fictitious manner. Any resemblance to actual persons, living or dead, or actual events is purely coincidental.

Copyright © GJ Stevens 2023-24

The moral right of GJ Stevens to be identified as the author of this work has been asserted by him in accordance with the Copyright, Designs, and Patents Act 1998.

All rights reserved.

Copyright under the Berne Convention

British Library Cataloguing-in-Publication Data
A catalogue record for this book is available from the British Library

ISBN: 9798327592179

Other Books by GJ Stevens

James Fisher Series

Fate's Ambition
Their Right to Vengeance
Shattered Destiny

Post-apocalyptic Thrillers

IN THE END
BEFORE THE END
AFTER THE END
BEGINNING OF THE END (Novella)

SURVIVOR
Your Guide to Surviving the Apocalypse

Agent Carrie Harris Series

OPERATION DAWN WOLF
LESSON LEARNED
THE GEMINI ASSIGNMENT
CAPITAL ACTION (Novella)

Agent Carrie Harris – Undead Thrillers

STOPPING POWER – SEASON ONE

Part 1

1

"We'd just come off a three-month run transporting radiated chicken through the Mias disputed zone. You should have seen the size of the gunships we saw almost every day. They were beasts. Each ten times bigger than our rusty hulk and with vacuum blasters covering every surface," Archie said, stroking his thumb and forefinger along the white stubble around his mouth, whilst perched on a mess of white cotton sheets at the end of a hospital bed.

Enraptured heads nodded around the semi-circle of men sitting on the floor, each wearing the same white pyjamas and thin dressing gowns as Archie.

"They'd get so close, causing a blaze of warning lights and alarms throughout the bridge, hoping to hustle us enough to figure out if we were really just transporting food," Archie continued as he leaned forward, making eye contact with each of his audience. "With reports that both sides were as ruthless as each other, it didn't matter to us which side they were on. I'm not afraid to say they gave us the jitters, but that's why MegaFreight paid so well."

Archie cocked an eyebrow as a man's hand shot up whilst he bounced on the floor, a giggle not hiding his excitement.

"Yes, Darren," Archie replied.

"Were you really only transporting food?" the twenty-something teen with greasy, streaked-back hair said with his hand still in the air.

"You're not the star police, are you?" Archie said, leaning toward the man as he lowered his voice.

Darren burst out laughing and lowered his hand as he covered his mouth and shook his head.

"We might have had a few things stowed away, if you know what I mean," Archie replied, before looking at the rest of the men in turn. "Anyway," he continued. "With a well overdue couple of days off, we landed at the port in orbit around Vorgon, a planet not unlike Earth but long abandoned when an ice age hit, in the Third Nebula of Thairan.

"The port was like Vegas. You could get anything you wanted, and in any shape, size and breed," he added with a wink toward Darren. "All the crew left the ship with our accounts stuffed with credits. After hitting a few bars, before I knew it I'm stumbling about, half off my face. They long ago banned drinking onboard ship, so we were all gasping to let loose."

When a cough sounded from the other side of the room, Archie looked up, peering across the four beds to the only man in the ward not gathered at his feet. Eyeing the scowl from the dumpy guy who looked like a young Danny DeVito, but with jet-black hair across his scalp and around his chin, Archie smiled.

"Anyway, I knew I was on the edge, so I took myself away in search of the other type of action I craved."

Lips smacked around the gathered crowd and the men bobbed forward, a couple rocking.

"So I found a place I'd not been to before, but once you've been to one…" he said, his voice tailing off as he glared back at the man in the bed running his fingers through his thick beard. "You know what I mean. I took a seat and grabbed the menu whilst some stumpy little piece in nothing but a tiny G-string danced in front of me."

"Was she a proper dwarf like Mac?" Darren said with a snort, before his expression fell when he glanced across the beds.

"Yeah, but with more hair," Archie said, beaming over at Mac's reddening face. "She was so short she wouldn't need to get down on her knees, if you know what I mean." The men's eyes widened as at least one of them licked their lips. "But not wanting to spew up what I'd spent so many credits on, I shooed her away and this lime green Andorian bit..." His smile widened as he stopped talking, watching Mac shuffle down the bed whilst drawing up his sleeves.

Each of those gathered followed Archie's smile, but as Darren got to his feet, like a flock of birds the others stood, backing away as the man who rose to half their height came around his bed. He twitched and covered his face with his palms as he stepped back.

"Now, now," Archie said, sneering at the man whose large round belly swayed from side to side as he headed over. "If I call out, you're back in isolation."

"Not today, you focking turd," Mac replied, his voice gruff and low, the words spitting out with venom as he balled his fists, forming the word *hate* across both his knuckles.

"I keep telling you it's fuck, not fock," Archie said, his smile faltering as Mac drew closer.

"Not where I come from," Mac replied, drawing down his brow just as the ward doors burst open.

Archie glanced over Mac's shoulder, but rather than finding a nurse coming to split them up, a tall man with broad shoulders and mousey brown hair stood in jeans and a t-shirt stretching Luke Skywalker's face across his muscled chest. The bottom of a bright red tattoo was just visible below the short sleeve.

"I'm looking for a man," the newcomer boomed, despite being a little out of breath. His perfect white teeth shone out like a lighthouse.

Turning his head to the side, Archie raised his brow.

"I'm looking for a man who has travelled far and wide."

As if not hearing the new voice, and with his cheeks a deep shade of beetroot, Mac continued plodding towards Archie.

"Has anyone here travelled across the Pedrian Gap with their shielding wrecked, but somehow dragged their charge to port whilst having enough energy left to drink everyone else under the table?"

Archie peered back at the new arrival and then down to Mac, who, despite slowing, still advanced, the bands of muscle tight in his neck. The other men stared at Archie, lifting their outstretched fingers towards him.

"Is anyone here a skilled chef that can work with even the foulest ingredient and produce a masterpiece?"

Raising a brow, Mac paused, but not looking around, he took a last step before kicking Archie in the shin. As Archie called out with the pain, Mac turned to Darren, jabbing his finger towards him.

"I'm short, not a dwarf, and if I was, what business is it of yours?" he said, his grumbling voice low.

Darren shook his head, then tripped backwards over his own feet as if the finger had reached across the gap.

"And if you're going to steal my stories," Mac added, turning back to Archie, who rubbed his lower leg in silence, "tell them right. They were impregnated ostriches, you idiot, not chickens."

With a swift prod of his outstretched finger, Mac sent Archie toppling back before spinning around to face the man standing at the door.

"It's just a shame that most people I feed have a moron's palate that couldn't discern the subtleties of flavour if it hit them over the head," Mac said, raising a brow and turning his nose up.

"It's good to see you, Mac," the newcomer replied, his white teeth on show as he beamed with a warm smile.

"Ugh," Mac grunted, his lips curling into a scowl. "I'm glad you're not dead, Travis. What took you so focking long?"

Travis's smile widened, but hearing a sound from the other side of the door, he rushed forward, peering into each corner of the room. Finding no other way out, he picked up a plastic chair and raised it above his head.

"I'm busting you out. Move out of the way." As the chair left his grip, it bounced off the window and rushed back, catching the tall man just below his knee.

"Fock," he called out, hopping on his good leg before twisting around to the opening doors.

"Travis, you idiot," Mac said with a shake of his head.

"Mac, get changed," said a woman whose head appeared between the two doors.

"They're letting me out today," Mac said, glaring at Travis.

"Your cab will be here in five minutes."

2

Travis

"Six months," Mac snarled as the tall double gates at their back swung closed, concealing the orderly already heading away down long the drive, back to the series of low-rise buildings they'd left behind.

Jerking his head back, Travis stopped in his tracks and turned before grabbing Mac's arm.

"Get off," Mac replied, shoving Travis's hand away. Mac had changed into a white t-shirt so large it was as if the staff had not been able to find anything more suitable and had sown together a bedsheet instead. Beneath the top, he wore a baggy pair of black tracksuit bottoms he'd had to roll up to enable him to walk.

Mac swung his foot, catching the side of Travis's ankle with a kid-sized trainer.

"That's how long you left me in there," he spat, then walked off, ignoring the car with the fluffy dice hanging from the rear-view mirror, its engine idling.

"What the…?" Travis called out, rubbing at his leg as he looked between his painful limb and the man tottering away. When Mac didn't look back or show any sign he'd slow, Travis followed, thankful his limp eased with each step.

"Wait up. That can't be right. I got here as quickly as I could," Travis said, a little breathless as he caught up. They were halfway to the entrance and the main road before Mac stopped so abruptly it took Travis by surprise, forcing him to step back in case of a repeated attack.

"It was six months. Are you calling me a liar?" the short man snarled, curling his lip as he glared at Travis.

"I don't know what to say," Travis replied, raising his arms in the air and holding his palms out. "I still don't have a clue what's going on. I can't remember anything past waking up naked in the middle of a field about twelve hours ago."

"Twelve hours?" Mac shouted, narrowing his eyes as he peered up, concentrating on Travis's expression as if looking for a lie.

"Honest," Travis said, but the word sent Mac's eyes tighter. When he took a slow step forward, Travis flinched but didn't back away, instead reaching into his back pocket, the air filling with the kick of vinegar as he unfolded a grease-soaked torn sheet of newspaper.

"After I'd stopped panicking, I stole some clothes strung outside what I think was someone's house, and I convinced the owner of a food place to give me fried potatoes cut into thin strips. I found this staring back when I'd finished."

Travis held out the scrap of newspaper where in the centre photograph a tumble of people blurred in motion with Mac in the middle of the melee, his fist frozen in time as it connected with the chin of a man in a dark uniform.

Mac's brow relaxed, and so did his sneer as he concentrated on the greasy page.

"It says you headbutted a police officer in the genitals because he didn't believe you were a chef on a starship," Travis said, unable to stop himself from grinning. "I'd have known it was you even without the photo. It didn't take me long to find where they'd locked you up. You're somewhat of a local celebrity."

Snatching the page from Travis, Mac tore it to shreds before letting the pieces scatter across the ground. With a grunt, he turned and walked along the road, but at a more reasonable pace. Travis followed.

"What do you remember?" Mac asked after a moment without glancing up, his voice only a little less gruff.

Rather than answering, Travis stared at a white car with blue and yellow stickers along the side and a blue light box on the top as it came into view beyond the gates.

About to repeat the question, Mac held his tongue, spotting the car slowing with two pairs of eyes peering out along the driveway towards them.

"I'm the pilot and co-owner of the Mary May," Travis said when the police car sped up, disappearing behind the tall bushes lining the road on either side of the institution's boundary. His voice was tentative at first, but grew in confidence with each moment Mac hadn't laughed him down. "I guess something sent us from the ship," he said, swallowing hard as he looked around. "And back in time."

Travis watched as Mac's lip curled. After tensing for another attack, he relaxed when the short man shook his head.

"I know it feels like it's the nineteen thirties, although quite different to what we learned in school, but it's two thousand and twenty-four still. I'm certain," Mac said, watching when it was Travis's turn to shake his head. "We haven't gone back in time."

"I don't get it," Travis replied.

"What about the rest of the crew? Do you think the same happened to them? Do you remember anyone else?" Mac said, watching as Travis shook his head. "I can't believe you only lost twelve hours."

"At least you've been warm, and it looks like they fed you," Travis replied, looking him up and down, but regretting the words as Mac's flaring eyes met his. "Sorry. You know what I mean. I understand it must have been hard. I get it. When I came around yesterday, it felt like… I don't know. This place isn't unfamiliar, but I was sure I'd landed a hundred years in the past. Do you know what I mean?"

"It took some getting used to," Mac replied, his voice low as he nodded.

"Do you have any idea what happened to us?" Travis said, coming to a stop. Mac halted, turning around, and Travis breathed a little easier when he saw his expression had relaxed a little. "If it's not a time machine, then what could it be?" he asked, lowering his voice as he leaned closer.

"I don't know," Mac replied, shaking his head. "There are so many gaps," he added, tapping his finger against his temple.

"How much do you remember?" Travis said, turning to the side, but when he got no reply, the corner of his mouth rose. "Um… Out of interest," he said, pausing as if taking time to consider his next words, "do you still remember how to cook?"

Mac narrowed his eyes and glared over.

"I mean, I hope you're still a brilliant chef," Travis rushed to say as he lifted his hands and showed his palms, relaxing when he spotted the twinkle in Mac's eye. Travis softened his voice and leaned a little closer. "Do you remember the Mary May?"

Mac nodded, showing off his stubby white teeth.

"No way," Travis said, his expression lifting. "Do you know where she is?"

Mac nodded again, still with his teeth on show.

"What about the rest of the crew?" Travis asked, his voice tentative.

"I only remembered you when I heard your voice," Mac replied, shaking his head and walking again.

Arriving at the main road, he glanced at the red bus heading towards them.

"What do we do now?" Mac asked, turning to Travis.

"Let's get back to the ship. Maybe the others are waiting for us there," Travis replied, a new brightness in his eyes.

Mac nodded, pushing his hand out into the road.

"Is that a bus?" Travis said, peering along its length before staring at the wheels. "How do we…?" he said, but held back when the bus slowed.

Pulling up the billowing t-shirt, Mac pushed his hand into the pocket of the tracksuit, his pudgy fist clutching a few notes and a handful of change as the bus's air brakes hissed it to a stop.

"It's the money they gave me for the taxi. It should be enough," Mac said and Travis looked down in wonder at the spread of coins.

About to reach out to touch one of the metal discs, he looked up as the doors folded open, then yelped, jumping back when he spotted a straw-coloured Labrador waiting on the other side, the dog panting with its tongue lolling out of its mouth.

Mac tensed, Travis's grip on his shoulders at his back as he used the short man as a shield, whilst the dog led a wrinkled woman down the steps.

With the old lady gone and the bus checked for other animals by Mac, he coaxed Travis past the scattering of filled seats. Travis insisted they sat in the back row to give them a good view of any animals hidden under seats.

After a short while, Travis's shakes had calmed, and he'd tuned out Mac's low rumble of laughter, instead staring out at the lush green fields.

Thankful when his nerves had calmed, he noticed a spotty-faced man with bright ginger hair sitting a couple of rows ahead, who kept glancing over his shoulder at them.

With a jab of his elbow into Mac's side, the short cook's laughter subsided as Travis leaned toward him.

"Do you recognise that man?" Travis whispered, whilst Mac glared up at the interruption to his thoughts. Not relaxing his glare, he followed Travis's nod to the man who, by that time, had turned away.

Mac screwed up his brow as he peered over. When it seemed the ginger guy wouldn't look again, the man lifted his head and glanced over his shoulder, before hurriedly returning when he realised the pair were looking straight at him.

"I don't trust my memory," Mac said. "You?"

"Me either, but was that a glint of recognition I saw?" Travis asked and leaned a little closer, ignoring Mac's low rumbling growl. "What if he's crew and his memory is as bad as ours?"

Mac shook his head, then stood, Travis moving just in time to stop Mac's shoulder from smashing into his cheek.

"What if he's not? Come on. This is our stop."

Travis stood as the bus slowed, following Mac. Uncertain whether to approach the guy, as he passed he glanced down, holding his breath when he spotted the words *Starfighter* across his t-shirt with a spaceship emblazoned on the breast pocket.

3

"It should have been you locked up in that place, not me," Mac shouted over the bus's roaring engine as it pulled away from the kerb.

Without looking back, Travis held his palm up, concentrating instead on Colin, when all it had taken was a whisper in the ginger man's ear for him to step off the bus.

The bus stop sat beside a field of grass stretching out as far as the eye could see, whilst on the other side of the road, the view filled with a sea of tall trees.

"Twenty three," Colin replied to Travis's earlier question. "I'm a mechanic's apprentice for the bus company," he added, with a nod towards the bus as it passed a sign beside the road for *Oglethorpe* and a dilapidated house, which was the only building in sight. "I've been there for six months now."

"Six months," Travis exclaimed, fisting the air as he turned to gauge Mac's reaction. Finding his eyes narrowed and a scowl still wrinkling his forehead, Travis looked back at Colin.

"And your name is familiar," Travis said, his voice booming. "And he's a mechanic," he added, with a glance back down at Mac. "We'd need a mechanic. Wouldn't you think?"

Mac's stare lingered on Travis for a long while, glaring at his wide, toothy smile. When he relaxed his forehead, Travis turned back to Colin and spread his arm around his shoulder.

"Do you remember me?" Travis said, lowering his voice, watching as Colin's brow furrowed before the ginger-haired man shook his head. Tightening his grip on the man's shoulders for a moment, Travis let go and turned to him for a better look. "You're missing memories too," Travis said, narrowing his eyes and leaning closer. "Aren't you?"

The man stared back, taking turns to look them both in the eye before staring at the Jedi Knight stretched across Travis's chest. Pursing his lips, Colin lifted his chin.

"If I was, how would I know?" he said, raising his brow.

"Yes," Travis bellowed, turning to beam at Mac, but found the short man already doddering away, his ample butt swinging from side to side as he shook his head.

Clutching his arm around Colin's shoulders once more, and whistling to mimic the abundant birdsong, Travis led him along a dirt track between the tall trees.

"Don't freak out, but let me fill in some blanks. I hope some of this sounds familiar," Travis said, gripping the man tighter. "We're the crew of a starship, the Mary May," he said, nodding towards the logo on Colin's shirt. "But we're separated from each other and our memories are shot," he added, grinning and flashing his eyebrows at Colin's rapt attention. "I'm the pilot and Mac is the chef," he said, looking over at the man kicking out a surprising pace.

"Where are we going?" Colin asked, as they wound their way along the path beneath the thick green canopy.

"You'll see," Travis replied, but sounding distracted, he let go of the man's shoulders, looking high into the trees when he realised the birds had stopped singing. "Are we near?" he called out.

Mac nodded, then slowed to let them catch up.

"I can't believe I was so close," Travis said to no one in particular as he searched around wide-eyed. Shaking his head, he came alongside the chef, then spotted a vast clearing with light pouring across tree stumps which rose only to Mac's diminutive height. Bright, off-white sawdust and splintered lengths of wood covered the ground, filling the air with its provocative scent.

Halting side by side at the edge of the clearing, Travis marvelled at Mac's lack of a grimace just as a memory rushed into his head of the pair running alongside each other, each of them carrying a stout barrel full of Ivanic rum under their arms, whilst Mac shouted for them to go faster, despite his struggle to keep up.

Closing his eyes, Travis felt as if he could sense the rest of the crew, but he couldn't find their faces no matter how hard he tried, finding only a deep sense of a connection he knew was forged in the highs and lows of adventure.

The feeling turned to a dread that soon it would be time for Mac to cook, and with an awful smell already forming in his mind, he was thankful when a resounding thump pulled his focus back into the clearing.

Blinking, he watched as Colin fell flat on his back in front of a large rectangular indent in the ground, his eyes closed with a red lump sprouting in the centre of his forehead.

"Idiot," Mac said, scowling at the man laying on his back who neither of them noticed had continued walking into the clearing.

"Huh," Travis replied. "It's like he didn't know she's invisible."

"Sapphire. Reveal the Mary May," Mac snorted.

As the clearing shimmered, Travis held his breath, its

intensity increasing like a rising heat haze. Feeling static electricity making his hair stand on end, the area soon darkened, before much of the light went with a blink.

Anyone over the age of three would recognise what resembled the basic form of any flying craft. Cockpit windows waited high at the front of a long, dull silver, unpainted metal fuselage, much like a squashed cylinder with wings on either side. In the middle of each wing and breaking up the sleek lines of each span, stood a large rectangular engine with a yawning, scuffed red opening. Instead of a tail fin at the rear, two smaller engines waited above the main body where scorch marks covered the panels and dents peppered almost every surface. Different coloured sheets of metal clung on in various places with thick, hurried welds that promised their own tales.

On the beaten up panel below the cockpit, a faint row of shapes that were once letters appeared to show the craft's designation.

Keeping the ship raised above the ground were three large stanchions pressing giant metal feet into the soil. One waited under each wing, and another stood under the cockpit where Colin had walked into.

"She's a focking beauty," Travis said, not noticing Mac's raised brow as he stepped around Colin's unmoving body. "I remember falling for her the first time we met."

"She's not a focking person," Mac said, but with no bite to his words as he looked along her lines. "Do you remember how to fly?" he said, his voice a near indistinct murmur. "Focking bitch," he added, almost tripping over the trouser leg that had fallen around his foot as he tried to take a step.

"I'm sure it will come back. Right now I just have to

figure out how to get in," Travis said, peering up at what he hoped was a door. After nothing happened when he reached up and rested his hands on the cold metal, he glanced at Mac with a silent question.

"What am I now, your focking butler?" Mac said, standing after rolling up the trousers. But when he didn't bare his teeth, Travis felt a warmth in his chest.

"Sapphire. Open up."

4

As a ramp groaned down below the front wing, Travis gawked, open-mouthed, at the cavernous interior beyond, lit by low lights studding battered metal bulkheads.

With his hand covering his mouth and wide-eyed, Travis took slow steps up the incline, only noticing Mac as he pushed past and into the hold, the short man shuffling across the space before he slipped, his butt slamming on the deck, leaving him sitting upright and stunned in a puddle of liquid beside a dented metal cup.

"Fock," Mac bellowed, then climbed to his feet, kicking and sending the cup clattering across the metal floor, before storming off past what looked like a bundle of clothes further along the wide space, all whilst gripping the low hanging legs of his borrowed tracksuit bottoms to prevent himself going over again.

Mac's call sent a shudder down Travis's spine, leaving him with a dread he couldn't shake until the round man disappeared through the furthest of two doors which slid out of his way.

Alone, Travis peered around the vast space in awe of its extent. Remembering Colin, he headed back outside and, after checking for signs of a pulse at his neck, he dragged the still unconscious man up the ramp by his shoulders.

As the ramp raised behind him before sealing against the hull with a clank reverberating up through his feet, the familiar sound triggered a rush of recollections of the space where he stood.

He remembered caged birds shedding feathers as they squawked nonsense, and gilded boxes encrusted with jewels they were under oath not to open, piled from floor to ceiling. Battered crates filled the vast hall, each tattooed with acronyms and glorious, but indecipherable patterns. Packages of weapons, ore and gems filled his head too, and those were only the ones that stuck out.

Satisfied at what he hoped were memories coming back, Travis moved towards the only door at the front of the ship. The metal bulkhead swept to the side as he approached, grinding against the floor as it moved. The harsh sound made him step forward, giving it a swift kick.

Alarmed at why he'd felt the need to attack the ship, he stepped through, but his concerns melted away when the door closed behind him with only a light whoosh, leaving him to scan, open-mouthed, across the dim bridge spanning the width of the spacecraft.

After peering across every surface at least twice, he spotted the windows they'd seen from outside were black, but he soon let the thought drift away as his gaze settled on a pair of leather seats behind the bank of controls, each with a joystick and other levers in reach along with a sea of unlit lights, buttons, switches, dials and screens.

In front of the pair of seats and hanging from the low ceiling were a pair of highly polished silver stars each attached to purple ribbons mounted side by side on a square of what looked like cardboard.

Moving his feet just in time, he side-stepped a pile of spilt papers and the half-eaten remains of a compressed food bar he didn't recognise, shedding crumbs on the deck. A pang of hunger tugged at his gut, but reaching the first of the seats, he did his best to ignore the prompt and swallowed hard as his fingers traced the head rest. About to drop into the leather, he spotted a bundle of blue clothes abandoned at the foot of the seat.

Taking the heavy gauge material by the collar, he raised it up, finding a zip running all the way up the front, along with an array of coloured patches across the chest of what he soon realised could only be a flight suit. After folding the bundle, he closed his eyes and sighed as he settled into the seat, marvelling at its familiar hold.

A long moment seemed to pass before he opened his eyes, but as he did, he leaned forward, gripping the joystick and staring out across the confusion of controls.

"You've got no idea, have you?" Mac said from behind as the doors slid closed at his back.

"Not a focking clue," Travis said with a shake of his head.

"Well, that's just perfect," Mac grunted, murmuring under his breath.

Travis glanced over to find the short man leaning down and scowling at the food bar before he corralled the spilt papers into a pile.

"Don't worry," Travis said, jumping from the seat and pushing on a smile. "It'll come back to me," he added, leaning up to the closest set of buttons. But after staring for what seemed like an age, he shook his head, unable to understand the gibberish written on each label.

Despite this, and settling back in the seat, after walking in the world for a day with everything feeling a little alien, he couldn't help but revel in the sense of being home, even though memories were still scarce.

Grinning, he glanced over his shoulder and noticed Mac had changed. Still clearing up the mess into a black fabric bag, Mac wore a fitted leather jacket stressing the round of his belly and wide legged jeans that weren't designed to hug the body so tight. Dark, solid-looking boots capped with gleaming rounds of steel had replaced the white trainers.

"Better?" Travis asked.

"Like you wouldn't believe," Mac replied, raising a brow.

Travis didn't linger, his attention instead moving behind the pilot's seats. He stood and stared past the half-height glass partition separating another four seats mounted on a raised platform, surrounded by a myriad of controls with dark screens lining the walls and set into desks.

Stepping onto the platform, Travis spun the closest seat with his hand, as if by habit, whilst searching for anything that might trigger a memory. When the rush of a motor filled the air, he glanced back to Mac, who gripped the long hose of a vacuum cleaner and ran the head across the deck, grunting with each swing.

"Where did you...?" Travis said, but cut himself off when he spotted something he recognised amongst the panels.

Leaning up to the wall of switches and dials, he scanned across a line of buttons, each labelled with white lines forming different basic shapes. Realising they resembled the controls of a media player, Travis pushed play and his eyes lit up, his smile doubling when every screen came to life.

"What did you touch? Are you a focking moron?" Mac shouted. With the drone of the cleaner fading, he rushed over, shouldering Travis away as he glanced at the glow of each monitor around the bridge. "What did you press?"

Travis reached out to point at the button, but before

he could get close, Mac swatted his finger away. Rather than complaining, Travis stared at the digital clock on every screen counting backwards from 47:99:99.

Staring as the digits raced down, Travis tilted his head, wondering what would happen in just under two days. The thought vanished when on the bulkhead beside the closest screen he spotted an envelope taped with three words handwritten in capital letters.

OPEN ME NOW!

Swapping a glance with Mac, who'd also spotted it, Travis stepped up to the bulkhead and gingerly pulled it from the metal. As the paper came away, Mac tutted, licking his finger and rubbing at the sticky mark left behind.

Pulling out a single sheet of paper and avoiding Mac's glare, Travis read aloud.

"DO NOT…" he said, before deciding to finish the rest in his head.

TOUCH ANYTHING.
SAY THIS INSTEAD.
SAPPHIRE. RUN EMERGENCY PROGRAMME DELTA FOUR.

"Um," Travis said, his mouth dry, letting go of the paper as Mac reached up and snatched it from his grasp.

"What have you done?" Mac replied, shaking his head after reading the page then releasing a long sigh. "I guess we should find out how much you've focked up."

Letting his smile drop, Travis swallowed hard.

"Sapphire. Run emergency programme delta four."

5

The already low lights dimmed as a series of strips around the bridge's perimeter glowed blue and a large, disembodied pair of plump lips of the same colour floated midair above the pilot's controls. A rumble of bass rose from unseen speakers.

"I am the Mary May's synthetic autonomous processor for hyper-intelligent reconnaissance and exploration," the low female voice said in time with the moving lips. "You can call me Sapphire. Now bow before your master."

Sharing a look with Mac, Travis swallowed hard.

"I'm kidding, of course," the voice continued in a lighter tone. "Or am I?" she added, lowering again.

The pair swapped another look, but before either of them could speak, the lips moved once more.

"I'm sorry. It's in the script. I was compelled to say it."

Travis's smile returned when, although not recognising the words, he couldn't help but wonder if he might have been behind them. With a glance at Mac, his deepening scowl seemed to confirm his suspicions.

"I am the series four thousand craft AI responsible for the day-to-day operation of Cargo Ship Mary May built by Charon Industries Inc," the voice went on, its tone much more breezy. "I'll give you a minute to take a seat."

Without thinking, Travis sat in the closest chair before swivelling around to Mac and eyeing him with uncertainty, as the short guy scowled at the one next to him. Seeing Travis preparing to stand and offer his hand out, Mac leapt forward.

"Don't you dare," he called, before using the bar meant for resting feet to scramble up.

"The CS Mary May," the voice started again, "is a class four cargo ship and you are amongst the crew."

"How does she know who we are?" Travis said, speaking over her.

Mac shrugged away the question.

"I know this because only the crew's voices can interact with me in my current mode," the female said.

"Sorry. I thought this was a recording," Travis replied, staring at the disembodied lips as they continued to move.

"I am sure you have many other questions, but as this is a recording, you will have to hope we have thought of everything you might want to know."

Not hiding the confusion on his furrowed brow, Travis relaxed back into the seat.

"I am in hibernation mode and therefore only able to perform basic functions such as providing heat, power, minimal security and door control, and the playback of recordings. Like yourselves, the remainder of the crew scattered across time and whichever planet we are on. They are likely suffering from significant amnesia, amongst other symptoms."

Travis lifted his chin, concentrating on the lips, and was about to open his mouth when he remembered what she'd just said.

"Six Gregorian months ago, whilst working under contract within the Deltoid Sector Union, we retrieved a cargo for a new client. When the client failed to pay the fee on time, we retained the cargo, comprising repossessed equipment from a scientific research facility which went out of business. Amongst the consignment was an experimental quantum nexus travel system."

"A quantum what?" Travis said, frowning as if the words hurt his head.

"From what we know so far, the EQuaNTS was built to travel between dimensions. Based on the fundamental physics you learned in school, there are infinite dimensions, the bounds of which are defined by every decision made by a sentient being. This device bridges the dark matter barrier between them. I'll give you a moment," she said before the lips stopped moving.

"Dimensional travel?" Travis said, swivelling around to Mac, his eyes screwed up.

"It's another focking joke," Mac replied with a disinterested shake of his head. "I bet you a hundred credits you wrote this focking nonsense."

Travis's expression relaxed, and a smile bloomed from the corner of his mouth as he turned back towards the lips.

"This is not a joke," she said, but didn't give them time to react. "For the last five months, the crew of the Mary May have travelled to several parallel worlds."

"Is this for real? It sounds dangerous," Travis asked, looking between Mac and the disembodied lips.

"Whilst conducting compulsory safety inspections on the device as we tried to find a buyer and recover our expenses, a member of the crew inadvertently, and through no fault of their own…"

"Travis," Mac said over the voice.

"…connected the device to the ship's power supply."

"It was definitely you," Mac added, but Travis didn't look around.

"Incompatibilities with this ship's voltage regulation system caused an electrical surge which activated a jump and damaged the machine's interface, forcing the crew to wire it into the Mary May's control system."

"Wait for it," Mac said at Travis's shoulder.

"So far, we have been unable to determine how it is operated, but a simple way to understand what we know is to imagine there are an infinite number of index cards on a Rolodex. The dimension you're experiencing is the current card on display. The next few cards before and after are recent divergences, and would therefore be recognisable to the travelling crew. However, the divergence becomes greater the further away you get from the original.

"Continuing this analogy, to travel to another dimension using the EQuaNTS, you flick through the cards and find the one you want. However, in its damaged state, it is akin to manipulating the Rolodex whilst wearing boxing gloves.

"That, coupled with the creation of a new dimension with each decision made by every sentient being, until we can understand how it works, travel to the same dimension more than once is almost impossible. Likewise, to locate any specific dimensional destination."

Travis's mouth hung open as Sapphire went quiet. Swivelling around to Mac, he watched him glare back with narrowed eyes.

"If it's a joke, it's very specific," Travis said, but turned away as the voice continued.

"So far, we have made five jumps and concluded the human body is not compatible with dimensional travel. The bigger the step away from the starting dimension we take, the more significant the side-effects the crew suffers. These include extreme nausea, lateral and temporal displacement, along with amnesia. As my systems are based around a biological central processing unit, I am not immune to the effects and my safety systems push me into a hibernation state which only a technician from Charon Industries Inc, or the ship's mechanic, can painstakingly pull me out of."

"Colin," Travis said.

"Why the hell did we continue to use it?" Mac said, his voice gruff.

"You're probably asking why we continued to use it after the first time," the voice said. Travis narrowed his eyes. "During the first jump, it became clear that every parallel world is different in some way to the next. Even the smallest of decisions made by an individual can have significant consequences on the world around them. Put simply, the alternatives are not like your home. With a unanimous vote, the crew agreed to attempt to go back to the original point where you would offload the EQuaNTS device before picking up your normal lives again.

"However, we feared that, despite all precautions, the crew could scatter again during a jump. If this circumstance occurred, it is very important that all crew are onboard before you start the EQuaNTS's countdown."

"Countdown?" Travis said with a gulp.

"Here we go," Mac said.

"I will shortly go over the information you will need to gather the remaining missing crew and then to make the next jump. Once the crew is back together and your group's memories have returned, we will process the data collected and adjust the EQuaNTS settings before initiating the forty-eight hour starting sequence. Remember, once started, it cannot be stopped. At zero hour the ship will jump using the loaded coordinates.

"I repeat, it is imperative that you do not press the start button until you are ready, as once started, anyone not on board will be left behind and the chances are infinitesimal that you will ever find the dimension again to retrieve them."

Jumping from his seat, Travis rushed to the playback controls, jabbing the pause button again and again. But no matter how hard he pressed, the countdown continued its retreat.

"Shock and horror," Mac said, underlying his sarcasm with a deep sigh as Travis's head dropped into his hands.

6

"To assist with finding the remaining crew, we have prepared a brief presentation," Sapphire continued, causing Travis to look up from his hands to find a rotating three-dimensional image of a wiry guy in shorts and t-shirt had replaced the floating lips. Black-rimmed glasses accentuated the round of his face, the thick lenses making his eyes seem so large.

"Miles is the ship's navigator. Despite being equipped with intelligence in the top quartile, he has the social skills of a goat. He is always sniffing as if with a perpetual upper respiratory tract infection. Nevertheless, he wears shorts and t-shirts no matter the temperature, or the external weather conditions when planet side. He continually denies that his lack of clothes has anything to do with a constant need to blow his nose. You will probably find him in some academic centre, perhaps a library, or should all other attempts fail, check the local medical facilities for those with hyperthermia."

Travis spun around wide-eyed to look at Mac, pointing at the image.

"I remember him," he said, rushing out the words and watching Mac nod despite what appeared to be some uncertainty.

"Mac is the chef," Sapphire continued, and Travis looked away, filled with a sudden dread as to how the man might react. "He's a neat freak and an angry man. Watch out for his steel toe-capped boots because he likes to take his frustration out on anything at ankle height.

You'll find him hunting out ingredients, although it won't make a difference, or in a kitchen brewing up a concoction…"

"What do you mean?" Mac blurted out as the voice continued. Travis's new grin fell from his lips.

"If you still can't find him in these places, look for Mac either in a bar, jail or a looney bin."

"I'm going to kick your ass," Mac called out, jumping from the seat, but before he could cover the distance between them, Travis raised his feet from the floor, leaving the steel caps clattering into his seat's central pole.

"Sit down. You don't know I wrote it," Travis said, shooing him away. "There's more," he added, as Sapphire spoke whilst the image of a well-built woman rotated in the air.

Wearing black trousers and a black jacket zipped up to her chin, long blonde hair gathered in a tight plait came halfway down her back. Thick muscles bulged against the arms of the jacket, their bulk plain to see despite the size of the image.

"Don't fock with Princess. Ever. Look in gyms or back water bars where she'll have everyone's attention," Sapphire continued.

Pinching his eyes together, Travis nodded.

"Do you remember her?" he said, not looking at Mac. "It doesn't say what her job on the ship is."

Mac only replied with a grunt, the shake of his head reflecting on a dark monitor, but before Travis had time to think, the image changed to himself wearing a figure-hugging military dress uniform.

"What?" Travis exclaimed when Mac let out a long snort of laughter, but when the camera zoomed in on his own confident smile, Travis beamed with pride, mouthing the words as the female voice spoke.

"A military veteran who's distinguished service career was cruelly cut short in its prime by a combat injury, the lead pilot, Travis, is self-sufficient and will be the first to gather the crew. In the unlikely event he is not, you'll find him serving the local community as a fire fighter, or officer of the peace."

"Moron," Mac said, spitting out the word. "You focking wrote this, otherwise she'd have mentioned your stupid ass phobia of dogs!"

"Shut up. She's talking," Travis butted in, holding up his hand when the image changed again.

"Clutch is the ship's engineer, and the only one with a hope of bringing me out of hibernation."

Taken aback when the rotating figure wasn't a balding, middle-aged man, Travis leaned towards the man's dark, dirty skin and a thick dark beard wrapping around the bottom of his face as his stare seemed to follow Travis despite the image's rotation.

"He's perpetually filthy, in part because of his role, and glistens in the light with machine oil. He hates to shower, but somehow, whatever he's caked in keeps things reasonable for those around him. Clutch sleeps with his Universal Tool and you'll find him where machinery gathers."

"I know him," a voice said, cutting in from the doorway. Ignoring Sapphire's continued words, both Mac and Travis turned to find Colin lowering his pointed finger from toward Clutch's image.

Travis drew back, sucking through his teeth when he spotted the golf-ball-sized lump in the centre of Colin's forehead.

"What?" Travis exclaimed as he caught up on what the man had said. Jumping down from the seat, he turned back toward the front when he realised Sapphire had just stopped speaking, but rather than finding a figure floating in mid-air, the disembodied lips had returned.

"That concludes the details of the six crew, and emergency programme delta four. I look forward to the reunion."

The mouth vanished, and the screen went dark before returning to the countdown.

"Six crew?" Travis asked, twisting around to Mac when he realised what she'd said.

Mac scowled at Colin before turning to Travis.

"What?" Mac replied, easing himself out of the seat, his boots landing on the deck with a heavy thud.

"She said six crew," Travis said, and the chef lifted his chin, squinting in thought whilst holding out his stubby palm.

"You," Mac said, pushing out a finger. "Me," he added as he lifted another digit. "Miles, Princess, Clutch and Colin," he said, before glaring at his raised digits. "Six, you focking idiot. She didn't mention that jumping killed brain cells. Get a grip."

"Of course," Travis replied, nodding as he blinked several times. Then, as he spotted the countdown in the corner of his eye, a rush of energy raced through his core. Doing his best to push the anxiety at the seconds counting down away, he turned to Colin with a widening smile. "Now spill. Where did you see Clutch?"

7

Travis had changed into the bright blue flight suit that fit like a glove before they'd left the ship, filled with pride when he spotted the cartoon version of the Mary May embroidered on his chest, one half red and the other bright blue, which matched a tattoo on his upper arm.

Sitting on the city11 double-decker bus, he peered past Mac, who straddled the two seats of the row in front, and stared out of the window before turning his head to look up at a series of aircraft buzzing above. Some were just indistinct specks in the air, whilst at least one other, a helicopter, flew much lower, rushing into view one moment and out the other.

As each craft disappeared, whilst listening to Colin at the front of the long vehicle chatting to the man driving from beyond his protective partition, Travis turned his attention to the streets rolling past. The sights reminded him of his childhood, his days at school studying the vids and the old films his family forced him and his brother to watch when home for the holidays.

Those were snapshots of the past, but were so much more like this present than his own. The trees were the same colour. As were the patches of grass, of course, although rarely seen in his dimension. The people looked the same. That hadn't changed, but what they wore was different. Not vastly, but many details were off. In his home, people long ago understood the slow death the population was inflicting on the planet.

For the same journey back home, there were no

wheels that touched the road and so the destructive hydrocarbons mixed with crushed stone below them were just an artefact of the past, not needed to propel people along, replaced instead with an algae and recycled plastic mix. Its vibrant rainbow of colour adding brightness to the day.

The clothes would only be seen in a museum as gone were the bright, weaved plastics and man-made fibres.

As he continued to stare outside of the bus, he couldn't help but wonder which decision had caused his dimension to split. Perhaps it was a simple choice by some powerful leader to concentrate the efforts of a world-leading country on finding alternatives to destroying the place we all called home.

Travis smiled at the irony.

Perhaps it was such a simple decision that led to perfecting nuclear fusion, which then produced its eventual miniaturisation and gave their dimension the ability to build spacecraft that could reach out to the stars. When spaceflight became a causal occurrence, the technology to move almost as fast as light came less than a generation later, and so unlocked the resources of the galaxy and should have ended the slow death of the planet overnight. Instead, it meant people cared even less for the place that was the cradle of their civilisation.

The buzz of the helicopter's return pulled him out of his thoughts and he focused back on the road, where, because the sign at the front of the bus read *Out of Service*, they glided past every stop.

On the other two bus journeys they'd taken to find a colleague of Colin's willing to let them travel to the depot, he explained that the guy they called Clutch had worked at the company since before he joined. He was the man that could fix anything, and the person to go to with any mechanical issues they couldn't solve alone.

The twenty-minute journey ended with the raise of a barrier from across the road and a long, slow drive passing a tall building before coming around the end and parking.

Leaving the driver with a wave, they spotted giant doors on the other side of the hanger-like space, finding many with buses parked halfway in, whilst the others allowed them glimpses into the vastness beyond.

Without speaking, the pair followed Colin through a side door and into a cavernous area dotted with buses in various states of disassembly.

"It's Saturday," Colin's voice echoed as he scoured the garage. "He's the only one who works by choice on his day off."

A moment later, he stretched his hand out, pointing across the room before walking towards a pair of boots sticking out from underneath a red single decker bus with every conceivable panel open.

"Callum," Colin called.

"God damn it," a voice echoed out, followed by a clatter of metal before a wrench skittered out from under the bus.

As a library of memories flooded into Travis's head, he couldn't help but beam at the man he recalled was a wonder with anything but the living.

It didn't take long for the low-wheeled trolley to slide out.

"Yeah?" the man said, his voice deep and skin streaked with oil and grease. As the trolley came to a halt, he sat up with narrowed eyes and his right fist clenched. He looked just like Travis had expected, apart from the beard which hadn't been on the image they'd seen on the Mary May, and nor were the streaks of silver mixed with the blackness of his hair, or the crow's feet in the corners of each eye.

The man nodded at Colin whilst looking side on at the other two. "Are you off to a fancy dress party?" he asked, narrowing his eyes further as he looked Travis and Mac up and down.

"Clutch?" Travis said, his smile growing as he watched the filthy man's head turn to the side before he shook it.

"Give it a minute," Travis added. "I'm Travis, veteran pilot," he said, pointing to the crest of a slender starship embroidered on his breast pocket. "The stumpy guy is Mac. Ship's chef," he added, ignoring the short man's snort whilst trying his best not to twist his expression at the inevitable. "And you know Colin, your apprentice."

The guy turned away, placing a socket wrench on a tray beside him before wiping his hands on a rag that looked dirtier than his skin.

"Do you remember us?" Travis asked, pushing his hands into his pockets whilst the man got to his feet.

"I remember Colin. I saw him yesterday. Which one am I meant to be?" the guy said, raising his chin.

"Sorry?" Travis replied, his smile not wavering.

"You must be posh, and that's scary. Colin is ginger. So who am I in your Spice Girls tribute band?" the man said, cocking an eyebrow at his apprentice.

"I have absolutely no idea what you're talking about," Travis said, before glancing over his shoulder to Mac.

"We only need one mechanic," Mac snarled, before turning and walking away.

Travis's smile faltered until, pushing his hand deeper into his pocket, he felt the smooth edge of something metal.

"Catch," Travis called out, and with a step back, taking care not to trip on the tools and the containers scattered around, the man cupped his hands and caught the dark rectangular box wrapped in a central band of grey metal.

Rather than looking up to question what Travis had thrown, he ran a digit along the short face before moving his finger as if to press an unseen button he seemed to know would be there.

His eyes widened when a thin bar protruded with a round of metal at the end. Paying no regard to the two men watching, he settled himself back onto the low trolley, and still holding the box with the protrusion in his hand, using his feet he pushed himself back under the bus.

Travis nodded, grinning at Colin, who stared back with his brow lowered and an unspoken question on his lips.

But Travis didn't elaborate. Instead, he turned around to search for Mac. Unable to find him, and at the sound of the trolley wheels, he twisted back around to find Clutch rising to his feet with a satisfied smile. But rather than looking at the two still staring, he stepped to the bus's cab and within a short moment, the engine burst to life.

"It's a Universal Tool," Travis called out over the din before the engine cut. "You're never without it," he added, his voice echoing.

"I know what it is," the man snapped, his smile flattening. "It's the V23 and can form any one of four hundred heads depending on the job, and all controlled by thought impulses through the hand. This is the premium version that comes with a plasma amplifier cutting system," he added, his tone softening as he stared at the box before looking back up, his eyes glazing as he stared off into the distance.

"It's been ten years," he eventually said, turning back to Travis.

"Fock," Travis said under his breath as he stepped closer. But before he could take another step, the clatter of metal caused him to spin around.

"What the hell?" Mac cried out, his voice echoing before he appeared at the doorway, soaked with a dark liquid running down his face and leather jacket as he held a dripping can of cola.

"Please tell me he's forgotten he likes to cook," the mechanic said under his breath.

"Welcome back, Clutch," Travis replied, launching himself forward to wrap his arms around him.

8

Within an hour they were back at the clearing, Clutch having borrowed a minibus under the guises of a test drive following a repair. Travis and Mac used the journey to fill him in on their search for the rest of the crew, saving the news of the countdown's start until they'd arrived and he'd turned off the engine.

"Don't touch anything else," Clutch said, fixing Travis with a long stare and only looking away as the ship shimmered into view, a sense of static electricity coursing through the air.

Gripping the Universal Tool, he left the others behind. "I'll see what I can do for Sapphire," he called over his shoulder as he scrambled up the lowered ramp.

Before he'd disappeared across the vast hold and out of sight, the others turned left and made their way to the bridge, where Travis stared at the rushing seconds on the surrounding screens.

He shook his head at the three hours already gone.

"Sapphire, how do we find the rest?" Travis called out, but despite his high and optimistic tone, he wasn't surprised at the lack of response.

"We need to eat," Mac said, giving Travis a start and filling him with a dread as he glanced at Colin's unfaltering look back.

"Um, I need to speak to Clutch," Travis said, striding over to the door and calling over his shoulder. "Colin, see if you can find addresses of local gyms and libraries. Mac, we haven't got time for food. We'll grab something whilst we're out. You coming?"

"No," Mac replied. "I've spent enough time away from the ship for a lifetime," he added, pressing a finger into the tacky mess of drying cola down his front.

Only catching the tail end of a gruff warning not to leave without eating, Travis rushed away.

"Clutch, where are you?" he called out as he hurried across the vast cargo space, his words in part to drown out Mac's voice behind him.

Choosing the left of the two doors on the other side of the hall, it slid open to reveal a compact space with a bunch of stained and cracked leather seats, and two mismatched orange double-seater couches. A long table with benches bolted to the metal floor waited between a wall lined with cupboards and a counter stacked with rows of machines that looked like microwave ovens. The lingering stale air sent a shiver down Travis's spine.

Looking away from what looked like a small bundle of folded clothes laying neatly on the table, Travis found a door at the far end of the room. But instead of heading that way, he moved towards a large hole in the floor where the top of a ladder pointed down at a steep angle in the other corner.

"Clutch, where are you?" Travis called again.

To the sound of cupboards already slamming closed and the ping of buttons pressed above him, he reached the bottom of the steps, sliding his feet on either side of the ladder as if he'd done the same so many times before.

With relief, he savoured the thick odour of oil and the stink of chemicals he couldn't name, each a powerful reminder of the engineer.

Stooping for the low ceiling and finding the corridor, he nodded, already knowing it would run the length of the ship, recognising the series of contraptions on the right that were connected either with a shaft or a tangle of thick cables, their surfaces dotted with unlit indicators, their bulk leaving little room for him to pass.

Travis lingered on the once vibrant red covering much of what he saw, the colour faded and smudged with oil, the paint worn to bare metal in many places.

Hearing a low hum above, Travis tore his attention away to a series of bulkhead doors on the opposite side of the long space. With no sign of Clutch, and taking care where he stepped, he eased his way toward a door standing ajar about halfway along.

"Fock," Travis called out, as pain shot up his leg after only a few steps. "Fock," he exclaimed again as the agony sent him standing up straight and banging his head on the ceiling.

Rubbing his scalp, he couldn't shake a sense of déjà vu, and peered down to a metal upright in the centre of the walkway with its faded yellow paint only hinting at its warning. Glancing up at the ceiling as he rubbed his scalp through his hair, he spotted several dents in the same panel above him.

"I'll get to that soon," Clutch called out, startling Travis enough to send him up straight and banging his head in the same space again.

"Fock it," he called out, before finding Clutch standing up to his full extent and peering out of the doorway as he pulled the zipper of worn overalls tight up to his chin. "Why do I get the sense that's not the first time you've promised to fix this?" Travis said, narrowing his eyes at the man.

"What do you need?" Clutch nodded over, not answering the question.

"I'm taking Colin to look for the others," Travis said through gritted teeth, the pain already easing. "Have you remembered anything that might help find them?"

Clutch narrowed his eyes, running his hands through his hair, despite the dark stains covering his fingers.

"Someone is afraid of dogs. I mean terrified," he eventually said, his brow low as he turned to the side.

Travis tried his best not to scowl.

"Have you remembered anything useful?" he asked, giving in to a frown.

After another moment, Clutch shook his head.

"Never mind. I've got to go. Mac is threatening to cook," he added, taking care when he turned and glanced back at the ladder.

"I'll come with you," Clutch replied, his head twitching to the side with alarm.

"No. We need Sapphire back online," Travis said, and Clutch peered past him toward the ladder before looking back into the room he was half standing in.

"Yeah," he said, before disappearing inside and Travis was sure he heard a lock slide across the door.

Leaving the oily aroma behind, it was soon replaced with an acrid vinegar stench clawing at the back of his throat. Stifling a cough as he climbed the ladder, he took care not to make a sound as he placed his feet on the rungs.

Raising his head into the crew mess, he spotted Mac with his back to him whilst he stood on an upturned metal box which bowed in the middle, as he gathered jars and boxes from the cupboards whilst stirring something in a large pot every so often.

Somehow keeping himself from gagging on the pungent air, Travis arrived at the top of the ladder, holding still as Mac jumped to the deck. But rather than turning, he stepped to the side, scraping the box along the floor before climbing back on and reaching up.

Knowing Mac could turn around at any moment and force him to endure a bowl of whatever he'd created, Travis slipped through the door beside the hole in the floor.

9

Lights flickered on as the door slipped closed at his back and Travis found himself in a beige corridor where five doors waited. With two on either side and a single opening at the far end, other than a few scuffs on the walls it was unremarkable.

Choosing the closest, he entered a small space where he found a bunk bed on the left. A desk stood on the opposite side, its surface dotted with plastic containers, a thin tablet computer and trinkets not out of place. Along the back of the desk, and lined up against the wall, stood a series of dog-eared books, their spines worn.

Despite a vague glimmer of nostalgia, he couldn't shake the alien sense of where he stood. Still, he stepped a little further in, intrigued at the hint of perfume and the sharp edges of the grey bed clothes. Spread out across the lower mattress he stared at a flight suit much like his own.

With another step he leaned up, his mind racing in search of who had occupied the one-piece before they'd vanished, but all thoughts came to an abrupt end when, with a glance up, he found the wall beside the bed stuck with row after row of scattered photographs.

Unable to hold back a smile, he squinted for a better look when he found himself grinning back from a handful. He spotted Mac, too, but only in the background.

Closing his eyes, he tried to put himself in those moments, but finding only a cloud of frustration, his chest filled with a sense of loss, followed by a rising panic that maybe the memories were gone forever.

With another look, he spotted Clutch standing in the background of a few, as were many other faces. Some he recognised, but only from Sapphire's recording. There were more that triggered no recollection.

Making an effort to look at each of the pictures for a second time, he held on to a hope that soon the floodgates would open.

When after a long moment the deluge didn't come, he held his gaze on the frozen smiling stare of a blonde woman. With broad shoulders and a powerful swimmer's build, her dead-eye-look sent a shiver down his spine.

"Princess," he said to himself as he lingered on a similar shot where she stood with her arm around another woman, a stunning brunette a little shorter than her. A beautiful stranger captured mid laugh, and before he knew it he'd reached out, touching the glossy finish as a wider smile consumed his mouth.

Hearing a distant hum of a machine starting up, he leaned across the bed, and breathing in the delicate perfume, he closed his eyes and forced himself to calm. Feeling as if the memories were just out of reach, he plucked the picture from the wall, then stepped back, standing tall to take a better look.

Before he came to any great conclusion, he peered up, spotting a monitor at the end of the bed displaying the countdown, its seconds racing away so much faster than he thought possible.

Hearing footsteps in the corridor, Travis stepped from the room where he found Colin frowning as he looked around.

Spotting Travis, their eyes met, sending Colin's brow

high.

"Princess," Travis said, turning the photo for Colin to see, whilst inadvertently covering the other woman's face with his finger. "Do you recognise her?"

Colin stared in silence before shaking his head.

"Nor do I," Travis replied. "Is this my room?" he said to himself, as his attention focused on the door opposite which someone had once scrawled *Ace* in now faded black marker.

Colin smiled and followed him inside.

The layout and size of the room was identical to the one he'd just left, but with only one bunk on the side where two stood in the girl's space. A monitor counted down the remaining time, whilst in a line along the rest of the wall were photos of Travis in various forms of military uniform. In one shot, he stood in full formal dress whilst he shook hands with a man only a little shorter. They both stood in front of a pair of crossed flags as they smiled at the camera and the man handed over a rolled sheet of paper held together with a blue ribbon.

The others had Travis in military flight suits, some with groups of others wearing the same, whilst some showed him beaming at the camera as he stood next to a spacecraft much smaller than the Mary May, its sleek, aerodynamic lines making it look like it went fast.

On a shelf were several scaled models of similar craft that Colin couldn't help but step forward and examine, his eyes pinching as he marvelled at their detail.

Filled with the warmth of familiarity, Travis watched Colin enjoy his surroundings.

"What was the military like?" Colin asked, his gaze lingering on Travis's graduation.

"Some of the best times of my life, and full of so

much promise," Travis replied, his voice tailing off. "Look around for as long as you want, but don't touch anything. I'm going to see if I can find a photo of Miles," Travis said, before leaving Colin behind.

He found Miles's room was the next one along, and with the stale smell of oil and two beds, one on top of the other, he figured he shared the space with Clutch. The room couldn't have been more different to his. Instead of his neat ordered surfaces, the desk was cluttered with maps and charts weighed down by lumps of metal milled into intricate parts.

There were no photos on any walls, and nothing personal to help recognise the men. Catching sight of the ever-present countdown on the monitor he'd found in each room, Travis stepped into the corridor, but stopped himself mid stride when he heard Mac's low tones close by.

"I don't know why you look at him like he's a god," Mac grumbled.

"I don't," Colin replied.

"You were. Your mouth hangs open like he's the second coming," Mac said as a bubble of laughter engulfed his voice.

"Well," Colin said, his voice tentative at first. "He's impressive. He's still so young but achieved so much. Isn't that something to look up to? He used to fly star fighters, and now he's your pilot. Don't we all dream of doing that?"

Travis couldn't help but smile to himself, despite Mac's scoff.

"Do you know how long he was in the military for?" Mac said, and Travis closed his eyes, stepping back just a little. "He aced the academy, sure, but on the first day out of training, they scrambled the squadron. As he rushed to his ship, he tripped over the umbilical cable and went down. He shattered his knee, obliterating the bone into ten pieces, and ended up spending four months in medicare whilst it healed," Mac said, not holding back a laugh.

Travis stared at the worn metal of the deck.

"How's that funny?" Colin asked, his tone flat.

The laughter slowed.

"Well, it's ironic, at least," Mac replied, his voice a little lower. "Anyway, it turned out to be for the best."

"What do you mean?" Colin asked.

"You don't remember anything, do you?" Mac said, as Travis pictured Colin shaking his head. "Within a week, his squadron mutinied and attacked Caldron Port, killing three hundred civilians in some ill-thought out attempted coup."

"That's awful," Colin replied. "But why was Travis's injury for the best?"

Travis stepped backwards and leaned against the wall, closing his eyes.

"His parents were at the port," Mac said, his voice so low Travis could barely hear it.

"Oh," Colin replied.

"Those medals on the bridge are theirs. The people that attacked trained alongside him. They were his friends. They were like his brothers and sisters. To him they were good people, but to the chain of command they were tools who followed their orders without question," Mac said.

No one spoke in the long silence that followed.

"Now Travis won't carry a weapon, or let us use them, either. He's against any use of force."

"I don't blame him," Colin said, his voice almost a whisper.

"Anyway, I can't stand around shooting the shit all day. Lunch won't cook itself. And if you mention any of what I just said to him, I'll snap your legs off at the knees. You understand?"

"Yeah," Colin replied. "And I better get back to the bridge to see if I can find those gyms. There's no signal down here."

Stepping away, Travis shoved past the door that opened at his back and he tucked himself into the room before letting it slide closed. Unable to bear more than a minute of the numbers ticking away, moving from the corridor with light steps and grateful for the cacophony from the kitchen, covering his mouth, Travis held his breath until he was out of the corridor.

"Colin," Travis snapped, arriving at the bridge to find the apprentice mechanic sitting in his chair and marvelling at the unlit controls. The ginger-haired man jumped from the seat, but Travis was already staring at the thirty-nine hours remaining.

Climbing into the driver's seat of the minibus, Travis pushed the key in the ignition, stopping its turn when the lights came on across the dash.

"Do you want me to drive?" Colin asked from beside him, but just as the ship shimmered out of sight, each light flared on before blinking out.

"Where are we going?" Colin asked as the engine came to life.

Having swapped seats, but ignoring the question, Travis stared out of the window and across the fields.

A moment later, and with the engine idling, despite his mouth opening, nothing came out as he listened to the distant thump of rotor blades.

Leaning up to the windscreen and into the clear blue sky, he couldn't find the source.

"Did you find what I asked?" Travis said, still staring up, only looking over when Colin pulled his phone from his pocket and scrolled down the screen.

"There are two libraries and four gyms within a twenty-mile radius," Colin replied.

Travis nodded, raising his hand and motioning along the road.

Within two minutes of arriving at the first on the list, a prim librarian in a plaid skirt and frilly blouse asked them to leave. Travis's excitement was too loud for the small space when they thought a man in shorts seen only from behind was their navigator.

Deflated once Travis turned the old man around by the shoulder, they left with no complaint, walking the short distance to the second floor gym above a line of shops.

"We're thinking of joining," Colin spoke up as they stood at a reception counter manned by a tall guy who, if it wasn't the bulging arm muscles, looked like he should be at school. "Can we have a tour?"

The young man behind the counter nodded, then called out toward the open door at the side, but before anyone arrived to take over, the guy led them through a barrier as it slid out of the way. They only half listened to the teenager's practiced monologue as he wafted his hand about, instead checking out each face they found.

With the place quiet, they didn't find Princess pumping iron or running on the rolling road. She was neither in the group class jumping up and down in the large room beyond a glass partition, nor the co-ed changing rooms.

Arriving back at the reception counter, the guy slipped behind the wooden partition and smiled. Then, after Travis pulled out the photo he'd taken from beside the bunk, he handed it over to Colin, who angled it toward the guy.

"Thank you," Colin said, ignoring the man's question about how they'd like to pay.

Poised to continue, he stopped himself when a young woman stood from where she'd been reaching down, hidden from their view. The woman glared at Colin, who seemed unable to stop himself from staring at the figure-hugging Lycra that left no room for his imagination.

Colin's mouth hung open.

Shaking his head when Colin didn't speak, Travis took the photo back.

"Have you seen this woman?" he said, waiting only a moment before the man took it and lifted his brow. The gesture sent Travis's heart speeding.

"They're fit," he said, the corner of his mouth lifting.

"But have you seen her?" Travis asked.

"Which one?" the man said, handing the photo back.

Remembering the other woman in the shot, Travis took it back and folded it in half so it only showed Princess.

A phone ringing in the office beside the counter sent the woman off just as the guy shook his head.

"Let's go," Colin said.

After peering over, Travis nodded and led them back out onto the street.

Deflated, within an hour they'd been to each of the other places on the list, but although busier, no-one had recognised their crewmate.

"What if we don't find them?" Travis said, as if to himself as they walked side by side down the street in the middle of a town he didn't know the name of. "What if we have to leave and they remember everything? Will they spend the rest of their lives searching for us, only to realise we'd left them behind?"

Colin stared back, his brow bunching with a frown, but Travis knew there was nothing the man could offer.

"Right," he said, making Colin jump. "What do people in this world have to do to get a drink? I'm pretty sure it'll help me think."

10

"What are you having?" Travis asked Colin, who'd followed him into the Boozy Beeches after a short drive further into the town.

"I'm driving," the ginger man replied with a shake of his head as he glanced out of the window at the minibus parked on the street outside.

"Suit yourself," Travis said, stepping up to the long bar before peering at the side profile of a grey-haired man in a white shirt and black trousers. With a navy blue tie loose around his neck, his head hung low as he stared into a glass with a finger width of brown liquid at the bottom.

Dismissing him from his search, Travis scanned the rest of the men perched on stools at the bar, but when none of their faces triggered recognition, he glanced across the booths at a pair of couples sitting at each end of the long room, with three empty places in between.

With a shake of his head, he turned to the array of bottles behind the bar, his vision swimming when he found they ran the length of the narrow room. After reaching his vision's extent to his left, a flash of light made him turn to where he found a TV hanging on the wall.

Although no sound came from the large screen, he watched the images of tall electricity pylons filmed from the air as words scrolled along the bottom.

"I missed Coronation Street last night because of that," a man's deep voice said, and Travis turned to find an overweight man standing behind the bar. Wearing a black t-shirt with a faded skull on the front, he tipped his head at the pair.

Travis lifted his chin, then turned back to the screen.

"What's that all about?" he replied, glancing back at the man to find his eyebrows raised.

"You're from out-of-town then?" he asked, and Travis nodded. "They're calling it the biggest blackout since the miner's strikes in the eighties. Almost all of Oxfordshire lost power. They only got it back on this morning. I wasn't sure if I'd be able to be open today."

Travis nodded, only half listening as he read the scrolling words.

Massive power surge knocked out main substation just outside Oglethorpe.

"However, we're open, as you can see. There's been a few more power cuts, but those only lasted a few seconds. Anyway, what can I get you?"

Travis glanced back at the screen.

National Grid are working to stabilise the electricity supply whilst they investigate the cause of the continued surges.

"So what would you like?" the barman asked.

After glancing over his shoulder at Colin, Travis stared at the closest bottles before gesturing to the man on the stool beside him.

"What's that?" he said, and the man looked up, his eyes ringed red as if he'd been crying.

"Whiskey on the rocks," the man replied in a hoarse voice, before returning to hunch over his glass.

"I'll have one of those," Travis pronounced, his voice booming.

As the barman gathered the drink, Travis turned to Colin.

"Do you recognise anyone?"

"No," Colin said, shaking his head.

"That'll be four pounds ninety, mate," the bartender said, setting the drink down.

Travis jerked his gaze to Colin. With a narrowed brow, Colin shook his head again before reaching for his wallet and sliding out a plastic card.

"We were lucky with Mac and Clutch," Travis said, stepping away, the ice cubes clinking in the glass as he swirled the brown liquid and raised it to his nose. "I just don't know where else to look."

Colin nodded as he watched Travis put the glass to his lips, then open his mouth wide after taking a sip.

"Yeah. It's like looking for a needle in a haystack," Colin replied, watching Travis scrape his tongue along his teeth as if trying to get rid of the taste.

"That tastes like something Mac came up with," Travis said, placing the remains of the drink on a nearby table before stepping into the doorway. "Wait. What did you say?" he added, glaring at Colin.

"I said it's like looking for a needle in a haystack."

"Huh," Travis said, cocking his head to the side before turning onto the street. "Do you think they're working on a farm?" he added, as he peered along each side of the road.

"No," Colin replied, bunching his cheeks. "It's just a phrase."

"I've never heard that before," Travis replied, glancing back.

"I wouldn't worry. We're survivors. The crew I mean. Look at Clutch," Colin said. "He's been here for ten years and he found a job. He seemed happy. Well, sort of, I guess. Mac found somewhere safe that kept him warm and fed for six months." Colin paused, unable to stop himself from smiling as he watched Travis smirk. "I don't know how long I've been here, but I was doing just okay."

Travis's smile dropped, his eyes narrowing as he looked off into the distance.

"And it's only been a day for me. I just hope the others are as lucky."

"I'd never have you down as a worrier," Colin said, placing his hand on Travis's shoulder.

"I'm not," Travis snapped back, raising himself up tall and forcing Colin to withdraw his hand. "It's just…" He paused for a long moment, staring along the street before looking back at Colin. "Even though I can't remember the details, or even their faces, I can feel them. Like we're connected…" Stopping himself short, he stared back off into the distance. "They're family, and it's my fault, I think."

A silence hung over the pair as their stares followed a car driving past.

"Why don't we search the Mary May?" Colin said as the car rolled out of view around a corner. "Perhaps we'll find some clue to where they've settled."

"Great idea," Travis said, turning on the balls of his feet and slapping Colin hard across the shoulders.

"Plus, I'm starving," Colin said with a nod after recovering from the playful hit.

Travis glanced back.

"You don't remember anything, do you?" he said, stifling a laugh.

11

"At the bar. Did you see where the news report was from?" Travis asked, stepping with Colin at his side and pointing to a black and white sign further up the road.

"Oglethorpe," Colin said, nodding as the word came out.

"A coincidence?" Travis said, cocking a brow and tilting his head to the side.

Colin turned to Travis, his eyes narrowing as he held his gaze, but when neither of them spoke, Colin shrugged and Travis turned down the dirt path.

"Just remember," Travis said, glancing to Colin after walking for a few minutes between the trees. "Don't let Mac see you refuse his food."

Colin regarded him for a long moment, speaking only as Travis found the Mary May shimmering into view.

"Why?" Colin asked, shaking off the shiver running down his spine. "Even if it's as bad as you said? What's he going to do to me? Do I need to sleep with one eye open?"

Travis shook his head and came to a stop as he glanced over again.

"It's not like that. He comes from a family of famous chefs, but they all died in the Massacre of Butang. You know, the one that started the third colonial war."

At Colin's frown, Travis reached out and placed a hand on the apprentice's shoulder.

"It'll come back to you," he said, his voice softening.

"I'm remembering more all the time. Visual prompts help, so let's hope looking around the ship will start your process."

Colin nodded and turned to admire the ship as they walked again.

"What do you remember about the crew?" he asked.

"Pretty much everything," Travis replied, his tone more relaxed as they walked side by side. "At least I think. I remember a lot about Mac and Clutch. You not so much," he added, his cheeks bunching with an apology as he tipped his head to the side. "I remember a time, and it wasn't long ago, when Mac's cooking was exceptional. We'd look forward to mealtimes, and I mean they'd be on our minds all day. Clients and suppliers would invite themselves aboard just to taste his food."

"What happened?" Colin asked, glancing over as Travis slowed and turned towards him.

"Consider yourself lucky you don't remember that," Travis replied, lowering his voice and staring off into the trees over Colin's shoulder. "Although I'm not sure you were there. I can't remember the date you joined."

The other man shrugged.

"Arriving in port after a long haul, the thrusters malfunctioned and caused us to hit the loading dock. There was only a little damage to the Mary May, but we'd grown a little lazy on how we stowed the cargo, and maybe we weren't so discerning about what we transported back then.

"A few barrels of an unknown chemical spilled and hit Mac. We had to wear full atmosphere suits just to get to him and when we did, he was out cold. He spent a week in medicare and it was touch and go at one point. When he woke after a couple of days, he'd lost all sense of taste and smell," Travis said, stopping short of the clearing.

"Oh wow," Colin replied. "That must have been hard on everyone."

"Yeah. We were all pretty tough on ourselves. There was so much we could have done better," Travis replied, looking at the browning sawdust at his feet. Coughing into his fist, he turned away.

"He must have realised he couldn't cook with his condition?" Colin asked.

"Well…" Travis replied, bunching his cheeks and frowning. "He was so upset, and someone might have told him he should give it a go, and perhaps when he did, they also said the food was as good as it had always been."

"And that someone was you?" Colin said, raising a brow.

"Maybe," Travis replied, looking away.

"And that's why no one tells him about his food?" Colin asked, his voice quiet as they approached the Mary May.

"We tried to a few days later," Travis replied, his voice almost a whisper. "But it didn't end well. I can't remember exactly how it went down, but no one wants him to get hurt."

"How do you put up with it?" Colin asked.

"We cope," Travis replied. "It's been a few months now and everyone has their own strategies. I've almost blurted it a few times, but somehow we've all held our tongues."

"Is the problem with his taste why he's so grumpy?" Colin asked, raising a brow.

"Nope. He's always been a curmudgeon," Travis replied. "But if you're around him long enough, you'll see his softer side."

Colin narrowed his eyes as the ramp lowered from the silvered metal siding.

"Really?" he whispered, leaning forward.

"No," Travis chuckled, shaking his head.

"The way you guys are with him, I'm surprised you keep him around," Colin said after a long moment, but Travis shook his head.

"If you ever mention this, I'll push you out of an airlock," he said in a low voice. "But he's a good guy to have on your side in a tight spot. He's loyal and a hard worker," he added, before falling silent. At the top of the ramp the stench of sweaty socks hit them both, but it was the four fewer hours missing from the countdown that turned his stomach.

12

"Eat," Mac ordered after ladling a green, soup-like liquid into bowls in front of Travis and Colin, who both sat beside each other at the bench.

"Mmm." The pleasure-filled sound slipped from Travis's mouth, knowing Mac watched whilst leaning his back against the counter. Smacking his lips, Travis stirred the creamy liquid, chasing chunks of orange rising to the surface before they fell back under. Only the stench of year-old footwear wafting up with each move of the spoon stopped him from lifting it to his mouth.

Spotting Mac's attention turn to Colin, grinning from ear to ear, Travis eyed the ginger-haired man's smile that didn't quite cover his grimace. With a swift tap of his foot against Colin's under the table, Colin forced his mouth wider, but he still couldn't push the expression to his eyes.

As he lifted his spoon, Travis turned to face Mac in the hope he could force down the need to chuckle.

"How's Clutch getting on?" Travis asked, loud with excitement.

"It's still hot," Colin said, almost under his breath.

"Getting Sapphire up and running, I mean?" Travis added, letting go of his spoon then picking it up again when Mac frowned. Regretting the waft of rising odour, Travis waited for an answer.

"I haven't seen him," Mac grunted, turning away when a machine along the wall chirped for his attention. "I think he's locked himself in down there."

"He'll be getting hungry. Do you remember how he forgets to eat when he's busy? Perhaps you should take him a bowl," Travis said, grinning.

"I can do it," Colin interrupted, but Travis shot him a glare before Mac shook his head.

"No. You two finish up. Is it good?" he said, cocking his brow.

Travis nodded without delay before glancing along the table.

"It should be cool enough now, Colin," Travis said, his cheeks bunching as Colin slowly lifted the spoon. Feeling his stomach tighten as the metal touched the man's lips, Travis's eyes widened in time with Colin's as he swallowed hard, the cords in his neck straining.

"Is it okay?" Mac said, leaning forward, seeming not to notice Colin's face reddening.

"It's yummy," Travis added, leaning as far back on the bench as he could manage whilst stirring the bowl again. "What about Clutch? He'll work quicker on a full stomach."

"Yes, yes," Mac replied, turning to face the counter and ladling more liquid into another bowl.

Travis smiled at Colin, who glared back, squeezing his lips tight as he pleaded with his eyes.

"Eat up. There's plenty more," Mac said with a grunt, before heading across the room to the ladder in the corner with another bowl. To the sounds of metal clinking against the side of the bowls, Mac lowered out of sight whilst balancing the soup one-handed.

Waiting a breath for him to be out of sight, Travis jumped from his seat, grabbing both of the bowls. Taking care not to spill a drop, he rushed around the table, upending the contents into the sink then pressing down the orange lumps into the drain with a finger.

Hearing a distant call of Clutch's name, Travis ran the water before rushing back to the table as feet clanked on the metal rungs again.

"Ahhh." Travis let out a satisfied breath, leaning back in his seat as he let the spoon clatter against the side of his empty bowl.

"More?" Mac asked, back at the counter.

"No thank you," Travis said, climbing from the bench, then pressing his hand against his stomach as it rumbled. "Colin," he snapped, much to the man's surprise, as they both looked away from Mac's narrowing eyes. "Let's see what we can find to jog our memories," Travis added, before leading him out through the doorway.

Savouring the relief of the cargo bay's stale air, after a quick glance to orient himself, Travis stepped through another door in the wide space he hadn't been through yet. The space beyond was much like where they'd just left; a smaller version of the main cargo bay, but filled with the faint acid sting of burnt electronics.

Walking towards another door at the far end of the room, at first glance Travis thought it was empty, until, in the corner, he spotted something almost as tall as him.

Like a dark, five-tiered cake of equally thick layers, ventilation grills covered the base. The next three cylindrical layers, each decreasing in width, dotted with unlit lights, round dials, and buttons. A silver disc, the smallest of the five, its surface unblemished with adornments, sat on top.

A metal table stood at its side complete with a fold-up chair, whilst a keypad and screen rested on the tabletop with cables snaking down to the floor, before disappearing around the base of the tall object Travis only had a vague recollection of.

Unable to look away as he walked closer, he spotted a thick cable coming out from the side of the base before it snaked across the floor and rose to a socket in the ship's bulkhead at waist height.

Looking away as Colin's stomach rumbling reminded him of his own need to eat, he pressed his palm on Colin's back and guided him to the door at the rear.

"It's here somewhere, if I remember right," Travis said, as he pulled out a metal box from a stack of similar containers lining the far wall. Moving boxes of all shapes and sizes out of the way in the small room, he soon beamed back at Colin as he clutched a battered metal container covered in the remains of bright yellow paint.

Snapping open the catches on either end, he glanced over his shoulder at the closed door, then pulled out two foil-covered packages, handing one to Colin before taking care to replace everything as he'd found it.

Colin's fingers mirrored Travis's as he pinched the package at the side, then peeled the foil to reveal what looked like an oat bar. Taking a bite, their eyes rolled back in their heads.

"What is this? It's delicious," Colin said between mouthfuls.

"I live on them," Travis replied after swallowing hard. "They're from a neat little place on the Peribellum Peninsula. I've got quite a stock, but I hope the next dimension also has them."

"Is this all we eat?" Colin said, after stuffing down half the bar.

"Pretty much. At least when we're on board. These little delights contain everything the body needs and more. Everyone apart from Mac has their own selection of food hidden away, but we're not beyond shar…" Travis cut himself off at what he thought might be footsteps.

As the lights above their heads flickered, Travis stuffed the last of his bar in his mouth, then snatched the packaging from Colin, which, with his own, he pressed into the pocket of his flight suit.

With a quick glance around as the door to the storage room slid to the side, he stepped back into the cargo space, where his gaze fell to the ever-decreasing countdown above the entrance.

"Is that the EQuaNTS?" Colin asked, stepping closer to the tiered object.

"It must be," he replied, stepping around to its side, following the cable from the base to the plug socket in the wall. "Why did I ever plug it in?" he said, his voice quiet as he moved to the bulky socket.

"What are you doing?" Colin asked, his voice rising as Travis reached for the plug.

"Maybe if I pull the power, the countdown will stop," Travis said, gripping the cable. But before he tugged, a deep voice came from the doorway.

"Or maybe it will end any chance we have of getting home."

13

"Let's not fock up again," Clutch added as Travis and Colin turned to find him standing in the doorway.

Letting go of the cable and wiping the soot from his hands down his flight suit's legs, Travis dipped his head.

"I'm sorry," he said, unable to look Clutch in the eye.

"Don't sweat it. By the state of the Mary May, it looks like we've all done some crazy things," Clutch replied, his tone rising. "I came to find you because I've got some news."

Travis lifted his head.

"Sapphire's on her way out of hibernation. It should only be a few hours before she's fully operational again."

Travis nodded his enthusiasm, spotting the clock's continued countdown over Clutch's shoulder.

"Plus," Clutch continued, his eyes brightening and pulling a black plastic rectangle from his pocket, then wiping his oil-stained fingers across the surface. "With more of her systems coming up, I found something that might help." After his cheeks bunched with a flash of frustration, he opted to wipe whatever it was across his overalls.

Seeming satisfied with the result, he pressed a button on the side of the rectangle whilst pointing it at the monitor.

Travis squinted when a bright light engulfed the clock's black background before darkening almost as quickly and leaving behind an image of the room they stood in.

It took Travis a few moments to realise it wasn't a live CCTV feed showing him standing in the same place. Instead, blinking the image into focus, he stared at a man in glasses with unkempt long hair and a thick beard, wearing shorts and a t-shirt.

Remembering the three-dimensional images from the bridge and Sapphire's words, he realised the man shown jumping up and down with joy on the screen was their navigator.

"Miles," Travis whispered, but said nothing more when the man in the video's excitement calmed and he lowered into the seat. When somehow he pulled the chair in with some unseen force, Travis realised the video was playing backwards. Landing in the seat, the man's eyes went wide as he stared at the screen, but with the monitor turned at such an angle, they couldn't see what it showed. The guy's expression relaxed as he tapped at the keypad, then sweeping his fingers across a separate tablet resting on the desk, his mouth moved as if he was talking to himself. With no sound coming from the screen, they had no way of knowing what he was saying.

Out of the corner of his eye, Travis spotted Clutch raise his arm, pointing the control at the screen before the image sped.

"There's a serious amount of this," he said, but their stares remained transfixed on the rushing scene, watching his jerking motion as the navigator focused on the screen, his lips moving with only an occasional shift in his seat as he tapped at the controls.

Within a blink of an eye, the man disappeared from the monitor, only to return a moment later dressed in different shorts and t-shirt as he sat back at the desk, tapping at the controls once more. His mouth didn't stop moving.

"How much of this is there?" Travis asked, without looking away.

"Weeks," Clutch said.

"We haven't got time to go through all of it," Travis replied, turning from the image when it showed nothing new. Neither Clutch nor Colin replied as they stared at figures flashing in and out of view but too fast to make out who they could be. Food and drink containers appeared on the table but were gone the next moment.

Soon the chair went, and Miles hunched over the desk, but continued to tap at the screen and talk to himself. Next, the table was gone, the monitor resting on the floor and Miles held the tablet sitting cross-legged on the deck in front of the tiered machine.

Travis shook his head, unable to look away even though he knew they were wasting precious time that they should use to search for the rest of the crew. By that point, the only movement Miles made was to lift the tablet closer to his face.

A thought hit Travis as he watched.

"Slow it down," he said, still looking at the screen.

"Huh?" Clutch replied, with the control by his side.

"Slow the video down," Travis said, reaching for the control, but before he could grab it, Clutch seemed to realise what he meant and lifted the rectangle of plastic and pressed a button.

The image slowed to normal speed and Travis stepped forward, squinting at the picture. "Have we got any bigger screens?"

"The mess room," Clutch replied. "What have you seen?" he blurted out, already walking to the door and not slowing before it slid to the side.

Ignoring the remains of the sweaty sock smell, the trio formed up in the mess in front of a monitor almost the width of the double seater sofa. It didn't take Clutch more than a few clicks of the control before the image they'd left behind in the rear hold appeared.

"Play it," Travis said, paying no attention to Mac looking up from the sofa they stood in front of. His eyes were sleep-narrowed and his face puffy whilst his entire body engulfed the seat.

Each of the new arrivals stared at the image, as every so often Miles's lips would stop moving and he'd press the tablet's screen. Before he talked again, he'd press once more.

For another few minutes, they watched Miles repeat the same process.

"What's going on?" Mac asked and they all looked down, watching the short man turn away from the screen as he struggled to raise himself.

"Is he recording on the tablet?" Colin asked, drawing everyone to look back up.

"Is this the tablet?" Travis asked, pointing to the device Clutch held.

"No. This is mine," he replied.

"So where is it? Did anyone see it on the table?" Travis asked, his gaze finding Colin and then Clutch. They both shook their heads before each of them turned down towards Mac, who was still trying to stand as he shuffled his feet on the deck, trying to find traction.

"Where did you put it?" Travis asked, his narrow-eyed expression matching that of the other two.

Mac glanced back at the screen, then shrugged.

"How am I supposed to know where I tidy all your shit up to? If I didn't clean up after you lot, this place would be a pig sty," Mac replied. "When I was in the fleet…"

"We haven't got time, Mac," Travis cut him off.

"Think. It's important."

Glaring back after a moment and without a word, Mac raised his hands out and Travis and Colin helped him up.

Still not speaking, he scurried out of the door to the cargo bay, arriving back a few minutes later with what looked like the tablet they'd seen on the screen as he wiped its face with his sleeve.

"Where was it?" Clutch said, frowning at the device as Mac handed it over to Travis, but the chef didn't reply before all heads turned to the handheld where Travis touched the screen, double tapping an audio file on the front page and pressing play.

Swapping looks, a wet intake of breath came from the speakers, followed by a young man's nasal voice.

14

"It's been so long since the first inter-dimensional jump and the toll on the crew is obvious in everyone's mood. Although no one complains, each time the countdown ends only for us to realise we've taken a step further away from home, our loved ones and the lives we knew, I can see the change."

The slurp of the man drawing up snot rushed from the speakers, contorting the faces of those listening.

"It's still hard for the crew that didn't leave anyone behind and getting more difficult as the differences between our dimension and where we arrive grow. Even the slight differences don't sit right and it's obvious we're all desperate to get home.

"The last jump was the worst. Not understanding how to set the controls means we've pivoted further away than we've ever been before. I tried to send us in the opposite direction but ended up overshooting. At least I don't need to break the bad news. They can see it for themselves how far we are from home if they walk planet side, or read the sensor report.

"What was our home in our own dimension doesn't even look the same. Sure, the shape of the continents are familiar, but the vibrant blues and greens are like an animation and the moon is almost barren with only four colonies. The space between the stars is empty, not bustling with traffic. Mars is a graveyard of failed attempts to ready the place for when Earth dies. I don't doubt there are many more differences we haven't yet seen.

"After telling the rest of the crew I wasn't willing to make another jump until I'd figured out how to fix the faulty dimensional controls, or at least how we can safely use them in their current state, Travis says we need to go planet side to gather resources, but I'm not sure that's the right thing to do.

"The air is just the same as we're used to breathing, but teeming with fourteen billion people, the conditions will be worse than where we're from. The same head count of our species, but crammed together on one planet. Perhaps there are bacteria and viruses we've never been exposed to.

"But if he's right, and the others seem to agree, then it's better than making another blind jump before solving the major navigational problems. One of the more recent phenomena we've experienced is what I call scattering. We first encountered it on the second to last jump.

"We were planet side and after the countdown ran out, we woke to find ourselves away from the ship, each crew member flung across the horizontal and through time. They'd each suffered short-term memory loss, and it took us a couple of hours to reunite.

"Clutch's account was the most disconcerting. We'd landed the Mary May in a field fallow for the winter and he found himself walking around naked amongst the cows. It was lucky he hadn't wandered off too far before his memories came back and he could find the ship.

"Over the course of the next two hours, each of the crew found the Mary May, returning to find Clutch had laid out their flight clothes to spare their dignity. One by one, they arrived from a different direction.

"As far as I can tell, the scattering is a safety mechanism designed to prevent anything living from materialising inside a solid object. I hope it only affects us when we're planet side. I can't imagine what would happen if we were outside of an atmosphere, or stranded on the ground whilst the Mary May was in orbit."

Only the sounds of breathing came from the speaker for a long while, until a cough punctuated the silence.

"The memory loss is probably a side effect. That, along with the power surge sending Sapphire into hibernation to protect her organic centre and memory banks, adds to the risk of things going wrong.

"I also worry that whilst planet side, we're a target for the people indigenous to their dimension. If they don't have the same technology, we'll stick out like a sore thumb. We'll be so vulnerable. I'm not sure how many of Sapphire's systems will be available to protect us.

"I fear that the larger the number of dimensions we cross, the bigger the scatter and the longer it will take Sapphire to get back online. At least we can ease the issue by only jumping when outside a planetary atmosphere. I wonder if sticking to Travis's orders not to carry weapons might bite us in the ass.

"But enough of this opinion. I need to get on with figuring out how this thing works, or at least how I can control it. I need to experiment with alternating the phase modulators and uploading a new execution pattern…"

The voice cut off as Travis tapped the screen.

"We haven't got time to listen to it all," he said, taking the tablet from Clutch and pressing the fast-forward button. The two arrows flashed in the centre of the screen, sending the progress bar along the bottom edge travelling faster until Travis tapped again and the voice came from the speaker.

"I just can't seem to understand why the frequencies

change…"

The voice cut off as Travis tapped again, before waiting for a beat and repeating the gesture, cutting him off after barely a sentence.

"This is getting us nowhere," Travis said, frustration bunching his cheeks before touching at the slider and moving it to the far right.

The others leaned in closer, watching as Travis slipped his finger to the left a little.

"Maybe he makes more sense at the end," Travis said. Without looking up, he pressed play.

"It's like we're doomed never to go home. Despite getting closer to understanding the principles of this machine, Clutch tells me we've developed an engine fault. He says it's fixable, but it will take a few days for his mech-printers to manufacture the parts we need, so in the meantime I can't do any testing because we're stuck on the planet's surface."

"Did you know this?" Travis said, catching Clutch's eye but already finding him shaking his head.

"No. I've spent all my time working to get Sapphire up and running," the mechanic said, just as each of their gazes landed on a screen above the door showing the decreasing numbers.

"If Miles is right, we have to be off the planet in just over thirty hours," Mac said and all eyes turned to Clutch.

"Otherwise we're back to square one," Colin added to nods around their huddle.

"I'll check what the mech-printers have produced," Clutch said, turning away, but stopped when the familiar voice came through the speakers.

"Shit. No. No…"

A loud bang and commotion cracked out from the

tablet before silence followed. Everyone in the room held their breath, leaning closer to the handheld when it remained quiet.

After a few seconds, a breathy voice came from the speaker, but only the last few sounds formed words they could recognise.

"Oh no."

Its pitch rose higher than they'd heard before and an alarm sounded in the background, followed by a long hiss of air. After a few seconds, the alarm silenced and everyone in the room stared at the tablet, peering at the thin rectangle of glass and plastic even though they could only hear the odd indiscernible sound.

"It's another short out," Miles said, his tone devoid of all optimism.

Travis looked up, locking eyes with Colin.

"I think the Mary May's electrical supply isn't high enough quality for the device. I want to turn it off, unplug it from the wall, but I'm afraid then it will lose any useful information and we'll never get it going again. We'll be stranded.

"The fault has started the countdown. I don't know to where or when, but I've bypassed some of the faulty equipment by plugging it into the ship's controls and rewiring an audio playback interface on the bridge. This should stabilise us before we next jump. I need to tell the others."

Silence filled the space, but they each continued to stare, holding their breath.

"At least we're prepared this time," Miles said, his voice still flat, the edge of panic tempered. "We're going to do our best with the situation, and I've figured out an equation we can use to track everyone's location when the jump happens. If I've got this right, it appears the horizontal displacement shouldn't be too vast, but when it comes to the how far back in time they end up, I haven't figured that out.

"This should at least give everyone a head start on getting back to the ship. But I implore you, if you're listening to this, Travis, Clutch, please find me first so I can get back to work and help find the others. I'm close to figuring out how we can get back home."

After a moment in the silence that followed, Travis spotted they'd reached the recording's end. Minimising the window, he scoured the desktop and found a file named *Scattering Calculation*. Double pressing the icon, he held his breath when the screen filled with numbers and equations that made his brain hurt as he tried to follow the mathematical symbols.

Tilting the screen, he shoved the device in front of Clutch.

"Can you solve this?"

It didn't take long for Clutch to shake his head, but soon after, he raised his brow.

"No. But I bet Sapphire can. She'll be available soon," he said, grabbing the tablet and rushing down the ladder in the corner of the room, his feet clattering on the metal as he touched down on the deck.

Travis spotted the smoke rising on the new morning's horizon as Colin slowed the minibus, guiding them to the side of the dirt track. Feeling butterflies in his belly and the stench of animal waste in his nose, passing a verdant copse of trees, Travis found a gap in the thick, fruit-laden hedgerow. Noticing a green tent with bright-orange doors, the shelter within a car's length of the calculated coordinates, Travis couldn't shake the sense of relief.

Mesmerised by the crackle of a fire set a little way back from the canvas, it took him a moment to realise no one warmed their hands against the flames.

"Miles," he called out into the light wind.

When no answer replied, Travis stepped closer to the tent, finding the fabric doors tied to the side, giving a clear view of a sleeping bag and blankets weighed down with a rucksack.

As he peered for more clues, the snap of a twig caused him to turn, and he looked over to the trees where a man in black-rimmed glasses and long hair matted together in dreadlocks, his chin engulfed in a beard, stood wide-eyed with his hands pulling up shorts.

"Miles?" Travis asked, standing up straight with his mouth hanging open as the word died to nothing. "We found you," he added, unable to hold the silence for any longer.

"I guess so," the man replied, sniffing, his voice the same as the recording as he took slow steps towards them.

A smile rose again on Travis's lips until, out of the corner of his eye, a shadow moved. His head twitched to the side and he froze on the spot at the sight of a pitch-black Alsatian rushing from the trees.

With a sharp breath, Travis stepped back as the dog leapt towards him. Before he could run, the Alsatian was on him, pushing Travis to his back as he screamed, pressing his arms across his face to block the savage attack.

"Quark, no," Miles called out, and the animal pulled

away, withdrawing his tongue slick with saliva whilst rushing to the navigator's side.

Still panting, Travis scrambled to his feet, touching his face, then inspecting his fingers. Despite finding thick slobber where he'd expected blood, he repeated the gesture. With no pain or skin out of place, Travis stepped back whilst staring at the dog sitting at Miles's side, its tongue lolling out of its mouth.

"I'm sorry," Miles said. "I know you're afraid."

"I'm not scared," Travis said, rushing out the words as he glanced at Colin, who had finished parking the minibus.

"He remembers," Colin said, his expression uncertain and Travis held his breath, his eyes going wide as he stared at Miles.

"Do you?" Travis asked, his voice high and hopeful.

Miles nodded before drawing up snot with a sharp sniff.

"That's a relief. I had this whole crazy story to tell you," Travis added. "It's great to see you."

"You too, Travis," Miles replied. "Who's this?"

Travis cocked an eyebrow beside him.

"Colin. Second mechanic," he said, the corner of his mouth rising. "Everything else should start coming back to you now."

Miles narrowed his eyes as he looked at the ginger-haired man.

"I can't believe you stayed here," Travis said, pulling the navigator's attention away. "How long have you remembered for?"

Miles raised his chin. "A while. But I didn't know where to find the Mary May. Something told me I should stay here until someone came."

"Great," Travis said, looking around the campsite

before glancing at the dog, a flash of white across its left ear the only detail in his jet-black coat. "Is there anything you want to bring before we get going? By my reckoning, we have about sixteen hours to find Princess whilst you sort out where we're jumping to. You said you were close to figuring it all out."

"I was," Miles replied, but he didn't move. "Has the countdown started?"

Colin and Travis both nodded.

"Does that mean we're going home?" Travis asked, his lips turning into a grin as he looked Miles in the eye.

Miles swallowed hard, glancing at Colin, then down at his side as he ran his hand down the dog's back.

"Travis," he said, his voice low. "I'm not coming back."

15

"What do you mean, you're not coming back?" Travis blurted out as he looked up from staring down at the black Alsatian, whose tongue hung out of its open mouth. If it wasn't for the beast, he'd walk up to Miles and put his hands on his shoulders.

"I'm happy here," Miles said, the words stilted as he pushed his glasses up his nose. "I have a new home, and all I have to worry about is gathering firewood."

"What?" Travis blurted out. "Your home is the Mary May."

Miles lifted his chin, the muscles in his jaw tensing until he let it all out with a breath and a shake of his head.

"I remember everything about the Mary May. I loved being part of her crew almost as much as you do. But I also remember how hard the last six months on board were. I know we all had a difficult time, but it almost broke *me*. Here I do odd jobs for a couple of days a week and the farmer leaves me alone."

Travis peered around before his gaze settled on the chaos of the campfire. Forcing himself away from staring at the hypnotic flames, he lingered on the tent's sagging canvas before moving his gaze to a pile of dried-out dung only a few steps away.

"If it's a simple life you want," Travis said, catching Miles's eye again, "we can cover one of the rear holds in straw and smear shit on the walls. You can bring your tent and sleep in there if you like."

Miles tilted his head, his eyes narrowing as his lips

turned into a thin smile.

"Thank you," he said, raising a brow. "But I've found something else I've been missing all my life," Miles said as he crouched to run his hand down the dog's back.

"What?" Travis exclaimed, frowning as he searched the surroundings again. When Miles didn't reply, he looked around once more, unsure of what he'd missed.

"Companionship, Travis," Miles said after a moment. "Or call it love, whatever you like," he added.

As Travis turned back, he noticed Miles kneeling with his face up to the dog, who licked his cheek.

"What? That?" Travis said, spitting the words out as he drew back. "You're in love with that beast?" Shaking his head, he drew himself up straight. "I always knew you were different, but an animal?" Travis said, forcing a laugh as he turned to find Colin's shoulders slumped and his head lowered. "Did he hit his head? Was his brain scrambled when we scattered?"

Travis turned back, peering between the dog and his navigator.

"I know you don't understand. I get it, but she's my friend," Miles said as he stood. "More than that, she's always there for me. I won't leave her behind."

"But we're more than your companions, I'd like to think. At the very least, we're your shipmates. Friends even," Travis said, his voice lowering as he glanced back to Colin.

"How much do you remember?" Miles asked, catching Travis's eye.

Travis swallowed, hoping the gesture wasn't too obvious.

"Enough," he said, despite being unsure what were memories and what the others had said.

"I can see it in your eyes," Miles replied. "It's not

enough. *I* remember pretty much everything and I want more than I had."

"Okay. Maybe there are still blanks," Travis replied, tapping his finger against his temple. "But was it that bad?" he added, dropping his hands to his side.

"No. It wasn't bad," Miles said, shaking his head.

"Well then. I know my memories will come back. I remember so much about Mac and Clutch already. Miles," Travis implored, taking a step forward before glancing at the dog and holding himself back. "I've listened to your recording. You were close to getting us home. Are you really going to leave us stranded so you can live in a tent with that mutt? Am I hearing straight?"

"You are," Miles said, his voice low. "I know how you feel about dogs, so I won't ask."

"Too right you won't," Travis replied, then turned away before pivoting back around. "It's not too late to put this madness behind you. Come on," he added, beckoning him over.

"I made my decision a long time ago. I'm not changing my mind," Miles replied, locking eyes with Travis's glare.

Travis opened his mouth, about to speak, when the low thump of a helicopter sounded in the distance. Instead, he stared at Miles as the sound grew, only breaking eye contact when the thud of a double rotor helicopter rushed overhead.

As the heavy noise receded, and not looking back at Miles, Travis turned away and stormed off. Only as he settled in the passenger seat of the minibus did he realise Colin hadn't followed.

"Colin," he bellowed, pushing the door open.

A moment later, the ginger-haired man appeared from the gap in the hedge and ran over. Out of breath, he started the engine, and they drove for five minutes without either of them speaking.

"Are you really going to leave him behind because you're afraid of dogs?" Colin said, unable to stand the silence any longer.

Travis glared across the seats, and Colin twitched his head to the side.

"What?" he said when Travis remained silent.

"How old were you when the Anglo-Franco war started?" Travis asked after a pause, his voice deep but monotone.

Colin shook his head.

"Well I was ten. I don't think you were born, but you'll soon remember. They drilled it into everyone at school. Maybe you've watched the vids." Turning to stare out of the window, Travis closed his eyes as old memories he wished he could forget rolled through his head.

"My family lived on the south coast in what used to be Southampton. TV news spoke of troops massing off the coast one evening. The government thought they were posturing to apply pressure as part of a recent trade battle. The following morning in the early hours, we woke with our door smashed down to find the Francs had attacked and hit the coast with everything they had. They were rounding up everyone from our neighbourhood and parading us in the street. We were the lucky ones, and all because we came out of our homes without a fight."

Colin glanced over, then back at the road, swerving to correct the steering.

"The soldiers were cowards. They wore armour from head to toe and carried guns so big they were anchored to their bodies like extra limbs. They were too bulky to go inside the houses and bring out those who hadn't answered. Instead, they sent in beasts of all sizes, many of them dogs augmented with tech connected to an exoskeleton. Still, everyone knew they were once pets, albeit starved and frenzied, as if jacked up on drugs.

"They lined us up in the street and forced us to watch our neighbours, kids my age and younger, and women and old people dragged out in shreds. The screams drowned out our tears until silence was all that was left along with a bloody mess I'll never forget."

"I'm sorry," Colin said, pulling the minibus to the side of the road.

"Now ask me again if I'm afraid of those animals," Travis added, not looking over.

Colin stared back, and when Travis didn't speak, he shook his head.

About to say something, Travis looked away from Colin, his gaze following to an olive drab truck behind an army Land Rover Defender with a flashing orange beacon on its roof, both moving past at a crawl. On a flatbed pulled behind and held from the road with more wheels than he cared to count, stood a light-grey dome that looked like that of a plane's nose cone.

Tall poles rose high from each corner, where cameras pointed in every direction.

Feeling a deep bass hum run through his chest, his gaze followed cables snaking from under the dome to a metal cabinet laying on the back, its doors covered with flashing lights and dials. Before Travis could focus, it was gone, along with the vibration and another Land Rover following.

Travis watched as it wound its way along the road and out of view, leaving them with the queue of cars forced to crawl behind it.

"What's that?" Travis asked.

"Nothing good," Colin replied with a shake of his head.

"Let's go," Travis said. "We need to find Princess. Where did the algorithm say she appeared?"

16

"Have you seen this woman?" Travis asked, nodding towards the folded photograph he'd taken from the bunkhouse.

The middle-aged couple's conversation came to an abrupt halt as he stepped in front of them, but rather than peering at the glossy paper, they turned to each other.

After gawking at Travis and letting out a combined huff, they stepped to the side and shuffled away along the High Street.

"What are you doing? You scared them off," Colin said, joining at his side from the minibus parked close by. Travis paid him no attention, already seeking the next person walking his way, a thirty-something guy whose eyes narrowed as he watched Travis attempt to intercept him.

"We should have brought Mac if this was your tactic," the apprentice added before reaching for the photo. "May I?"

Scowling, Travis handed it over and stepped out of the way, watching as Colin forced a smile and moved from the man's path, standing instead at the side of the narrow pavement whilst angling the picture toward him.

"Have you seen my sister? She's missing," Colin asked, his voice low as the guy neared.

Much to Travis's surprise, the man stepped closer, his brow furrowing as he examined the photo of the tall, blonde-haired and blue-eyed Amazonian woman.

After a moment he stepped back, paying Colin as much attention as the photo until his gaze lingered on his unkempt mop of ginger hair.

"Stepsister," Colin said, widening his smile as his words cut the guy's thoughts short. After the man lingered on the photo for a few seconds more, looking him in the eye, he shook his head.

"I'm afraid not, but I hope you find her," he said, then walked away.

Snatching the photo from Colin's offered grip, Travis strolled along the High Street, repeating the words to everyone he saw whilst doing his level best not to glare back each time the recognition didn't rise in those passing by.

After an hour, and about to give up to form another plan, they arrived beside the kerbside seats of a cafe, the slight widening of a bald man's eyes whose arms interlocked with an older busty woman at his side jolted him with excitement.

"Sorry, no," the man replied to Travis's practiced question.

"Are you sure?" Travis asked, leaning toward him.

Rather than looking Travis in the eye, the man turned to his female companion whilst Colin stepped out of Travis's shadow, pointing at the photo, but without saying a word.

Travis glared at Colin when he refused to speak.

"Look again, please," Travis implored, softening his voice. "Our mother is distraught."

Colin nodded but stayed silent at his side as the dumpy woman glanced over, her eyes narrowing on the glossy page. She shook her head and looked up at her bald companion, but his lips were already moving.

"I've never seen her before," he replied, before

pulling at the woman's arm and guiding her around Travis and away down the street.

"He recognised her," Travis said, his breath almost gone as he stared at the man's back before they disappeared into a shop a few doors down.

"You're right," Colin replied as Travis slumped into a chair outside the cafe.

Colin took the seat beside him.

"Why wouldn't he say? Shall we go after him?" Travis asked, but before Colin could respond, the high pitch of a woman's voice came from nowhere.

"What can I get you?"

Spotting Colin's flinch, Travis looked up and found a woman standing at his side in a black apron covering the tops of beige trousers and a white blouse as she held a pen and notepad whilst waiting for an answer.

"Have you seen this woman?" Travis replied, pushing out the photo as he rounded on her reaction.

"Why?" the waitress snapped, stepping back and standing up straight, her eyes narrowing. Before he could reply, she glanced in through the cafe's open doorway.

Not saying a word, Colin pointed to the photo.

"Our sister," Travis said, frowning at Colin. "She's been missing for weeks," he soon added as he looked up at the woman.

The waitress peered back at the pair, her expression relaxing a little as she stepped closer.

"No, sorry," she said, peering down at the woman's image. "I haven't seen her around here," she added with a shake of her head before glancing back inside again. "These seats are for paying customers," she added, but without looking back.

Following her gaze, Travis lowered the photo, his eyes pinching together when he spotted who the waitress stared at. It wasn't Princess, but wearing the same uniform, Travis couldn't help but linger on the woman who hadn't noticed him. When she turned away, he felt an urgent need to check the photo, but as he did, he wasn't sure why.

With a huff of breath, their waitress was gone, stepping inside the cafe, and leaving him with a void in his chest and not understanding what had just happened.

Turning to Colin, the thought vanished as he remembered Colin's odd reactions.

"What's going on with you? Why do you keep making that strange face and pointing at the photo like you're a moron?" Travis said, but instead of pressing him for an answer, the bald man from earlier stepped into his personal space.

"I haven't got much time," he said, his voice no more than a whisper. "But you're not going to like this."

17

"I can't believe she's working in a strip club," Travis exclaimed, glancing at Colin rushing alongside him. "Where people take their clothes off on stage."

"At least we know why he wouldn't say anything in front of his wife," Colin replied, his face pale and a little out of breath with the effort of keeping up with Travis's long strides.

"How much do you remember about Princess?" Travis asked. "We would have remembered if we had a stripper on the crew, wouldn't we?" he added before Colin could reply.

Finding the street named by the balding guy as they rounded a corner, they slowed with Travis the first to spot the word Dazzle on an understated metal sign beside a pair of windowless black double doors. The two-storey building they led into was much like its other anonymous neighbours, apart from the blacked-out windows.

Turning to find Colin paler still and swallowing hard, Travis grinned before pushing at the door, a little surprised when the boom of bass greeted him, despite the midday hour. Finding Colin hadn't followed, he held back.

"Come on," Travis insisted.

"I… I…" Colin tried to say.

"What is it?" Travis asked after shooting a glance at the dark interior.

"I don't think I can go in," Colin said as Travis

glared, but Travis stepped back and grabbed Colin's arm, pulling him in behind him.

Bright lights washed down the dark walls of the anteroom and across a second set of double doors opposite. Behind a counter to the left, Travis locked eyes with a well-made up woman as they stepped in, her face fixed with a scowl as she looked the pair up and down.

"Free entry until six pm," she said, her eyes widening with what Travis wore. "But you'll have to leave before six. We don't allow fancy dress in the evenings," she added, snorting before nodding toward the double door entrance.

About to speak, Travis stopped himself when the lights flickered off as one, then returning to brightness within a heartbeat, he watched the woman roll her eyes.

"That's been happening since the big blackout yesterday," she said.

Travis glanced over his shoulder at Colin before returning to the woman.

"When did it last happen?" Travis asked, remembering what Miles had said about the Mary May's power surges that had damaged the EQuaNTS machine.

"Does this look like an information kiosk?" she said, curling her lip.

Travis raised his brow as he stepped closer to the counter.

"Okay," he said, forcing a smile. "We're looking for Princess."

The woman leaned back in her chair and laughed. "Which one?" she replied once she'd recovered.

Travis glanced at Colin, about to ask a question, but finding him more than a little green, he turned back to the woman.

"We have two Princesses on until eight," she said,

the curl of her lip softening. "Plus Verity, Daisy, Petra and Mistress Dawn."

"Uh, don't worry," Travis replied after a moment. "We'll find her," he added, but turning to the door, he found his feet planted on the spot, perhaps not ready to see one of his crewmates with no clothes on.

Forcing himself from staring at the door, he turned to the woman and found her still watching. He waited, their eyes locked as she glared, holding his gaze with her mouth slightly open.

With a glance at Colin and then back to Travis, she straightened.

"Are you sure it's a woman you're looking for?" she said, with no sign of humour in her voice.

Travis straightened up, raising his shoulders and puffing out his chest before he turned to the doors, then looked back at Colin.

Not giving him time to complain, Travis circled his grip around the man's wrist and pulled him into the tangle of bright disco lights and the flaring music. With the same dark walls as the room they'd stepped from, a bar stocked with bottles lit from above stood to the left. On the other side, a small dance floor waited in front of a raised stage, beside which stood a fat, balding man wearing headphones covering only one ear. He concentrated on something hidden behind a rostrum of sorts, with a light from a monitor highlighting the round of his chins.

Men in suits stood against the walls whilst others sat at tables at the edge of the dance floor. Each held a drink whilst their attention fixed on a short, topless blonde with a slight build gyrating around a pole in the centre of the stage.

Swallowing hard, then looking anywhere but the

dancer's bouncing flesh, Travis headed to the bar. Surprised to see Colin hadn't followed, he turned to find him still at the door with his mouth wide open as he gawked at the woman.

Watching his fixation, out of the corner of his eye Travis caught sight of the dancer's underwear flung into the air before landing on a bald guy's head. When the man didn't raise his hand to move the lace, Travis strode over to Colin and pulled him over to the bar.

A roar of applause rose from the thin crowd, and despite his best attempt, Travis caught sight of the naked woman running her hands over her body to whoops and hollers in the bar's backdrop, before gathering her things up and heading off stage. She disappeared through a door as the music quietened.

"Now put your hands together for the gorgeous Amazonian royalty, Verity," the DJ called.

Travis swallowed hard and turned with the music renewed, watching whilst biting his bottom lip as the door at the side of the stage opened and a young woman with broad shoulders in a thin red twin set of bra and knickers bounded out and up on to the stage, already moving her hips to the beat and grabbing the long silver poll.

Relieved it wasn't who they were looking for, he turned, and as he did, he bumped shoulders with a heavyset man in a black suit, whose arm muscles were as hard as concrete.

"I'm sorry," Travis said to the man's back, catching Colin still gawking at the stage as he offered his palms out in an apology.

Drawing a sharp breath as the man turned, Travis's eyes went wide when he realised not only was it a woman, but he'd stared at her photo all day.

18

"Princess?"

The question fell out of Travis's mouth as his eyes locked with the woman drawing back, her brow furrowed.

Only just noticing her black tie and dark suit, along with the lanyard holding an ID badge across her chest, he held her silent stare until a man, almost identical at first glance, arrived at her side, paying Travis no attention.

"You're first on the door," he said, and despite his deep monotone voice resounding through Travis's chest, she didn't flinch. "Sharon," he added, his brow knotting. As he stepped closer, for the first time the man noticed her staring. "Are you okay?"

The woman blinked as if she didn't understand the question, and she turned to the new arrival, but didn't linger, instead looking back at the man in the flight suit.

"Sorry," she said, acknowledging the other bouncer with a slight turn of her head whilst not taking her gaze from Travis. "Can you cover for me?"

Not waiting for an answer, she grabbed Travis by his arm. "I need a minute," she called back, not slowing as, with a tight grip, she pulled Travis across the dance floor, giving him little time to grip Colin by the arm. Neither paid any attention to his reply before hurrying through the doors at the side of the stage.

Arriving in the middle of a bright corridor, the woman urged Travis against the wall.

"Say something," she asked, fixing him with a stare, her brow bunched as she leaned closer.

With his back against the wall, Travis glanced at Colin standing out of arm's reach, then back at the woman whose hot breath washed over him.

"Like what?" Travis replied.

"It's you. Isn't it?" she said, her mouth hanging wide as she urged him to answer.

He nodded. "Yes. I'm Travis. Pilot of the Mary May."

"Fock," the woman exclaimed, stepping back as she raised her arms into the air. "Fock," she repeated, before spinning on the spot and looking up at the ceiling as she shook her head. "I'm not focking crazy."

"No, you're not. We call you Princess and you're a member of our crew," Travis said as they made eye contact again.

"What happened?" she said, almost breathless.

"We made an inter-dimensional jump that scattered everyone on board," Travis said, with Princess hanging on every word.

"I thought I'd gone mad," Princess replied, shaking her head with relief written all over her smile. "I need to know everything," she added, her breath still speeding, but Travis didn't reply as the music flared and the dancer who'd been on stage appeared in the corridor, not wearing any clothes. Neither of them spoke as they averted their eyes, listening to the padding of her feet as she drew closer.

"Alright, Sharon?" the woman asked as she neared.

"All good, Tracey. You're looking hot, as always," Princess replied when the woman passed behind her.

"Ah, thank you," she said, and both Travis and Princess couldn't help but cock their heads to watch her walk away.

"Not here," Travis said, as the woman disappeared through a doorway.

Colin squeaked as if desperate to speak, and Princess seemed to notice him for the first time.

"I don't know what's up with him," Travis said, but turned back to Princess. "How long has it been?"

"Two years," she said, her voice low as she pulled her gaze from Colin. "I woke up in a street without a stitch of clothing. I was lucky it was the middle of the night. My mind was blank. I couldn't remember anything from before. I didn't know who I was, and I couldn't stop throwing up. The police took me to the hospital, but apart from the memory loss and the nausea, the doctors couldn't find anything wrong with me. They gave me some clothes from lost property and a follow up appointment. The authorities put me in a bed-and-breakfast for a few weeks and enough money for food. I got this job and I've worked here ever since.

"Over the past six months, my dreams have been so lucid they've bled into the daylight. I'd dream about space travel and people I'd never met. You were there," she said, nodding as she stared at Travis and pressed her fingers against her cheeks. "Standing here, it's… it's all come back. Please tell me they aren't just fantasies. Please tell me there's not something wrong with me."

"You're not going mad," Travis said with a slow nod. "We're the crew of a private cargo starship, and we have an experimental device that transports us across the dimensions."

"I remember," she nodded, not hiding her excitement. "I remember Sapphire, Clutch and Miles, too. Oh my gosh," she replied.

Travis smiled.

"What happened to the rest of us? Is everyone alright? Have you found the Mary May?" she said, rushing out the words.

Travis nodded. "You're the last," he said, but couldn't make his excitement reach his eyes.

"What's wrong?" Princess asked. "Is everyone well?"

Travis tipped his head again. "We have the Mary May. Sapphire will be out of hibernation soon. Clutch is with her. Mac, too."

"I remember," she said, then held her tongue when a door opened and a dancer in purple lingerie appeared from the dressing room door.

"Alright, Sharon?" the woman asked as she passed.

"All good, Stacey. Have a good show," she replied, and only Colin didn't turn to watch the globes of the women's tight, bronzed butt bounce as she walked.

"The short guy," Princess said, looking Travis in the eye again when the music rose and fell. "Has he found a sense of humour yet?"

Travis laughed. "And he still wants to cook," he said, watching as Princess screwed up her face. "We found Miles, too, but he's not coming with us."

Princess stepped back, her expression falling. "Why?"

"He's in love with a dog," Travis replied, his expression darkening.

"Oh," Princess said, frowning. "I see," she added with a nod. "I've seen some things in my time, but... I always thought there was something odd about that boy."

Colin made another squeak, and the pair glanced over.

"Oh yeah, and Colin, too," Travis said, stepping to his side and patting him on the shoulder as Princess watched with a faraway look in her eyes.

"I bet I can make Miles change his mind," Princess said, and they both turned to find her clenching her fists.

Travis shook his head. "No. He's decided. It's hard, I know," he said. "He's burnt out, I think. He's done a lot for us."

"What good is that if we can't get home?" she replied.

"We'll find someone else," Travis said.

"Where?" she said, watching as Travis looked along the corridor as if peering past the double fire doors. "This place is like the dark ages. They've only just moved on from inventing the wheel. Where the hell will you find someone in this backwater to work on technology that's cutting edge in our time?"

"I don't know," he replied with a shake of his head.

19

"And with seven hours in hand," Travis exclaimed, beaming at the light shimmering in the clearing just ahead. About to glance over at Princess walking at his side, a shower of sparks beyond the ship caught his eye. For a moment he thought he saw horizontal lines running high beyond the trees, but as he blinked, the Mary May filled his view.

"Home," Princess said, letting out a deep breath before meeting Travis's gaze as he turned her way.

With a satisfied nod, he led her toward the already lowering ramp.

"Good job, Trav," she added, back in step.

With familiarity of the name, a warmth welled in his chest as he followed her up the incline.

"Oh, look who it is," came Mac's sharp tone, scattering his rush of memory.

"I see you've kept up with the exercise regime," Princess said, cocking her head to the side as she looked the short man up and down.

Mac turned up his nose and peered at Colin and Travis.

"Where'd you find her?" the cook said with a sneer.

"A strip club." Travis's reply sent Mac's brow rising high on his face as he rounded his attention back to Princess.

"Oh my God," he said with a shake of his head, offering his hand out as he spoke to her for the first time. "That must have been awful."

"Thank you," Princess replied, her face brightening with his concern. "But it wasn't too…"

"I mean those poor men who paid good money only to get you," Mac added, pulling his hand back and unable to stop himself from bellowing with laughter.

"She was security," Travis soon replied. "Thank goodness."

"Hey," Princess blurted out, knocking him on the upper arm with a bunched fist, but with no power behind it. "What do you mean, thank goodness?"

Travis stepped away from her glare, then raising his palms in surrender, he glanced at Mac.

"Would you want to see your sister jiggling her bits about?" Travis called out, before realising who he was talking to. "Well, maybe *you* would," he added, before taking a step away from Mac's swinging foot.

"Ah," Princess cooed, moving between them. "That's sweet, Trav. You're like a brother to me, too."

"And if I remember right," Travis said, cocking his brow, "they weren't your kind of clientele."

Princess narrowed her eyes, peering over as if deciding what to do. Then with a shrug, she looked down at Mac.

"Anyway," she said, leaning forward, "how are you, you stunted prick? I was hoping you'd joined Miles's commune of freaks," she added with a flurry of laughs, before Mac stepped up and took her in his arms, whilst Travis pretended he didn't see the cook closing his eyes to savour the embrace.

"Get a room," he called over his shoulder, then when after a few seconds they hadn't split, he headed to the dim bridge.

Finding Clutch laying on the floor face up with half of his body under the front dashboard, Colin and Mac soon joined him.

Light pouring through the windscreens stopped him from questioning the mechanic. Instead, his attention went to the trees dominating the new view. After blinking to the slight haze that wouldn't clear, and remembering what he thought he'd seen from outside, Travis glanced to the far right, glimpsing a pair of parallel cables almost touching the extreme of their starboard wing.

Scanning the remaining view of leaves rustling in the light wind, he peered to the port side and along the dirt track, but couldn't find the minibus through its myriad of twists and turns.

"Are we ready?" Travis eventually said. Clutch slid out and rubbed his hands down his streaked set of overalls, rising to his feet and peering around the controls and screens with their vibrant colours washed out by the day's light.

"Sapphire," Clutch called, flicking what looked like a random switch. As he spoke, he raised his chin high as if talking to someone on the next floor up. "Are we ready for transition when the timer runs out?"

"All indications are that the Mary May is at full operational capability, but following replacement of any part of the engine system, the manufacturer recommends a thirty-minute half power test burn," the disembodied female voice they'd last heard on the recording replied. "Welcome back."

Travis nodded, locking eyes with Clutch, both of them wearing bright smiles.

"Welcome back, Sapphire," Travis said, glancing over his shoulder and catching Mac's raised brow, before he spotted that where the monitors had shown the decreasing count, they were now lit with dials and charts, text readouts and CCTV camera feeds of the inside of the ship, whilst also pointing outside to give a three sixty view of their surroundings. Only a single screen at the rear showed the remaining seven hours counting down.

"Thank you, Travis, but I was always here. I was in a hibernation state," Sapphire said, her literal reply enhancing the warm glow Travis felt inside.

"Sapphire, what can you tell us about the dimension we're due to jump to?" Travis asked to nods of approval from Mac and Colin, who with Clutch, gathered around the pair of pilot's seats as they listened for the reply.

"I am not connected to EQuaNTS and I have no other information on which to extrapolate any details," she said.

Travis looked away as brows furrowed and expressions fell.

"It's just wired up to the controls, not Sapphire's interface," Clutch explained.

"Well, let's hope Miles's parting gift was only a small jump and we don't scatter across the universe again," Travis said, catching Colin's attention. "What else can we do?"

Clutch and Mac looked back, their mouths opening.

"We need to do whatever we can. There's no way I can do another ten years out there alone," Clutch said, glaring at each of them.

"Grey looks good on you." Princess's voice cut through the gloom and they turned to the door to find her standing in the flight suit Travis had last seen laid out in her bedroom.

"Sapphire, Clutch," Travis said with a renewed enthusiasm, "is there a way to track crew members outside of the ship if it happens again?"

Clutch's eyes narrowed to a squint as he turned his

head in thought.

"Good idea," he replied, nodding after a moment.

"Yes," Sapphire soon added, making Travis's eyes light up. "We have transponders. But the nature of the event will require them to be inside your bodies. Clutch, fetch your thickest set of rubber gloves and every drop of lubricant you can get your hands on."

"Huh?" Clutch replied, his eyes going wide.

"No focking way," Mac said, racing across the deck and jumping up to his chair behind the pilot's seats. "If anyone comes near me with grease, I'll ram my foot where the sun doesn't shine."

Erupting with laughter, Travis closed his eyes and put his head to his chest, but when Sapphire didn't speak, his laughter slowed.

"Sapphire, you're kidding, right?" he eventually said.

"Yes. I was making a joke," she said in her monotone. "The nature of the scattering event removes all non-organic matter from your person, rendering the solution unworkable."

Breathing a sigh of relief, Travis rubbed his head as he tried to think.

"Sapphire, is there a way to stop us from scattering again?"

"Not with our current level of technology," she replied.

"So without Miles we're at the mercy of what he's programmed into EQuaNTS?" Travis added, sending each of them looking at Clutch, who still nodded.

Movement caused them each to turn to Colin, who'd raised his hand as he stood from leaning against one of the few parts of the bulkhead not peppered with lights or controls.

Travis cocked his brow.

"What are you doing?" he said, but Colin just kept silent and his hand high.

Travis looked at each of the crew before his attention landed on Princess. A smile rose on his lips as he nodded.

"Colin has a little problem," he said, still looking at Princess.

Princess looked Colin up and down just as Travis stepped toward him.

"I think he has an issue talking around women."

"Yeah, that's right," Clutch said with a glint of recognition in his expression as Princess glared at Mac, who'd burst into laughter. "It caused a few problems at work."

"Listen, boy," Mac said as his laughter slowed. "You don't need to worry about Princess. She's not a real woman."

Princess stepped over and slapped him on the leg as Travis moved over to Colin, and leaned in to whisper in his ear.

"If only we all scattered to the same place," Colin said, his voice so quiet. "We'd at least be together and would stand half a chance of getting through this again."

Travis nodded as he repeated the message to everyone.

"Yes," Princess exclaimed. "Even if we were naked."

Mac grimaced and Colin went bright red.

"And we need to make a bigger sign for the audio controls," Mac said, glaring at Travis. "Maybe put it *next* to the buttons this time."

"Where were you standing, Travis?" Clutch asked, and Travis looked back, uncertain. "When we jumped, I mean. You lost the least amount of time."

"Right there," Travis said, pointing to the foot of his seat and where he'd found his overalls laying in a pile.

"Princess was in her bunk. Someone was in the main hold, going by the piles of clothes."

"I was in the mess," Mac chipped in.

"Sapphire's control space," Clutch added. "What about you, Colin?"

Colin shook his head and shrugged.

"Don't you worry, lad," Clutch said, nodding as he turned to Travis. "It's the only variable I can think of that was different between the six of us when we jumped."

"So let's all stay on the bridge when it happens," Travis replied, sending nods around the room before watching Princess turn. "Where are you going?"

"This is all well and good, but if it doesn't work, we're back to square one. I'm going to convince Miles to do the right thing," she said, raising a brow, as if inviting someone to convince her otherwise.

They each turned to Colin, who with his hand back in the air as he repeated his noise, they found him staring at a monitor and the view from the port side.

Travis stepped up to his side.

"I don't think that'll be necessary," he said as the pair stepped back, pointing to Miles on the screen in shorts and a t-shirt emerging from the dirt track.

20

Travis rushed past Colin to the far port side of the bridge, peering along the path where he spotted the unmistakable figure in thick rimmed black glasses.

"Sapphire, let him see us," Travis called out, then remembering what he'd seen earlier, he glanced over his shoulder to sparks raining down from cables as the haze fell away and the view rushed into sharp focus.

"I couldn't do it," Miles said, his voice low as he stared at the carpet of sawdust when the walkway landed a few steps ahead of him.

"Do what?" Travis replied, waiting in the opening whilst doing his best to ignore the man's downcast look.

"Strand you all here," Miles said, sniffing. "What Colin said played on my mind. Plus, it looks like it's going to rain and I hate getting wet."

"What did Colin say?" Travis asked, not glancing back despite the footsteps behind him.

"It doesn't matter now. Let's get you all home," Miles replied, lifting his head only enough to take a step forward.

"That's great, but why aren't you overjoyed? This is where you belong," Travis said, reaching out and slapping the thick steel of the Mary May's hull. "And it means you're going home, too," he added, before narrowing his eyes with a question to Colin, who arrived by his side.

"I'm fine. I'm happy," Miles replied before swallowing hard. "I mean, I guess I can be. Someday," he added, putting a foot in front of the other, stopping only when Travis drew in a sharp breath as he caught movement in the treeline behind Miles.

"What's that?" Travis asked, his voice raised, and he leaned out using the metal door frame as an anchor, only to draw back with a sharp intake of breath when he spotted the black fur of an Alsatian and the flash of white across its ear.

"What the hell are you doing?" he said, glaring at Miles before stepping backwards and into the hold.

"Oh shit," Miles said, almost under his breath as he turned. "Stay, girl," he called, his voice tailing off as he turned back to the ship.

Travis barely noticed, his thoughts instead filled with the memories from his childhood he was desperate to get rid of. A Golden Retriever's snarl. Its fur matted red with pink sinew stuck between its teeth.

"Quark," Miles snapped, a tone so sharp it pulled Travis out of his memory to watch the dog plodding toward them. "Stay there, Quark. Be a good girl."

After another step, the dog did as Miles insisted, settling on her stomach and resting her snout on the dirt with her paws on either side whilst staring at the navigator.

"She must have followed me. She was supposed to stay with the farmer. I'm sorry," Miles added, turning from the bottom of the ramp.

Still glaring at the animal, Travis stepped out of the hold's shadow, the silence hanging between the pair only broken as Miles sniffed and wiped at each eye.

"Good to see you, brain box," Mac called, appearing at Travis's side. Recognition flared in Travis's mind, bringing with it a flurry of memories of the man in shorts, many of them together in the mess room with a drink in hand as they set the universe to rights. "Ah balls," Mac added, spotting the dog just as Miles turned.

Travis looked away from the wet line down the navigator's cheek, glancing instead at the dog whose ears had pricked, her head lifting as Princess joined the group with a clank of metal under her feet.

"I can't wait to see what your kids look like, you freak," Princess said, and Travis found her lips curled with a warm smile, then without meaning to, his gaze fell on Miles.

He soon looked away from the deep setting of his eyes.

Heads turned as the dog rose to her paws, and Travis drew back, even though the black beast cocked her head the way she'd come.

Miles gasped, as if afraid she would wander away, but his breathing settled when the dog turned back toward them.

"Stay, Quark. Stay," Miles said, holding up his palm.

"Oh, man. She's cute," Princess said.

"No," Travis snapped as Princess stepped past him, heading down the ramp.

"Oh, come on. You're afraid of war dogs, not this cute little puppy. You said yourself those were augmented with tech and pumped up on drugs," Princess replied, taking another few steps before dropping to her haunches.

"No. Princess. Stay on board. Everyone must stay on board," Travis called out.

She glanced back with an eyebrow raised, holding his gaze for a long moment before lifting herself tall and stepping closer to the dog. Quark lifted her head as if sniffing the air before glancing back the way she had come.

Travis joined the others as they peered down the dirt track for what he might have spotted, paying little attention to Quark edging forward.

"My sensors detect a vehicle…" Sapphire's voice echoed out from the hold, causing them each to turn with a jolt back to the ship. "… With six lifeforms on board has arrived nine hundred and twenty-eight metres and fourteen centimetres off the port side."

Ignoring the dog, they each shared a look.

"The power surges," Travis said, glancing behind him as if able to see through the ship. "We landed near power cables and I think every time we cloak and de-cloak we send out an electrical surge which disrupts the local grid."

"Huh," Miles replied, but Princess nodded.

"That makes sense," she said, then leaned closer to the doorway. "Doesn't it?"

Despite them all sharing another look, no one replied.

"Sapphire, how long ago did we land in this location?" Princess asked.

"The timing varies dependent on your point of observation. Petroc's first law dictates that time is relative…" Sapphire said, until Princess interrupted her.

"Sapphire, from the indigenous people's perspective, when did the Mary May land here?" she rushed out the words.

"Sixty five earth hours ago," Sapphire replied. "Or Sixty point eight zero common time units."

"Two days," Travis blurted out, nodding. "The same time as the big power cut."

"Huh," Miles repeated with a frown.

"You've been too busy making hybrids to watch the news," Mac said with a flurry of laughter, which soon tailed off when no one joined in.

"And after that we started seeing loads of police, and the helicopters buzzing overhead," Princess added.

"That's not normal for this place?" Travis asked.

"No," she replied. "It's always been a sleepy little backwater since I've been here."

"Sapphire," Travis called out as he raised himself straight. "Initiate cloak."

"I am unable to comply with that instruction whilst the port side entryway remains open," she replied in her matter-of-fact tone.

Shaking his head, Travis took a step further down the ramp.

"Princess, back inside. Miles, if you're coming, then get your butt in the door," he said, stepping forward and about to reach out for his arm when he realised Quark was sitting at the navigator's heel with no one having noticed.

"Fock," Travis exclaimed, reeling back and almost tripping over his own feet.

"We'll keep her out of your way," Clutch's voice boomed out from the hold, startling Travis, who shook his head to clear his surprise. He turned to find the ship's mechanic stepping out and leaning over, rubbing his thumb across his fingers as he offered them out to the dog.

"You won't even know she's on board. We can keep her in the rear hold," Princess added.

Travis wouldn't meet her gaze, despite her manoeuvring to get into his eye line.

"You never go in there," Clutch said.

Not wanting to see the need he knew he'd find in each of their expressions, Travis peered past them all, searching the dirt track to ensure the new arrivals weren't already in view.

"He'll keep the rats away," Mac said.

"We don't have rats," Travis snapped. "And dogs chase cats, not rats."

"Okay. It will keep the space cats away," Mac quipped.

"That's not even a thing," Travis said, not realising until it was too late that he'd made eye contact with Miles and saw the glimmer of hope in his eyes. "You all know what I went through. So stop even thinking about that thing. We've got to go. I don't think these people are coming to offer us the keys to their planet."

"Ah, don't worry. It'll be engineers from the electricity board. We'll give them a fright of their life and they'll look like loonies when they report it. We'll be long gone before any cavalry arrives," Clutch said, watching as Princess nodded.

"The lifeforms will be in sight within forty-five seconds," Sapphire said. "And they're carrying devices capable of propelling metal projectiles at supersonic speeds."

21

"Oh fock," Mac replied. "Guns."

"Why didn't she just say guns?" Travis asked, turning to Clutch, his tone high as he shook his head. "Why is she so literal?"

Clutch shrugged, not looking from the darkness at the end of the trail.

"Come on. This is getting serious now," Travis called out, looking anywhere but his shipmate's eyes before turning and taking long strides back up the ramp. He told himself it wasn't time for emotion. "Sapphire, raise the cloak as soon as everyone is on board."

"Yes, Travis," she replied in her even tone, to the sound of footsteps echoing in the hold with Travis making his way to the bridge. "Cloak engaged," Sapphire said moments later as the bridge door slid almost silently back into place behind him.

For a long moment he stared out at the trees, relieved when he spotted the slight haze obscuring the leaves' fine detail.

After taking the pilot's seat and gripping tight to the armrests, everyone but Princess soon joined him, each of them, apart from Colin, taking a seat in the group of four on the raised platform without discussion.

Colin looked between the free seat in the same group, and the one beside Travis, but Travis looked away, as if making it clear that wasn't his place. His attention then caught on the controls and he realised he knew the purpose of each of the buttons, dials and lights, even though he still couldn't read the labels.

"Princess, give me an update on the new arrivals," he said, the words coming as a reflex when she walked through the door.

"They're coming into view now," Princess replied after a few moments. Gone was the playful tone, replaced with a professional, clipped reply. "Five persons. Human. All dressed in black and each carrying what Sapphire has identified as automatic assault rifle projectile weapons."

"Can she calculate if the weapons have enough energy to breach the hull?" Travis replied, unsurprised at her response.

"It's borderline."

"Miles," Travis called, his tone unchanging. "What do you need from us to finish your work?" When Miles didn't reply, Travis turned, swivelling the chair. Catching sight of the six hours shown on the countdown, he locked eyes with Miles. "You said you'd figured it out," Travis added with a raise of his brow.

Coughing into his fist, Miles cleared his throat and swallowed hard.

"I said I was close," he replied. "I think I've figured out how to control it. If we don't want to scatter, then we'll have to make a series of short jumps until we find the right destination. It will take a bit of trial and error, but I think it'll work."

Not waiting for Miles to finish, Travis glanced over at the CCTV screen Princess stared at, watching the group of dark figures stand up from crouching before wheeling around in circles. Eventually, their tight postures relaxed.

"That's great news," Travis said with a glance at Miles. "We'll get in orbit and leave you to get on with it," he added, before looking at the controls.

About to press a button, he paused and turned back to Miles. "How did you know where to find us?" he added, as the thought came from nowhere.

Miles turned and gestured to Colin still stood in the centre of the room, looking lost.

"Colin told me. In case I changed my mind."

"Thank you, Colin," Travis said with a smile before turning away. "Sapphire, prepare us for take-off. We haven't got time for the test burn. Are the people outside at a safe distance from the thrusters?"

"Yes," she replied. "If you raise the power to no higher than eighty percent."

"Roger that," Travis said, already reaching for a series of controls to his left. "Let's get well out of Earth's atmosphere before we jump."

"Are you sure you want to leave the planet?" Sapphire said, her voice causing Travis to pause and swivel in his chair, then question the room in silence for anything he might have forgotten.

"Yes," he said, his tone not filled with its usual confidence. "We're ready to leave, unless there's anything I've overlooked."

"If we leave now, we'll strand the remaining crew," Sapphire replied.

"We're all here," Travis blurted out, turning around in the seat and counting each head. "Six of us."

"Sapphire," Mac said, cocking a brow from his seat. "Run emergency programme delta four."

Without further word, the windscreen dimmed as did the perimeter lights before the familiar pair of blue lips floated above the flight controls with the message playing for the second time.

Miles's rotating image came first and each of them

glanced up to his likeness and then to the man in person, nodding as they confirmed it was him. Albeit, in need of a haircut.

"Miles, the ship's navigator, despite being equipped with intelligence in the top quartile, he has the social skills of a goat…"

No one laughed and continued to stare at the depiction.

"That's a dangerous game, Travis," Princess said, her voice low.

"What?" he replied with little vigour.

The image soon swapped to Mac, but other than a few tuts, the room remained silent when Princess's likeness appeared.

"This is Princess. Don't fock with her. Look in gyms or back water bars."

Travis relaxed as she smiled, sending bubbles of laughter around the others.

"A military veteran with a distinguished service career…"

The pilot's image came and went.

"Still a moron," Mac added when Clutch was the next to appear.

"…Is the only one with a hope of bringing me out of hibernation."

Travis leaned forward toward the mechanic's likeness, which highlighted how much the man had aged.

"And Colin is next," he said. About to turn, he held still when a brunette woman with a short, military style haircut appeared on the screen, his stare lingering on her stunning smile that made his heart heavy with a deep longing.

"Astra is the junior pilot with ten years of experience in the military. She's disciplined and a stickler for the rules and we don't know why she lowered herself to join this rag-tag bunch of misfits."

"Holy shit," Travis exclaimed, swivelling around and glaring open-mouthed at the crew, who each mirrored his expression.

Almost as one, they turned towards Colin, but didn't linger, instead fixing on the six hours remaining on the countdown, then to the loud bang from outside.

"Fock," Travis said, letting the word slip as his head filled with memories he hadn't known he'd lost. "She was in the cafe."

Part 2

22

Jabbing a button, Princess changed the camera feed, not looking up as Clutch scrambled past Colin.

Colin's dazed stare lingered on Travis, his mouth falling open. Whilst Clutch rushed to peer through the window at the source of the loud noise, Travis, oblivious to the sound, pulled out the photo from his breast pocket. He stared at the worn edges with Princess's image smiling back, then looked up at Colin, his eyes narrowing before he peered back down and turned the photo around, drawing a deep sigh as Astra's grin beamed back from the glossy paper.

"What are you seeing, Clutch?" Princess called, her attention switching between the monitor and over to the engineer leaning across the controls. "Sapphire, damage report," she added before he could reply.

"The Mary May has sustained no damage. As far as the sensors report, there has been no impact with the hull."

"Clutch?" Princess called out. "What's going on out there?"

"They're huddled in a group. It looks like they're arguing," he called, still concentrating on the view.

"Travis," Princess snapped. "Travis," she repeated when his head didn't lift. With a jab from Mac by his side, Travis looked up, his brows knotted as he peered over at the short guy, then followed his motion toward Princess.

"I saw her," Travis said, his voice soft and eyelids

heavy. "At the cafe. Only moments before we found you."

"We still have time, Travis," Princess replied, nodding, her voice low as she pointed across the bridge to the remaining monitor still showing the countdown.

Travis stared at the six hours and change, the fall of each second adding weight to his shoulders.

"Yes, we have," he replied, eventually looking back and standing tall. "Let's go get her."

"What about these jokers?" Clutch asked, nodding through the side of the windscreen.

"Jokers with guns, my friend," Miles added, his voice quiet.

"And what do we do about him?" Mac said.

Travis turned, unsurprised to find the stumpy man's finger outstretched to Colin. His eyes met with the ginger-haired man who looked back, his face as white as a sheet.

"We'll figure something out," he replied, lifting his chin before stepping up to Colin and patting him on the shoulder.

"What's the plan, Trav?" Clutch called, his voice rising in volume as Travis stepped across the bridge and toward the door. He stopped and turned to the mechanic.

"I'm not letting anyone stop us from bringing her home. We'll drop the cloak and scare the shit out of them," he said, his expression devoid of any cheer.

"I say we ramp the engines to full and get the heck out of dodge," Mac butted in. "Whatever carbonised mess we leave behind won't be our concern."

"Mac," Princess blurted out, glaring over, but turning away when Colin raised his hand.

"What is it?" Travis said, watching as Colin's eyes

flared, but when he didn't open his mouth, Travis drew a deep breath through his nose and stepped closer, putting his ear near Colin's mouth.

"No," Travis snapped, glaring as he pulled away. "We're a cargo ship. We don't carry weapons and we're not mercenaries."

"And," Princess quickly added, "there's no need to hurt anyone," she said, her voice low as she stared at Mac. "Let's calm the hell down."

Mac bunched the corner of his mouth, and with his eyes narrowing, he nodded. Clutch returned the gesture just before Travis turned and left the bridge, with Miles following.

"Sapphire, display the port external camera feed on the main cargo bay monitor," Travis called out as he arrived at the closed entry ramp door.

Miles passed by and headed through another door.

A split-second later, Travis spotted the five men on the screen, each dressed in black and standing in a huddle with their arms raised. Many of their fingers pointed at each other as if they were arguing. The tallest of the group wrenched the long gun from another man whilst two others in the same uniform held the guy back.

"Sapphire, decloak and lower the ramp," he said, pushing his back against the hull as light appeared from the ramp's seam, growing brighter as he concentrated on the video image. Their focus held on each other for a few seconds more until the eyes of the guy at the centre of the melee went wide and as his hands dropped to his side. His mouth moved, then one after the other, the rest of the men turned, their expressions soon mirroring his as they twisted around to face the ship filling the clearing.

"Put your weapons down," Travis shouted, leaning close to the doorway whilst keeping his back against the hull. As he spoke, each of the men rushed to grip where their weapons held slack on their straps, raising the muzzles toward the opening.

"I said put your weapons down," Travis snapped. "We don't want to hurt you, but I will protect my ship and crew." Despite his voice booming from the cavernous space, other than a quick glance to each other, none of the soldiers moved.

"Sapphire," Travis said in a near whisper. "Vent oxygen from the port exhaust nozzle in a one-second burst."

A short but high hiss of rushing air sounded from outside and the men flinched their weapons higher, taking a step back.

"Drop your weapons, now," Travis called again, concentrating on their every reaction. "I'm authorised to use deadly force to protect ourselves."

With a glance to the person on his left, the man in the middle was the first to respond, his movement tentative until his speed increased and he angled his weapon toward the ground. His lips moved, but Travis couldn't tell what he'd said.

"Sapphire," Travis whispered. "Repeat the last instruction."

With their eyes going wider still, one by one, they lowered their guns in slow motion.

"Place your weapons on the ground and take five paces forward," Travis shouted, watching as, with a glance at each other, four of them did as he ordered. "All of you," he snapped. "Don't let one man's stupidity get you erased from your Earth."

Two of the men turned to their colleague, shouting something Travis couldn't quite hear, but whatever they'd said was enough for the remaining man to set his gun down before forming up with his colleagues.

"Good," Travis called, nodding to the others who'd appeared at his side.

Princess looked back, her brow bunched, whilst Colin bit his lip. Mac and Clutch stared at the monitor with their eyebrows drawn together.

"I'm coming out," Travis shouted, turning back to the screen. "If you make a move, it will be your last."

"Travis, no," Princess gasped, reaching out despite not standing close enough to stop him.

As daylight hit his face, he spotted the sun was already behind the trees. With the light faded, he stared at the men, each of them gawking back with their mouths hanging open. Travis couldn't tell if they were staring at the ship or were gawking at him standing at the top of the ramp.

When none of them rushed to grab their weapons, Travis stepped down the incline.

"We don't want any trouble," he called after another step, raising his hand when his leading foot landed amongst the wooden chips.

As his weight settled, the man to the right who'd been reluctant to drop his weapon, shifted, then turned to run.

"Travis," Princess called, her shout echoing from inside the hull as his eyes locked onto the man. About to turn in hope he could scrabble up the ramp to safety, a shadow rushed past him as a call bellowed out from the hold.

23

"Quark," the call echoed out from the hold.

Already guessing it was Miles standing at the head of the ramp, Travis didn't turn. Instead, feeling as if time had slowed, he watched the dog racing across the sawdust as the man in black stooped, his gloved fingers touching the metal of his long gun before Quark barrelled into his side, knocking him away. Within the blink of an eye, an agonising scream filled the air as Quark clamped her mouth down on the soldier's arm and shook her head.

The pained call sent a shiver down Travis's spine as an image from his nightmares flashed into his head.

"Quark," Miles shouted again, pulling Travis back from the past. "Stop, or he loses the arm for good," he shouted at the top of his voice.

The men turned back, gritting their teeth as two of their number raised their arms to show their gloved palms.

Miles rushed down the ramp.

Travis glared at the five men as he followed, picking up their rifles as he passed by and throwing them into the tree line.

"Good girl," Miles said, his voice calm, despite the agonising cry from the man Quark had only just released. As the last of the weapons disappeared into the undergrowth, the piercing screams settled into a low moan.

"Is he alright?" Travis called over his shoulder as he

stared at each man, catching only a glimpse of Miles leaning over the guy on the ground.

"There's barely a scratch," Miles called back. "Good girl," he added in a more playful tone, as he kneeled in front of the panting dog whilst she slobbered and licked his face.

"On your stomachs," Travis shouted, forcing himself not to linger on the sudden switch in the dog's temperament. "Do anything stupid and she'll tear you apart. Do you understand?"

Despite not saying anything, in unison the men dropped to the ground as Clutch, Princess and Colin ran down the ramp to join them, pulling the men's pistols from their holsters and sending them to join the other weapons in the undergrowth.

"No, Colin," Princess snapped, but despite her quiet voice, Travis looked over, spotting Colin pointing a pistol at a man in front of him.

Princess stepped up, taking the gun and throwing it with the others.

"Who are ya?" the man who'd stood in the middle of the group said, his throaty voice thick with a Scottish accent.

Despite glancing at him, Travis didn't reply. Instead, he continued to search each of them in turn.

Pulling radio packs by their cables that wound inside the men's clothes, the small black boxes of electronics joined the weapons in the trees. Then using the long black zip ties they'd also found, one by one they ushered them with their arms behind their backs, securing their wrists whilst encircled around a tree.

"What are you doing to us?" the Scottish guy said, wincing as Travis tightened the ties around the man's hands.

"I just need you to stay here for a short while. We won't hurt you, if you behave," he replied as he stepped to meet the man's gaze. "We're not here for trouble, or to take anything of yours. We'll soon be on our way."

The guy stared up through narrowed eyes. "Where are you from?" the man said, his thick grey moustache rising and falling as he spoke.

About to leave, Travis paused, lingering on the question. "Southampton," he eventually replied, watching the man's brow twitch before he raised his chin.

"What is that?" the man asked, nodding with hooded eyes through the trees.

"It's better for everyone if you just forget you ever saw us," Travis said, glancing over to the Mary May looming in the clearing.

"That's a tough ask," the man replied, before Travis rushed away when he heard a sudden growl, followed by a shrill scream from the clearing.

Jogging from the trees, Travis realised the light had faded fast, but the thought fell away when he spotted Miles pulling Quark from another figure in black, with Princess glaring along the track.

"Any sign of anyone else?" Travis called out.

"No," Princess shouted with a shake of her head, already throwing the man's pistol aside and pushing him onto his front to tie his hands. "It's the driver," she added, as Travis stared at Quark, watching the jet-black animal relax from resembling the beast that haunted his childhood nightmares and morphing into the panting, sloppy pet lapping her long tongue across Miles's face.

"We'll talk about this later," Travis said, catching Miles by surprise as the man in shorts pulled Quark back toward the ship.

After strapping the sixth man to a tree with his colleagues, hearing the blades of a helicopter close overhead, Travis ran from the tree line towards the ship.

"Everyone back on board. We're getting out of here," he called, racing across the clearing.

"Do you think there are others coming?" Clutch asked, standing back on the bridge and watching as the view through the windscreen shimmered.

"It's only a matter of time. If they found us once, then they'll find us again," Travis replied, just as his gaze shot to the countdown, and the five hours remaining.

"Quicker than we can find Astra, I bet," Mac said from his seat.

Travis turned on the spot, his eyes narrowing as he peered at the short man. Although he knew his words were only a flippant remark, they lingered until Miles appeared at the doorway.

"She's back in the hold," Miles said, swallowing hard as Travis glared over.

"That's no family pet," he replied, forcing himself to keep his voice low as he looked to Princess and then Clutch. Neither of them responded.

"I…" Miles said, cutting himself off and swallowing hard. "I might have forgotten to mention she's a retired police dog."

Travis pinched his lips and lifted his chin.

"At least you can control her," he replied with a nod, realising everyone was looking at him. "Sapphire," Travis said, still concentrating on Miles. "Prepare for atmospheric flight. As soon as it gets dark, we're moving. And ensure the door to hold four is locked tight."

Colin lifted his arm.

"This is going to get boring very soon," Travis replied as he glared at Colin's sheepish expression, but still he moved in close.

"Why don't we just go now?" Colin whispered with a glance over at the countdown that had already lost the best part of another hour.

"We can't fly cloaked," Princess chipped in.

Colin nodded, not needing any further explanation.

"What are we going to do about him?" Mac asked, nodding towards Colin. "He's a stowaway of sorts."

Colin cowered, stepping back, but Travis patted him on the shoulder.

"He thought he was part of the crew, and I'm in part to blame for that," Travis said, moving towards his seat.

Mac lifted a brow and raised his chin, but Travis just continued to look at him.

"We'll think of something, but not right now. Colin has been a friend to us all and we owe him much," Travis said, then looked away, turning to the younger man. "You're more than welcome to stay on board. For now, at least."

Colin replied with a shallow nod and his lips turned into a deep smile.

"That's agreed then. You can help me look for Astra," Travis said, watching as Colin's nod grew more rapid.

With those words, the crew dispersed to their stations, apart from Mac, who settled back in his seat and closed his eyes.

Miles pored over maps on his screen, whilst Princess and Clutch left the bridge, leaving Colin marvelling at the array of controls and Travis flicking the switches and buttons spread out in front of him.

After ten minutes, Princess and Clutch arrived back just in time for Miles to raise a hand and beckon them all over.

"I've found just the place," he said, looking up at Travis, then at Princess standing at his shoulder. Tracing his finger across an aerial view of the surrounding area on the screen, he followed the road as the image moved beyond the trees, winding between a smattering of houses that grew in number. The buildings soon packed in side by side until the entire area was a mass of roofs of all shapes and sizes.

His finger soon stopped, hovering over a vast space covered in concrete with weeds between the cracks and spattered with rubble. Two giant dirt circles stood side by side in the centre of the site.

"It appears to be abandoned. The database shows it's some sort of old gas storage depot."

"Good find," Travis said, before stepping away to the starboard edge of the windscreen and peering out. "Sapphire, are we ready to launch?"

"We have not yet undertaken the manufacturer's recommended engine burn, but apart from that, yes, the Mary May is ready for atmospheric flight," Sapphire replied.

"Everyone strap in," Princess called out, even though all but Colin were already moving to their seats.

Colin remained standing in the middle of the bridge, trying not to make eye contact with anyone.

As Travis pulled at the belt attached to his seat, he clipped the four points of the harness at his crotch, then looked at Colin, lingering for a moment, before glancing over to the seat next to him and drawing a long breath.

"Go on," he blurted out. "But it's not yours," he added as Colin jogged across the bridge. "Is everyone ready?"

"Aye aye, Travis," they each replied, almost as one.

Travis glared over at Colin.

"Do not touch anything," he snapped, and Colin pulled his hands back from the edge of the console, tucking them into his armpits.

Travis leaned forward and pressed a button to the side of the nearest console, which edged his seat forward, pushing him right up to the joystick and an array of surrounding buttons and dials.

"Miles, lock in the coordinates," Travis called.

"Coordinates locked in," he replied.

"Going dark," Travis said, and after pressing a switch, the strip lights around the bridge fell dark, then all but a cluster of dials and instrument lights close to where he sat went dim. Finally, the slight glow from outside that no one had taken notice of disappeared. With another press of a button, a low rumble vibrated through the ship, but it soon rose in pitch, then faded into the background.

"Clutch, status report," Travis said, his voice low.

"Both main engines are in the green. Thrusters, too," the engineer replied.

"Sapphire, de-cloak," Travis said, noticing the lack of the shimmer as he pushed the handheld throttle forward and a vibration rose through his seat. "I'll take it low and slow," he said, not directing the words to anyone in particular, as they each felt the slight unsteadiness of leaving the ground.

With the joystick gripped in one hand and the thruster held in the other, which he only let go of to press a button or twist some dial, he stared at the CCTV feed and watched the ground fall away. Rising above the trees, he lingered on the branches blown to the side by the engine's thrust, and with a press of his hand, they tipped forward and headed in the motion's direction, leaving the clearing behind.

Swinging the ship through a turn, Travis eased them over the canopy of leaves until he made out the dark road where he guided them along its path, glancing between the controls, the CCTV feed and through the windscreen where the darkness punctuated with the distant glow of lights across the horizon.

A split-second pause in the vibration, and a rattle that followed through the ship pulled Travis's attention away from the monitor.

"What was that, Clutch?"

"All green. Just a slight dip in output from number one. She's just bedding in," Clutch replied, his voice giving Travis the confidence he'd hoped for.

Looking ahead, he concentrated on a green line superimposed on the windscreen, guiding him to their destination as the dim lights grew brighter on the horizon. Almost mesmerised by the view, Travis raised his brow when a voice spoke from his side.

"Have you got enough light?" Colin whispered.

Travis turned, surprised to hear him speak, even quietly.

"I've trained for these conditions, don't you worry," he said, just as the blink of red light in his peripheral vision and the sharp ping of an alarm broke the calm.

"Military aircraft on an intercept course detected," Sapphire said, her tone devoid of any urgency.

24

More blinking lights joined those already seeking attention across the bridge just as an orchestra of sounders added to the calls to action.

"Sapphire, silence the alarms," Travis called, and almost before he'd finished the words, the high noises were gone but the myriad of lights continued to flicker, flaring bright in the low light.

Each of the crew craned their necks, straining to peer out of the windscreen into the dark night, despite knowing if they saw something approaching it was already too late.

"Sapphire, time to intercept?" Travis called out. "Princess, can you track it?"

"Twenty seconds," Sapphire replied.

"I have it on our port side," Princess said. "She's coming in quick."

"Can they see us?" Clutch called out.

"There's no way of knowing," Princess replied.

"How good is this Earth's tech?" Travis said, his voice stern as he shot a look at the seat beside him.

Colin shook his head, his whole body shaking as he opened his hands to show his palms.

"What does that mean?" Travis snapped, but seeing Colin's eyes wide, he breathed out a sigh.

"He's a bus mechanic. How would he know?" Clutch said from behind.

With a shake of his head, Travis turned back to the windscreen. Leaning forward, he pressed a button beside a second screen, the table of numbers replaced with a series of green concentric circles and a line projecting from the centre. As the line swept clockwise around the circles, small triangles surrounded with a series of numbers illuminated.

Travis counted five elements, but picked out the triangle rushing from their port side with ease.

"Miles, find me somewhere to set down quick smart," Travis called.

"Already on it," Miles replied, his words distracted.

"Sapphire, shall I take her in lower?" Travis asked as he scanned the dark horizon.

"Engine flare has a high probability of attracting additional attention from the ground if you reduce altitude below twenty-five," she replied.

"Got it," Miles butted in, just as his radar screen replaced with the daytime aerial view of a wide patch of grass at the rear of a house.

Travis blinked at the sudden light ruining his night vision.

"Are you sure it's big enough?" Mac blurted out, his chair creaking as he leaned to look at Miles's console.

"It'll be tight, but she'll fit," Miles replied, just as the guide projected on the windscreen moved, pointing to their new course with Travis already leaning on the joystick to send the Mary May to follow.

"Sapphire, deploy landing shield and initiate cloak as soon as we're on the ground," Travis said, his words clipped as he leaned in the opposite direction of their inertia.

Their stomachs lurched as Travis wasted no time dropping them through the air where they slowed just above the ground, a flash of white rushing across the windscreen which soon vanished, replaced with a space obliterated in a section of wooden fence.

No one spoke as if afraid the Mary May's hull were paper thin. Instead, they leaned forward in their seats whilst Travis looked up high through the windscreen and then at the triangle rushing past the dead centre of the radar screen. Hearing nothing through the hull, its die-straight course tracked to the other side of the monitor.

"Whatever it was, it's gone," Travis said, letting go a long breath as he peered at the row of houses with just the width of their extensive gardens between them and the ship.

"We can't stay here," Mac whispered, and Travis slowly twisted in his seat, rolling his eyes and shaking his head as their gazes met.

As he turned back to the windscreen, light engulfed the bridge.

With his vision settling to the brightness from the port side, Travis held his hand up against his eyes in hope of protecting against the worst of the floodlight.

"Here we go," Travis said under his breath, as a silhouetted figure stepped into view less than a length of the ship away. The figure leaned forward to examine where the ship stood, sending panic flaring in his chest that Sapphire hadn't initiated the cloak.

Taking a slow, deep breath, he wrapped his fingers around the throttle and took hold of the joystick.

About to give the command, he held his tongue just as the figure turned and disappeared, the light going out a few moments later.

"Sapphire, decloak," Travis called out, and wasting no time, he pushed the throttle, thrilling their stomachs as they shot into the air, leaving behind the space in the fence, the bark of several dogs and three indents in the ground that would be difficult to explain.

The thought of the owner scratching his head when in the morning he spotted what had happened to his garden made him grin, and by reflex he turned to his right, the smile growing larger on his lips. But it melted away when he saw Colin sitting in the chair beside him and not who he'd expected.

Angling the joystick, he turned away and pushed down the feeling.

"Sapphire, threat analysis," he called.

"The population destiny of the surrounding area means the Mary May is at significant risk of being spotted," she replied, and Travis pushed the thruster forward a little more as he guided the ship through the night.

As the ship settled on its giant legs five minutes later, Travis blew out a breath that the cracked and neglected concrete held underneath her weight.

"Sapphire, repeat threat analysis."

"No significant threats detected whilst the vessel remains cloaked. Lifeforms litter the landing site, but their heat signatures remain small and offer no risk," she replied, as a long yawn pulled air deep into Travis's lungs.

"Sapphire, what's the local time?" Miles asked, and they each turned to the four remaining hours on the monitor.

"Nineteen hundred hours," Sapphire replied.

"Let's hope the cafe's still open," Princess said.

As each of the crew unbuckled their restraints, Travis jumped from his seat and rushed across the bridge.

"Shall I come with you?"

Travis shook his head as he rushed toward the door. "You're the only one here that can fly if you need to get away," he said.

"You didn't call it flying last time," Princess replied,

her brow low with concern as he glanced back.

"Take this," Clutch said, intercepting Travis halfway to the door, and walking beside when he hadn't slowed.

Travis glanced at the metal watch Clutch held out and with the time piece strapped to his wrist, he stared at the screen as it filled with digits matching those of the countdown.

"Shit," Miles called out as the bridge door slid out of Travis's way. "I've done it," he added, and Travis stopped himself, turning along with the rest of the crew toward the navigator, where they found him leaning over his screen as he tapped at the surrounding keys with a fervour.

"Done what?" Princess said, the first to join at his side.

Miles shook his head as all but Mac gathered around.

"Yes. Yes," was all the navigator said, but the words were meant only for himself. "It's right," he added, looking up for the first time as his head bobbed up and down.

"Miles," Travis snapped, his voice booming around the bridge. "Start talking. We haven't got time for this."

Miles continued to nod as he caught Travis's eye.

"Of course. Sorry," he said, rushing out the words, then sniffing as he rubbed his nose. "Yes. I had to be sure I'd done it. And I have."

"Done what?" Travis replied, doing his best not to shout.

"Sorry," Miles said, pushing his glasses up his nose, then looking back down at the screen. "I've figured out the co-ordinates for the jump."

"To go home?" Travis asked, his eyes widening as he locked eyes with Miles.

Miles nodded, his cheeks flushed.

"Straight home?" Mac said. "None of those little jumps you mentioned?"

Miles continued to nod, his mouth fixed with such a wide smile it looked almost painful.

"I found a way to access the data stored in the EQuaNTS' memory and from there I figured out each jump's relationship to the others. Using Fourier analysis, I modelled the ship as a series of waveforms, and then applied it to the data…" he said, continuing to hurry the words.

"Miles," Travis interrupted. "The short version, please."

"Sorry," Miles replied. "I can get us home in one jump by using the data stored in the EQuaNTS."

Travis looked up and caught Princess's eye, then he turned to Clutch, his smile bright.

"Great job," Travis said, his smile falling away as he glanced at his watch face. "Now I've got to go."

Distant light glowed across the horizon as the end of the ramp clanked onto the concrete, and feeling a chilly breeze across his face, Travis stepped out from the hull's protection.

With the moon a quarter full, he took in the view, listening to Colin's steps behind. With no light shed by the Mary May, and with the lamps on each tall pole dotted around the abandoned compound unlit, he couldn't make out the surrounding high brick wall he knew lay beyond the thriving weeds, some of which stood taller than him.

The view to the left was much the same, but on the other side, a single bungalow stood in the distance with its windows lit but obscured in the most part by a tall wooden fence.

Already peering into the night for a route through the undergrowth, as their feet touched the cracked ground, Travis felt the shiver of static down his spine.

About to take his first step in the dark, a flicker of light by the house caught his eye, and he spotted a pair of small faces in the low moonlight watching out from a missing fence slat. Their stares soon turned from the invisible ship, falling instead on Travis and Colin as their petite mouths hung open.

"It's just kids," Colin whispered at his side. "No one will believe them."

Not looking away, Travis replied with a single nod, then raised his index finger to his mouth as the two small faces watched the pair in the low light disappear between the weeds.

It took them five minutes to find and navigate a route, tracing the lines in the concrete before they arrived at the crumbling brick wall.

"I'll give you a boost," Travis said, already dropping and bending to his knee.

With only a second of thought, Colin lifted his foot to Travis's cupped palm, before Travis hoisted him into the air and Colin hooked his hands over the edge.

"All clear," Colin whispered after peering each way, before Travis boosted him higher and he disappeared, followed by the sound of his feet slapping on solid ground.

Travis wasted no time in following, reaching with a jump to catch the edge. After drawing himself high, he soon dropped on the other side, and was about to pat Colin on the back when a flash of blue lights reflected off the wall, sending his attention instead to a police car drifting toward them.

25

Tearing his gaze away from the blue lights as the police officers pushed open their doors, Travis glared at Colin. It didn't take long to know by the shake of Colin's head that running wasn't an option. Instead, Travis glanced at his watch before turning to the approaching men.

Ten minutes had already passed since they'd left the ship, and his shoulders dropped, knowing the pair walking over would eat into so much more time than they could afford.

"Hi," Travis said, looking at the portly man on the right with silver hair and a black moustache, his skin leathery and tanned, even in the moon's dull glow.

The other man stood taller, with a more athletic frame and his face clean of hair. Glowing with youth, Travis couldn't help but wonder if it was his first day on the job, or if his voice was yet to break.

"What are we up to, gentlemen?" the older officer asked, flicking his gaze between the pair whilst Travis marvelled at the myriad of attachments strapped to each of the bulky protective vests.

"We just looked over the wall. That's all," Travis replied, glancing at Colin nodding at his side.

"A look?" the officer said before squinting at the top of the high wall, then turning back to meet Travis's eye as a question hung on his cocked brow. "And what did you find?"

"Nothing," Travis said, shaking his head. "It's too dark," he added as the officer glanced at his colleague.

"Are you on your way to a fancy dress party?" the taller officer said.

"No," Travis replied, looking down at his flight suit before shaking his head. "Are you?" he asked, his face straight.

"Are you being funny with us?" the older officer replied as he took a step closer. "Have you been drinking?"

"When I get a chance," Travis replied, his head tilting to the side, not hiding his uncertainty at the question.

"He means alcohol," Colin said, leaning close.

"Of course I mean alcohol. Have you been drinking alcohol?" the older copper snapped.

"Not since this morning," Travis replied.

The officer lifted his brow.

"Are you known to Police?" the thin officer asked as he pulled out a notepad and pen.

"No," Travis said, chuckling to himself. "Look, we've got somewhere to be. It's just wasteland. I don't think we've done anything wrong."

The older officer narrowed his eyes, staring at the weathered brickwork as if he could see straight through.

"What's your name?" the younger cop said after a long moment and in a voice deeper than Travis had expected.

"Travis."

"Full name," the man said, scribbling.

"Travis Baxter," he replied.

"Date of birth?" the policeman asked.

"Thirteenth February, nineteen ninety-one," Travis replied, peering over the officer's shoulder as a pair of large green trucks rolled past, before staring into the open backs where four rows of soldiers sat, each dressed in black like the men they'd left behind in the woods.

Colin and Travis shared a look.

"Have you got any ID?" the older officer asked, leaning forward and raising his chin as if it wasn't the first time of asking.

Before Travis could reply, the young officer held his hand up when a voice came from the radio hanging from his loaded stab vest.

"All officers on this channel. Bronze command requests urgent assistance at Claremont Drive. I repeat all available officers to Claremont Drive on the outskirts of Oglethorpe."

As the tinny female voice quietened, the cops looked at each other, the younger one lifting his chin with an unspoken question.

"Claremont Drive," the older guy said. "That's about fifteen minutes away, isn't it?"

His colleague nodded, closing his notepad before he turned and ran to the driver's side door.

"We've got your name," the round officer said, glaring at Travis. "And if I hear reports of something untoward happening again tonight, we'll find you."

Giving the pair no time to reply, they watched the round man rush back to the car before it u-turned and raced away with the siren screaming.

"This way," Colin said without prompt and Travis followed at his side, silent as he focused on the road ahead. Rounding a corner, and with houses and low-key shops bunched together along the street, they found the route choked with a sea of red lights as the white of exhaust fumes trailed into the night.

"It's late for a traffic jam," Colin said, the first to speak since they'd left the cops.

Travis peered along the road as they walked, moving past cars that, despite still crawling along, couldn't overtake them. Knots tightened in Travis's stomach with each step, desperate to get to the High Street and contact Astra.

Taking a deep breath and after what felt like an age, they turned into the road, relieved to find chairs and tables still laid out on the footpath, most filled with customers sipping drinks from mugs and long-stemmed glasses whilst plates of food spread in front of them. With the rest of the High Street shops dark, the cafe's lights spilled out into the street through its tall window.

"Let me do the talking," Travis said before laughing to himself. After jabbing Colin with a playful punch on the arm, he quickened his pace across the road whilst glancing at his watch, reassured when he saw there was plenty of time left to convince Astra.

With a spring in his step, Travis led the way inside, noticing the waitress they'd spoken to that morning. She'd spotted them too, her head twitching his way whilst glancing between a table of four animated middle-aged women she pulled plates from and the new arrivals.

Ignoring her hurry to finish her task, Travis peered around the room, soon repeating his survey with a frown when he couldn't see any other member of staff, let alone Astra. His eyes lit when another woman, a short blonde with her hair in a ponytail and pale skin, pushed through a curtain of beads across an opening in the rear wall.

Spotting the pair, she beamed a wide smile from over the counter.

"What can I get you?" she said, her voice high and sweet as she showed off a set of perfect white teeth, but before Travis could open his mouth, the other waitress rushed in from the side, clattering plates onto the counter.

"Thank you," the first waitress said to the other

woman, who seemed to understand she'd been dismissed and began gathering up the soiled crockery. "How can I help?" she said to Travis, her voice brisk.

"We met this morning," Travis said, forcing on a wide smile.

The woman lifted her chin, but her expression didn't change.

"We're looking for the other waitress. She was here this morning," he added, doing his best to ignore her stone-faced expression. "Is she around?" he continued when the woman didn't speak.

"We were outside," he added, turning and pointing through the door as if it would help. "She was inside," Travis said, whilst tilting his head when she still hadn't answered. "Short, dark hair. Tall. Do you know who I mean?"

"Weren't you looking for another woman?" the waitress replied, her brow wrinkling as she crossed her arms.

"Yes," Travis said, his eyes lighting up. "That's us," he added, glancing at Colin at his side. "And we found her."

The wrinkles in the waitress's brow deepened.

"What's her name?"

"Astra. It means star," Travis replied. "But she might be using a different name."

She narrowed her eyes as she turned her head as if unsure what to make of what he'd said.

"Why would she be using a different name?" she said, leaning a little closer as her eyes narrowed further.

"Uh, it's complicated," Travis replied.

"No. No, it's not," she said, shaking her head and standing up tall. "You're not welcome here. If you don't leave right now, I'm calling the police."

Not hiding his confusion as he looked at her side on, Travis felt Colin's grip on his shoulder, pulling him back as he leaned up to his ear.

"We should go," Colin said.

"She's our friend," Travis added, shaking his head and raising his hands, but lowering them when the waitress flinched.

Stepping backward, guided by Colin, Travis fished out the photo from his breast pocket and turned it over.

"You're disgusting," she shouted. "It's you. You bastard. When I found her, she was in a mess. She was sick for days. Traumatised. You're scum," she said, her voice shrill. "Jessica, call the police. Now."

26

"Fock," Travis shouted, paying little attention to Colin pulling him onto the dark street, or to the people looking up from their conversations as he pushed him along the road.

"She knows where she is," Travis replied, still resisting Colin guiding him away.

"I know," Colin replied, hurrying him along the High Street as a siren grew louder in the background.

"I can't believe she called the cops. Why was she so upset?" Travis said, peering past Colin as the background call rose, soon spotting the haze of flashing blue somewhere beyond the buildings.

"We'll have no chance to find her if the same officers stop us again," Colin replied, still blocking his way as he tried his best to usher him along.

Travis locked his legs as he gritted his teeth.

"Maybe if we talk to the police, we can explain that we don't mean her any harm," he said, as Colin pushed against his chest, before stepping back and shaking his head.

"Really?" Colin said, raising his brow, his sharp tone causing Travis to turn from the blue and look him in the eye. "So, what do you plan to say? Are you going to tell them you're from another dimension? A dimension where people fly spaceships like we drive cars?"

Colin turned side on to point back the way they'd come. "Oh, officer," he said, waving his hand about. "Did I mention that on our journey to your world we mislaid our crew, but don't worry," he continued, turning back to Travis and pointing at his face, "we've found everyone, but we still have to convince the waitress that we're not perverts and we're not trying to kidnap her colleague. Honest. Oh, and we've only got a few hours to do it in, so please can you help?" he said, his brows knitting together.

"Huh?" he added, folding his arms across his chest when Travis continued to look back at him.

"Are you finished?" Travis replied, tilting his head to the side and watching Colin's expression stiffen, as if with a sudden fear of what he'd said. Still, he nodded and Travis replied with the same gesture. "I take your point."

Colin let out a slow breath as Travis reached out and pinched his shoulder.

"I like this side of you," Travis said with a grin. "Who'd have thought you could be so assertive?"

Colin's eyes widened, but as if remembering what was going on, he glanced around with Travis's gaze following as they spotted a police car in the distance.

"We need to go," Colin said, and together they hurried along the street, sweeping around a corner, then turning down the first side road.

"She said Astra was a mess," Travis said, slowing and scratching at the back of his neck. All the joy in his expression had fallen. "And sick for days. Do you think she's alright now?"

"Sapphire said jumping affected people in different ways," Colin replied, walking at his side. "Anyway, you saw her. How did she look?"

"She seemed fine. Radiant, even," Travis said, a little unsure. "I think. I didn't see her for long."

"Where now?" Colin asked as he nodded, then peered around a dim junction where the road headed in three directions.

Travis stopped and glanced back the way they'd come, lingering on the short section of the High Street he could still make out.

"Maybe we should wait until the cafe closes," he said, his eyes lighting up as he glanced at the couple of hours counting down on his wrist. "Then we follow her home. Perhaps Astra is staying with her? It'll be cutting it fine, but…"

"Have you heard yourself?" Colin said. "That's called stalking. On this version of Earth, at least."

"I suppose," Travis replied after a moment's thought. The enthusiasm in his voice drained. "But what other choice do we have?"

Colin looked along the road, then turned to Travis with a shake of his head.

"That's settled then. I'm waiting here and watching the cafe for as long as we have left," Travis said, and before long he peered along the road's bend and toward the cafe.

"Fock," he called out, stepping back into the building's shadow when the word came out louder than he'd hoped.

Colin edged past him, his stare fixing on the police car parked outside the cafe.

"What now?" Colin said at his shoulder whilst staring along the road. "It gets worse," he added, before making room for Travis at his side where they both squinted to get a better look as the waitress followed the two cops they recognised, each holding white paper cups as they led her to the police car.

"There goes our best chance," Travis said, his voice flat, watching as the car turned in the road before heading off in the opposite direction.

"That's it," he added, standing up tall. "We've got no other choice. We'll have to tell the others."

Walking in silence side by side, urged on by the time racing down on his watch and despite his empty stomach throbbing with despair, Travis couldn't stop himself lingering on every face they passed and peering down every road as they retraced their route back to the Mary May.

Glancing into cars and through any windows not obscured, several times they'd slow, both their heads turning to a woman with short hair waiting at a bus stop, or a figure they found to be a shadow when they searched for detail.

Each sighting brought with it a flash of hope, but each letdown excavated the pit in his stomach to another depth.

"Maybe Miles has figured out how to delay the jump by now," Colin said, but Travis didn't respond, his attention instead on a police car heading towards them in the opposite direction, followed by a convoy of green canvas-sided trucks.

"Huh," he said, when the vehicles cut in front of them and headed down another road.

Colin replied with a shake of his head as they continued to walk. It wasn't much longer before they arrived at a pair of rusted iron gates with the familiar tall weeds on the other side.

Placing his hands on the risers, for a moment Travis couldn't bring himself to climb, but remembering the countdown, he did.

As Colin landed beside him, he spotted the solitary house, which they used as a beacon to guide them through the undergrowth until they saw the space cleared by the landing shields. Neither of them spoke as the Mary May shimmered into view.

Shaking his head as Colin followed him up the ramp, Travis avoided eye contact with both Princess and Mac, who waited in the hold, their expressions falling to match his with no need to ask a question.

"It was her," Travis said, his voice low as he slumped into his seat on the bridge. "She's somewhere close, but we don't know where," he added, staring at the remaining ten minutes on the screen. "I just needed more time."

"Is there any chance we can delay the jump?" Princess asked, looking around the bridge before her gaze fell on Miles.

The navigator was already shaking his head. "I checked and triple checked. If we ever want to go home, now is our only chance."

"We have options," Mac said, but when Princess looked over, he didn't elaborate.

"He's right," Clutch added, tapping his fingers on the seat back.

"Yes, you do," Travis said, not looking up from the deck. "But my only option is to stay and find her."

"That's not what I meant," Mac replied.

"Nothing anyone can say can make me go without Astra. I'm not leaving her behind," Travis said as he stood and looked up from the deck, his shoulders lifting. "I'll grab some of my things."

"What?" Clutch blurted out.

"You can't..." Mac said, but ran out of words.

"No," Princess added, stepping toward him.

Miles stayed quiet, his head lowering.

A squeak came from by the door, and everyone turned to the foreign noise to find Colin standing with his hand raised.

"Just spit it out, Colin," Princess said.

Colin's eyes flared wide, but he stayed quiet.

Travis let out a sigh and stepped over, leaning close. After a moment, he shook his head.

"No," he replied. "I can't ask them to do that."

"Do what?" Princess asked, her voice low as all eyes darted between Colin and Travis. When Travis shook his head, Clutch rushed up to Colin and leaned in close, nodding as he listened.

"He's asking why don't we all stay," Clutch said, turning back to the group, cocking an eyebrow. "We could, you know."

Travis turned back to the deck in silence as Princess, Miles, Mac and Clutch looked at each other.

"I'll stay," Princess said, lifting her chin and followed by nods from around the bridge.

"We can't let the Mary May jump on her own," Travis said, looking at Miles and then Princess, his brow low.

"We'd lose her forever," she added, shaking her head, and Colin turned back down to the deck.

"But maybe…" Miles said, leaning up to the console and peering at his screen as he ran his finger down the glass. His movement grew more energetic with each pass until, with a shake of his head, he glanced over at Travis, then to the five minutes remaining on the countdown. "The only way we can do it is if we unplug the EQuaNTS."

Travis's expression lifted as he stepped to Miles's station, then his eyes narrowed, uncertain why his expression lacked any form of excitement.

"What does that mean?" Travis said, but it was Princess that replied.

"The only way we can get home is using the data from the previous jumps," she said. "That's right, isn't it?" she asked, looking over at Miles.

"The machine's memory is volatile," Miles said, nodding.

"So if we unplug it, we lose all its data?" Princess said, as Miles continued to nod.

"It would mean my algorithm has no reference points to plot the new course once we've found Astra," he replied, his voice growing quieter with each passing moment.

"You all should jump. I'm staying here," Travis said, lifting himself tall. "With or without you."

"Me, too," Princess said, and drew a deep breath as she moved to stand beside Travis.

Without saying a word, Colin stepped in at her side, his cheeks going bright red and his eyes wide as she put her arm around his shoulders and pulled him in close.

"I'll come, too," Miles said, jumping from his seat and tucking in beside Colin.

All eyes turned to Clutch, who remained standing at the opposite end of the bridge.

"Are you coming or going?" Travis asked.

Clutch swallowed hard, then looked at Mac. But as the chef caught his gaze, Clutch turned to Travis.

"We haven't got time not to be sure," Travis said, his eyes narrowing on the two minutes remaining.

Clutch swallowed hard for the second time, then he closed his eyes.

"I've had ten years away from you guys and I don't care for another minute apart, but if we're not going home soon, then it means it's back to the one thing I haven't missed. I don't know if I can…" he said, opening his eyes and glancing again to Mac before quickly turning back to Travis. "…Go back to the same routine."

Travis paused, his brow lowering with thought, but as Clutch nodded to the back of Mac's head, he raised his eyes.

"I understand," Travis replied. "And I think you speak for everyone. We can deal with that."

"Really?" Clutch said, turning his head to the side.

Travis nodded.

"It's overdue."

Clutch's face lit up, then after glancing at the countdown, he jogged to Miles's side.

They all stared at Mac.

"What?" Mac replied, raising his hands as they continued to glare. "Of course I'm sticking with you idiots, but do I have to get down from my seat?"

Before the last of the words came out, Travis ran across the room, his feet clattering on the deck as he raced through the hold, only slowing as he arrived at the door behind which the EQuaNTS waited.

When it didn't open, he glanced around, but finding no one had followed, he looked back at the door in fear he was in the wrong place. Then he remembered his earlier command.

"Sapphire, unlock hold four," he said, rushing out the words just as a tone rang out from the watch, showing one minute remained.

Drawing a deep breath, he reassured himself there was still plenty of time as the door slid open.

And there it was, the cone-shaped machine that had caused so much trouble, but just as Travis took his first step past the door, he spotted the dog lying beside it.

As the door closed at his back, Travis's feet fixed on the spot.

"Oh shit," he said under his breath, unable to do

anything but stare at the animal looking right back.

Despite not needing to check the watch to know their time was almost up, all he could do was stare at the drool hanging down from the beast's mouth.

Amidst his terror, his thoughts flashed to Astra, and how she must have felt waking naked and alone. With no memory, she must have been distraught. Despite recalling her iron will and a sense of her true warrior nature, waking up with no idea of who she was or where she came from, she must have been so lost. He couldn't bear to think of it any longer.

That was genuine fear, and here he was about to leave her isolated for the rest of time because he was scared of an animal. He shook his head, and from nowhere, laughter bubbled up from his chest.

"Look at me," he said under his breath, and the dog turned her head to the side, her ears pricking up. "Such a big man who can't face his fears," he added, puffing out his chest as if to prove his point.

Looking at his wrist, his gaze held on the ten seconds remaining.

He drew a deep breath, clenched his fists, and let out a guttural scream. The dog jumped to her feet, bounding forward.

Focusing on the power cord, Travis dodged to the right, then surging towards the cable, he reached out, ignoring the pressure of the grip at his ankle until he tripped just in reach.

Falling, he pulled as hard as he could, knowing he couldn't forgive himself if he didn't at least try his best.

27

Travis's vision darkened as his head hit the floor, sending stars across his view as everything stilled. Blinking, a warm, stale breeze rushed across his cheeks. Unsure what he'd find when he could see again, his lids creaked open to find the panting dog up in his face.

Adrenaline forced his eyes wide, pushing back only to find her weight upon him. When a warm wetness touched at his chin, still blinking, he remembered what he was there for.

As thoughts of the timer counting to nothing overtook his fear, he sought his hand somewhere beyond the animal.

Letting go of the plug, a surge of elation pushed the panic away when he realised he'd disconnected the machine, until a question reared its head.

Had he done it in time, or had they lost Astra forever?

Having to settle with the fact he'd have the answer soon enough, he couldn't help but smile with relief at the dog still in his face, her mouth clamped around a bright yellow tennis ball. The ball released as she opened her mouth, and it fell to his chest before bouncing across the floor.

"Have you been eating your own shit?" Travis asked, unable to stop himself from laughing as the dog's head twitched to the side.

"Quark," a voice snapped from behind, and in an instant the weight pressing down left Travis, allowing him to sit up and wipe the slobber from his face as he sought the monitor by the door.

SIGNAL LOST.

"Did we jump?" Travis blurted out, confused at the message flashing back.

Spotting Miles kneeling and stroking Quark's dark coat, he hurried to repeat the question.

"No," Miles replied, although the uncertainty in his brow seemed to stop his expression settling either on a smile or a frown.

Travis stood and dusted himself off.

"Fock," was all he could say, the word elongating in his mouth as he watched the man and his dog sitting on the floor. He looked away only as a long yawn forced his mouth wide.

"We all need sleep," Miles said, not taking his eyes from the dog as his hands ran down her back in a slow, repeating rhythm.

"There's something I promised I would do first. You'll want to see this," Travis said, striding towards the door before stopping and turning to catch Miles's eye. "Oh, and you need to clean that dog's teeth, or change what the hell you're feeding her," he said, leaving Miles knitting his brow as he stared down at the animal.

"Right. I'll put the dinner on then," Mac said when the door to the bridge opened and Travis strode in, followed by Miles.

Finding everyone where they'd last been and the lone monitor displaying the same flashing message as in the hold, he raised a hand.

"It's done," Travis said, watching nods follow around the room before glancing over to Clutch and his slumped shoulders as he turned toward the deck.

Mac was the only one to move, jumping from his chair.

"Wait," Travis said, and Mac looked up, his brow rising with a question.

Travis glanced at Princess and then at Miles at his side, watching the almost imperceptible nods he'd hoped for.

"Mac," Travis said, turning back to the short man. "You're a valuable member of the team," he added, trying his best not to glance at the steel toes of Mac's boots. "But you can't cook anymore," he said, fighting his instinct to back away.

When Mac didn't launch into a tirade of abuse and instead cocked a brow, Travis narrowed his eyes and shot Princess a look, where he found her expression matching his.

He turned back to find the corner of Mac's mouth raised.

"You little shit," Princess said, just as a bubble of laughter filtered around the room.

"How long have you known?" Travis asked, taking a moment over his words, uncertain, but hopeful he'd read the situation right.

Mac still hadn't spoken, only opening his mouth as if about to speak. Instead he burst out in a gravelly laugh, holding his belly as tears streamed down his face. One by one, the others couldn't help but join in.

"Your first mouthful," Mac said when his laughter slowed enough for him to speak. "You're a terrible actor."

"Why didn't you say anything?" Clutch called out, the only one not laughing as he stepped into Mac's eye line.

"You all deserved it. You're too soft," he said, the laughter bubbling up again. "And once I'd started, I thought I'd see how long you'd put up with it. Never in a million light years would I have thought you'd let me do it for so long."

"We were trying to spare your feelings," Travis said, his voice hardening.

"Feelings?" Mac snorted. "Since when have I had feelings?" he added, as the rumble of laughter rose again.

"It's been months," Travis said, shaking his head whilst looking over at each of the others doing the same.

"For some of us it's been a long time since…" Clutch said, but stopped himself as if not wanting to push his luck.

"Serves you all right. Get a backbone," Mac said, his smile dropping.

"So you won't mind if someone else cooks?" Travis replied.

"I don't give a toss. I still have no focking clue what anything tastes like," he said, his words tailing off just as he shook his head. Travis thought he saw a glint of something in his eye.

"Okay. I'll take your word for it," Travis said with a shallow nod, then glanced at Princess, who'd raised an eyebrow. "Well, just because you won't be the chef anymore, doesn't mean you get a free ride," he said, watching as Mac's chin raised. "We'll find you some additional responsibilities. We can't have you lounging around all day."

Travis was almost sure he saw the start of a smile, but it soon turned back to a scowl.

"Do whatever you need to," Mac said, turning away before heading through the bridge door.

"Right. Okay," Travis said, not ready to think about what the changes could mean. "I know we're all keen to find Astra, but we all need sleep. In the morning, let's get down to it. Miles, I don't care what you say. Spend as much time as you need to figure out what we can do with the EQuaNTS. I know it will be harder…"

"Near impossible," Miles chipped in.

"Near impossible," Travis corrected himself with a nod. "I know it's going to be tricky, but other than navigating, I need you to spend as much time as you can figuring out how we can get back home."

Miles nodded, and it was then Travis spotted Quark sitting at Miles's heel as the navigator leaned to stroke down her back.

"And at some point," Travis added, raising his brow. "We need to decide what we do about that," he said, nodding towards Quark. The rest of the crew stiffened. "Clutch, I'm sure you have plenty to do."

The engineer nodded.

"Tomorrow, Colin and I will bring back Astra, whatever it takes," he said, locking eyes with Colin. "Then we'll climb into orbit where it's safe whilst we work out a new plan."

Standing around the bridge, they each looked back at Travis, but none of them made any effort to move.

"Travis," Princess said, her voice soft, a weak smile on her lips. "We'll make it work."

Travis pushed out his chest. "Too right we will," he said, lifting his voice and raising his clenched fist up high. "Now go get some rest," he added. "I'll sleep here. Colin, you take my bunk."

"Do we need to set a watch?" Princess asked. "We might need to leave in a hurry."

"Sapphire will keep an eye out," Travis said. "And we're not going anywhere without Astra."

With each of the deserted bridge lights dark, Travis reclined in his seat, staring at the photograph resting on the dashboard, the rectangle of paper lit from below by a cluster of dimmed switches.

Concentrating on her smile, Travis trawled his memory for the woman staring into his eyes, her arm over Princess's shoulder. Despite finding nothing but a jumble of feelings and the odd snapshot, those were enough to know how special she was to the crew and that he'd made the right decision to do everything in his power to get her back.

Swallowing hard, he shook his head as his thoughts turned to how she must have felt during those first few days.

With an ice-cold pressure against his chest, a memory of her sitting in the seat beside him flashed into his head, as together they swerved and cajoled the Mary May through an uncharted asteroid field, one of the many birthplaces of the scars in her steel.

The plate underneath the nose came from hiding in a debris field, forcing the ship's vast hulk behind a mass of moving rock as they tried to stay in the shadows and where Sventic pirate's sensors couldn't reach. They'd found the pair of ships stalking a sector they'd plotted a course through to shave a couple of days from a trip.

Travis took ownership of that mistake, a little eager on the right-hand thruster when a boulder half the size of the Mary May, but far more pointy, confronted them as if from out of nowhere. With a joint effort, they were lucky to leave with only a slice through the ship's primary hull, which missed all the sensitive electronics housed behind the secondary skin.

They'd hoped one day to have her repaired with more than the hastily-welded titanium plate, but as their order book grew, the months the repairs would take were too much and it faded to a pipe dream, growing further out of reach with each new scratch and scrape that added to her character.

The rest of the imperfections… well, their responsibility was under more debate. A rogue laser blast from a pair of mercenary border control fighters more interested in shooting first than checking out their credentials was something he'd like to have forgotten about.

Astra had threatened to hunt them down and repeat what they'd done to the Mary May but to their faces, and despite being much faster than the cargo ship, it didn't stop her and Miles tracking them to port. Whilst she found the pair and kept them busy in a bar, it was Princess and Clutch who broke past their ship's meagre defences to make a few modifications to the controls that would see them getting their own back when they next needed their weapons.

Focusing back on the dim controls, Travis was about to say something, but remembering he was alone, closed his mouth. Still, he looked over to the empty seat, but wished he hadn't. His smile had fallen a long while before he glanced around as the bridge door slid open.

"How much of her do you remember?" Travis asked.

"She's my best friend," Princess replied. "She's everywhere I look. You?"

"Bits and pieces," Travis replied as the woman's silhouette stood beside him, looking at the photo. "More feelings than anything."

"I get it," she replied.

"Were we...?" Travis asked, but stopped himself.

"Together?" Princess asked when he hadn't finished.

"I guess," Travis said, watching her shake her head from the corner of his eye.

"No. But I don't know why," she said. "Although you fought like cats and dogs."

"What, like you and Mac?" Travis replied with a snort.

"No," she said, letting a laugh escape. "Nothing like that. Anyway, I came to make sure you were getting some sleep."

"I will soon. Hopefully," he said. "I sense tomorrow will be an interesting day."

28

With the morning sun rising high, and wearing the Luke Skywalker t-shirt and jeans from the previous day after Travis took up Colin's suggestion to be less conspicuous, the pair were about to step down the ramp when Clutch called over, rushing from the mess door.

"Take this," he called, his voice echoing across the hold as he reached out. Unable to see what he offered, other than something that would fit in his palm, Travis twisted around for a better look.

With each step of Clutch's scuffed, heavy boots clattering on the metal floor, Travis's intrigue grew as he stared at the man's stained hand.

"What the...?" Travis said, scratching at the back of his neck, startled by a glimpse of the metal band across the object curled in Clutch's grimy fingers.

Rather than speaking, the mechanic bunched his cheeks and offered out his open palm where the metal around the middle of the Universal Tool reflected the overhead lights.

"But that's..." Travis said, the rest of the question sticking in his throat.

"If there's a chance it might help," Clutch said, still holding out the dark rectangular metal box, which was featureless other than the metal band.

Travis took a careful hold with his thumb and forefinger. Then, resting it in his palm, he examined it.

"How do I use it? What can it do?" Travis said, stopping himself from asking more questions as Clutch reached out and took it back.

"It can do pretty much whatever you need, with a few limitations," he said, watching as Travis frowned. "A plasma cutting torch might come in handy," he said, holding it out one handed and pressing a button Travis hadn't noticed on the base. As he did, the shorter end seemed to liquify, glinting in the light, but rather than it dripping to the deck, it formed a point, the tip glowing white once it settled.

Travis turned away.

"Don't worry. It's safe to look at," Clutch added.

Travis nodded, his mouth hanging open as he leaned closer.

"Or something simpler," Clutch said, as the light blinked out and the end of the point transformed into a cross, growing bigger as if for different size screws, before shrinking to nothing.

"So how do I...?" Travis asked as he blinked away his stare, forcing himself to look at Clutch, where he caught a glint in his eye.

"It will know," Clutch replied, glancing out to the weeds swaying in the light wind. Travis's brow lowered. "I've kept you too long already. Good luck. If you need us, send us a signal," he added, placing the tool back in Travis's palm and patting him on the upper arm.

With a glance and a nod over to Colin, he ushered the pair away.

Stepping down the ramp, and placing the tool in his jean's pocket, Travis peered across the tall weeds to the house at the boundary. Nodding to himself when all seemed quiet, and with no space in the fence for children's faces to stare out from, he turned to the wall he could just about see before movement on the ground made him look to two fluffy tails disappearing between cracks in the concrete.

Glancing at Colin as he felt a shiver down his spine, Travis found him smiling a moment before the air erupted with the thunderous roar. The pair looked up to where a pair of low-flying jets rushed overhead, but turning as they followed their path, with relief they found the Mary May was out of sight.

Taking a step forward, they stopped when the shiver came again and a voice they recognised called from behind.

"Travis," Miles shouted, pulling him from picking a course through the undergrowth, and turning to find the Mary May in full view with the ramp lowering before Miles and Princess rushed out towards them.

"What is it?" Travis called, meeting them halfway back to the ship where the ramp was already raising and the Mary May soon disappeared.

"Sapphire has detected a continuous nine gigahertz radio signal," Princess said, her eyes wide.

"And?" Travis asked, lowering his brow, unsure which of the two to look at.

"We think it's a short range radar system," Miles said, rushing out the words between heavy breaths. "They might be trying to find us."

"Who?" Travis said, looking between the pair shaking their heads.

"The people we captured at the other landing site," Princess replied, then looked at Miles, who already nodded.

"But she's cloaked," Travis said, glancing over Princess's shoulders to make sure he couldn't see the Mary May.

"The cloak only disrupts wavelengths in the visual spectrum," Princess replied.

"Plus a little ultraviolet and infrared," Miles chipped in. "But nowhere near nine gigahertz."

Travis remained quiet as he turned to look off into the distance.

"I guess they believed them after all," he eventually said, looking at each of them.

They all nodded their replies.

"Sapphire reviewed her recordings since she first detected the signal and reports its strength varies," Miles said.

"When did she first find the signal?" Travis asked.

"Yesterday evening," Princess replied. "The timing fits."

"We're assuming the varying signal means whatever is generating it is on the move," Miles said.

Travis turned to Colin, fixing him with a thoughtful stare.

"I think we've seen it," he eventually said.

Colin nodded, but remained quiet.

"We saw a big dome on the back of an army truck. Cameras on poles surrounded it. If they're driving all over town at that same slow pace, maybe that's what's causing the traffic chaos." He turned to Miles. "Could that be it?"

"It's clever," Miles replied with a nod, before peering off between the weeds, his eyes narrowed.

"What is it?" Princess asked just as Miles turned back.

"From what you said, it sounds like they could use the cameras to compare visual information with the data the radar collects," he replied.

"So maybe we don't have as much time as we'd hoped," Princess said, raising a brow.

"You guys need to go," Miles said, rushing out the

words. "We're monitoring the signal strength now and if it gets too close, we have to assume they'll spot us."

"You'll have no choice but to leave," Travis said, nodding.

"We're not leaving you behind, Trav," Princess said.

"You can't anyway," Travis replied. "You barely know how to fly," he added with a smirk as he turned and picked a path through the tall weeds.

After retracing their steps and finding the High Street quiet again, Travis glanced at Colin, not needing to ask if he'd also noticed the empty pavement outside the cafe, clear of the tables and chairs they'd expected.

Without speaking, they continued along the opposite side of the road, not stopping as they glared at the darkness beyond the tall window.

About to give into the urge to step across the street and check out what he hoped were the opening times beside the closed sign hanging on the glass door, Travis felt Colin's hand on his arm. He looked along the road and spotted the waitress who'd called the police, walking at a brisk pace towards the shop.

Averting their gaze from the woman, they continued walking and stopped only as they arrived at a bus stop, almost out of view of the cafe.

"We can't wait here all day," Colin said, as they craned their necks to watch the waitress unlock the door before stepping inside. "I've got the feeling Astra won't work today."

"Me too, but what else can we do?" Travis replied,

his voice low.

"I don't know," Colin said, forcing a smile, leaving them to sit in silence and watch as the lights flickered on from behind the tall windows.

"Anyway, how are you doing?" Travis asked, just as a bus drew up. After waving away the bus, Colin pulled his gaze from down the street and frowned back. "It must have been hard finding out you weren't crew."

"Oh, that," Colin said, raising the corner of his mouth and relaxing his brow. "I'm okay," he added with a nod, although his voice remained flat. "I think I knew in the back of my mind it was too good to be true."

Travis didn't reply straight away, mulling over the words instead. "At least there's a new opening for a chief mechanic at the bus depot," Travis said, his face filling with a smile before he jabbed Colin in the ribs.

Colin shook his head. "Maybe in twenty years. If I'm ever that good," he said. "And I'm not sure it compares with tinkering with the Mary May all day."

"I guess not," Travis said. "Don't let Clutch hear you call it tinkering," he added with a chuckle. When he'd stopped laughing, he pulled the rectangular block of metal from his pocket. "But imagine if you had one of these?" he said, flashing his eyebrows.

"Yeah, right," Colin scoffed, looking away from the Universal Tool. "I think Clutch would hunt me down if you gave it to me. Unless, of course, you have a spare?"

"You're right," Travis replied. "I'm shocked he let it out of his sight. There's no spare, I'm afraid. We took it as part payment when someone couldn't cover our bill. It's the only one I've ever seen."

Colin nodded, but soon the motion slowed and he turned to stare through the window of an empty shop opposite.

"Somehow I'd convinced myself, like you, that I'd forgotten everything about my real life. The only problem was that I remembered my childhood. My parents. School. My first job, and starting work at the bus station. Every time you mentioned memory coming back…" Colin said, his eyes narrowing, "…something told me the flood gates could open at any time. I'd hoped it would all make sense soon, and I'd find…"

"Find what?" Travis asked when Colin didn't continue.

"This is going to sound lame," Colin replied, looking away so Travis couldn't see his face.

"Just tell me," Travis said, shuffling closer and peering around to get a better look at him.

"It's nothing," Colin said, twisting further away.

"I don't believe you," Travis replied, nudging him with his elbow.

After a moment of silence, Colin turned back, his eyes damp and mouth hanging open.

"Just spit it out," Travis urged, resting his hand on Colin's shoulder. "I'd like to think you could talk to me about things, even though we've only known each other for a short amount of time."

Colin dipped his head. "I don't fit in this place. This dimension, I mean," he said, shaking his head. "When you told me about the ship and the crew, I thought my life had all been a nightmare, and I was on the brink of waking up to a life I'd dreamed of. A life that would make so much more sense. I thought those dreams could be memories."

"Is that true?" Travis replied, his voice soft. "And it's got nothing to do with Princess? I've seen how you look at her."

Colin looked up and laughed, pushing at Travis's

shoulder with his own.

"No," he said, shaking his head, his voice high as his cheeks reddened.

"Good," Travis replied. "Because you'd only be disappointed. She likes girls, and even if she didn't," Travis said, looking him up and down and laughing, "she'd destroy you."

"It's not that, I swear," Colin said, raising his palms.

Travis let the silence settle before he spoke again. "What's this about you not being able to talk with women around?"

Colin shrugged. "I don't know. Have you ever walked into a public toilet and found other men standing at the urinal? You're dying for a pee, but there's only one space. You take it because you're about to burst, but you can't go with everyone else around and you have to wait until they leave. That's what it's like."

"No. That's never happened to me," Travis said, his brow rising. "And no one's asking you to piss in front of Princess," he added with a smirk.

"But you know what I mean," Colin said, his voice low.

"I get it," Travis replied. "But I can piss in front of anyone. It's my superpower," he said, and they both chuckled. "Look," he added, the laughter gone from his voice. "We'll work on that together, right?"

Colin glanced over for a long moment before nodding.

The pair settled into another long silence as they shuffled backwards in their seats and further under the canopy as a helicopter ambled overhead.

"Do you remember everything now?" Colin asked, as the noise of the spinning rotors faded.

"Not everything," Travis replied.

"About the crew at least?" Colin asked.

"There are still blanks."

"Like what?" Colin said.

"If I knew that, they wouldn't be missing," Travis said, looking over, his brow raised.

"Yeah. I guess," Colin replied, and they fell back into silence.

"Take Mac, for example," Travis said after a few moments. "I remember when he joined. His food before the accident and the places across the galaxy we've travelled together. It's so vivid."

"But?" Colin said.

"But… I don't know… It feels like there's a big part of him I just can't remember, and it's bugging the hell out of me."

"That's weird," Colin replied. "What about the others?"

"Not so…" Travis said, but cut himself off when at the other end of the street he spotted a police car heading down the road before it came to a stop outside the cafe.

29

Remaining standing at the bus stop only long enough to know it wasn't the cops from the night before that pulled themselves from the car, Travis and Colin left down a side street, where Colin peered up at each high-mounted CCTV camera.

"What now?" he asked, glancing up and down the road lined on one side by three-storey flats, opposite a yard at the rear of the shops.

"I wish I knew," Travis replied, before stepping under the canopy of a tree, pulling Colin with him as the drone of rotor blades came into focus. "We should find a bar and check out the news. Maybe they'll mention that radar thing?"

"Not at eight in the morning, we're not," Colin said, glancing at his watch.

Travis narrowed his eyes.

"But I have another idea," Colin added, stepping out of the tree's shadow as the thump of the helicopter retreated.

Within a few moments they stared through a shop window full of TVs of all sizes, each tuned to the same news station with a young male reporter in a suit stood beside a road packed with olive-green trucks rolling past him. The camera swept to his side and to where another man stood, his head bald except for errant strands combed over the top, along with a flamboyant moustache which filled the space above his upper lip. A series of colourful medals were pinned to his chest.

Travis stared at the scrolling subtitles.

With the MOD not commenting on the influx of military vehicles, soldiers and air power, I'm here with retired army Major Oliver Bennett-Smythe.

Despite cowering as fast jets rushed over their heads, Travis kept his attention set on the largest screen in the centre of the window.

Major Bennett-Smythe, you served in a rapid response unit of the 16 Air Assault Brigade until two years ago. What do you make of what we've seen over the last few days?

It's fabulous, isn't it? he said, beaming with a broad, yellow-toothed smile.

The reporter's stern expression hadn't changed as the camera cut back.

I mean, doesn't it fill you with pride to see the might of the British Army working hand in hand with the Royal Air Force, the major added, the camera on him again just as he dropped his shoulders and lowered his head when a pair of jets rushed out of focus. The major straightened up before the camera cut to the reporter, who swept a loose tuft of hair back in place.

But what is it all about? he said, pointing to the slow-moving convoy. *The MOD is tight-lipped on the matter.*

The major continued to smile.

Have you heard bombs dropped? Has your audience reported shots fired? No. It's an exercise. The guy up top clearly has bigger balls than my last CO to stage these awesome manoeuvres as a show of force to the Russians, and right in our back yard. It's a proud day to be British.

The camera cut from the military man's broad grin to the reporter.

I'm sorry for the language, he said, glancing at the camera before turning back to the man. *What makes you so sure it's just an exercise? There are rumours it's a manhunt for pilots from a downed military jet, maybe those of a foreign power. Our newsroom received several reports of strange objects in the sky last night, only a couple of miles from here. Could it be something to do with the wide-ranging power cuts yesterday?*

That's all nonsense.

The words appeared on the screen quicker than the camera could move.

Next, you'll be saying it's a blasted UFO.

Travis and Colin looked at each other, but quickly turned back to the screen.

But, correct me if I'm wrong...

The major's lips hadn't moved, and they assumed it was the reporter speaking out of the shot.

...wouldn't 16 Air Assault Brigade be the unit called to attend a crash of that nature?

Well...

The screen changed to a smartly-dressed man and woman sat on a couch flicking through newspapers before they could see the response. The other screens followed as lights came on behind the TVs.

"If only he knew," Colin said, standing from a stoop. Travis nodded, glancing over his shoulder when he realised how engrossed he'd been. Finding no one paying attention to them, together they moved away from the shop window and walked toward the cafe.

"We're going back?" Colin asked.

"What else can we do?" Travis replied. "It's our only lead."

"I don't think it'll do us any good," Colin said, staring down the road as his gaze darted to every movement. "If your memories were still blank, and you thought someone was searching for you, but you had no idea why, how would you feel?"

Travis stopped and turned to Colin. "I'd want to

know," he replied.

"But now put yourself in the shoes of a woman found naked and vulnerable," Colin replied.

Travis didn't speak as his eyes locked with Colin's.

"She's not some vulnerable woman," Travis replied, raising his voice.

"Maybe not before, but what are we without our memories?" Colin said, keeping his voice soft.

"Okay," Travis replied after a pause. "Maybe we should have brought Princess with us," he added, before walking again. "Where'd she get the shoes from?"

Colin frowned, and noticing he'd stopped, Travis did the same and turned to face his frown.

"What?" Colin asked.

"You said she was naked. So where did she get the shoes from?" Travis said, but before Colin could open his mouth, he saw Travis's rising smile and they carried on walking.

"Do you remember anything useful about her yet?" Colin asked, as they peered along the road and its sweep to the right.

Travis shook his head.

"Remind me how you found Mac?" Colin asked, and Travis turned to meet his gaze.

"He made the news and I found the details in the paper wrapping up chips. Whereas we were lucky with Clutch. Thanks to you," Travis said, watching as Colin nodded.

"Maybe Astra made the paper as well," Colin said, lifting his chin.

"How much food will we need to buy to find her?" Travis asked, his brow low.

"There is an easier way," Colin said, laughing as he turned away. "But you have to be quiet."

30

Settled side by side at a library computer, Colin pulled the keyboard in front of him as Travis watched him type.

Naked women in Oxfordshire.

Hitting the enter key, the screen flashed red.

Inappropriate content! Continued violation will result in being asked to leave.

After slamming his finger on the back button, Colin peered around, only turning back when he couldn't see anyone glaring over.

He edited his search.

Naked Women found in Oxfordshire.

The screen flashed red again; the banner accompanied by a cough from the reception counter. After tapping the back button a second time, the pair glanced over to a middle-aged woman glaring back at them.

Woman found naked roaming the street in Oxfordshire.

Colin stared at the screen as he read the phrase over and again while he held his finger hovering over the return key. With a last glance at the counter, he pressed enter, relieved when the screen remained white with a series of text results filling the page.

With a look at Travis, who'd leaned closer, Colin pressed the first link and read aloud in almost a whisper.

"In the early hours of Wednesday morning, a woman was found naked wandering Oatlands Road Recreation Ground. Reported to police by concerned dog walkers, she was taken to hospital, apparently suffering from the early stages of hypothermia. A man who was amongst the many who called in the sighting, but who asked to remain anonymous, said, 'I was watching Missy, my Cockapoo, doing her morning business when I looked up and thought I was having a dream. There was this beautiful woman with short hair staggering about as if she was unwell, or had too much to drink, but not wearing a stitch of clothing. When she vomited, I called the police'."

"That could be anyone," Travis said, equally quiet.

Colin raised his hand for him to be quiet and continued to narrate the article.

"The woman, who has yet to be identified, received treatment in John Radcliffe Hospital A&E department, where she was confirmed as suffering from amnesia in addition to other conditions. Police have issued the following statement: A woman thought to be between the ages of twenty-five and thirty-five was found in the suburbs of Oxford at five fifty-two this morning. When officers arrived, they found her disoriented and unwell, and with no recollection of what had happened to her. With short brunette hair, her only identifying marks were tattoos on each of her upper arms."

Travis cocked his head to the side and Colin arched an eyebrow.

"What is it?" Colin asked, watching as Travis drew up the right sleeve of his t-shirt, revealing a cartoon version of the Mary May tattooed on his upper arm, although the depiction was missing the repair patches added to the hull over the recent years. A line down the middle split the ship in two, with the top half coloured blue and the bottom half red.

Travis closed his eyes as a memory filled his head. He sat on a couch next to Astra, her eyes bright and cheeks flushed with pain as the high-pitched vibration of the laser pressed against her upper arm. Despite the discomfort, she smiled at him whilst trying her best to stop herself from laughing each time Travis flinched when another man leaned the tattoo laser close to his skin.

Shaking his head, he remembered the shit he got when his version took double the time it had taken for hers.

"It's Astra," Travis said, not keeping his voice low as he watched Colin lift his brow.

"Lots of women have tattoos," he replied, glancing between the tattoo and the lines of text on the screen.

Travis followed his gaze and read the description for himself, unable to shake off the thought of her stumbling around the park with no clothes on as she threw up.

"It's her," he reiterated when he came to the end of the written words. "Scroll up."

Colin did as he asked, and Travis pointed at the date.

"Three months ago," Colin said, nodding, and they shared a look before turning back to the screen where Colin clicked a few more links, speed reading what he found. "There are no more details."

Travis stood, ignoring the side-eyed look from the wrinkled receptionist before he burst out through the library doors and into the fresh air, stopping only for Colin to catch up.

"Which way to the John Radcliffe Hospital?" he said, his voice tailing off as he spotted a long queue of traffic on the main road ahead.

"This way," Colin said, charging after him and pointing along the path.

Together they walked without speaking, the pair seeming deep in thought, and it was a good five minutes before Travis glanced at Colin, where he sensed him eager to ask a question.

"What is it?" Travis said.

"It's nothing," Colin replied, shaking his head and looking away. He soon turned back.

"Just ask," Travis said, spotting the man's eyes pinched together.

"I was just wondering. Well, it's something I've been thinking about for a little while," Colin said, letting the words trail off. "Since I saw the Mary May for the first time, in fact."

"Just ask," Travis repeated as he looked along the road, glancing at the passing cars whilst trying not to make eye contact with the drivers passing on the other side of the road.

"Since I'm from this dimension, and you're not, I wondered other than causal space flight and invisibility cloaks, force fields, and, of course, liquid metal," he said, nodding down to Travis's pocket. "What else has your dimension got that we don't?"

Travis glanced at the pavement and then at Colin.

"I've not seen enough of your world to know what we have that you don't," he said, cocking his head.

"What about teleportation?" Colin blurted out, almost before Travis has finished speaking, as if he'd been longing to say it.

"People have tried it, but let's just say the results were…" Travis said, shaking his head as he searched for the right word. "…messy."

Colin frowned, but it wasn't long before his eyes went wide.

"Laser guns," he said, then raised his hand and mimed pulling a pistol's trigger before looking at Travis.

"We have energy weapons in our dimension. If that's

what you mean," Travis said, his voice lacking Colin's enthusiasm.

"Cool," Colin replied, nodding. "Can I see them?"

Travis shook his head.

"We don't have any weapons on the Mary May, remember?" he said, watching Colin deflate, until his shoulders lifted again and his eyes went wide.

"Bionics?" Colin asked, lowering his eyes and glancing at Travis's arm before raising a finger and prodding at the man's bicep.

"Stop that," Travis said, drawing himself away and swatting at the outstretched finger. "There are people using tech to improve themselves, or to replace limbs."

"Coooool," Colin said with a grin. "What about robots?"

Travis nodded but looked away, hoping Colin would understand he was done talking about it.

Colin took the hint, and they continued to walk with the back-to-back traffic ebbing and flowing beside them. Within ten minutes filled with little talk from either of them, they spotted more military vehicles, trucks and Land Rovers joining the traffic, along with more police cars as they closed the distance to the hospital.

As the John Radcliffe's tall blue and white buildings came into view, Travis's focus switched to the ambulances parked beside large dark green containers waiting on the side of the road with pressurised doors built into either end. Soldiers in fatigues wandered up and down in pairs, pointing long rifles towards the ground as they made eye contact with each person walking past and the occupants of every passing vehicle.

Glancing at each other as if with the same question, they watched the foot traffic grow with each step, until almost bumping into a woman in a nurse's uniform coming towards them. Travis stopped.

"What's going on?" he asked, pointing along the road as a truck roared past them, spilling out diesel fumes across their path.

"Bloody fascists," she said, coughing into her fist. "They've taken over half of A&E and there's nothing wrong with the people they've brought in."

Travis and Colin swapped a glance. Pushing away the thought, he looked back at the woman, afraid she'd walk off.

"Do you work here?" he said, and she raised her brow before peering down at her uniform.

Colin leaned up to Travis and whispered in his ear.

"I mean," Travis added, "do you work in A&E?"

She turned from looking at Colin with her brow cocked, then nodded at Travis, with heavy, tired lids.

"Do you remember a woman the police brought in three months ago?" Travis blurted out. "It would have been in the early hours?"

Colin leaned up to Travis's ear again.

"She'd lost her memory," Travis soon added, and they both watched the woman's brow rise. "And she was naked," Travis said. "It made the news."

Colin nudged Travis's arm.

"She's our friend," Travis rushed to say. "That's the only reason we're asking," he added, glancing between the woman and Colin in the hope he'd not said the wrong thing.

"I've only worked there for a couple of months," she replied, her expression softening as she shook her head. "My colleagues might know, but good luck with getting in there," she added, and by the time the pair looked back from following her glance over her shoulder, she'd walked away.

Looking back towards the hospital, the pair stood in the middle of the path as people streamed either side of them. As someone tutted loud enough for them to both hear, they spotted the pointed helmets of two police officers walking towards them from the hospital.

"It's them," Colin said, catching Travis's eye. "The coppers from before."

"They won't notice us," Travis replied, standing on tiptoes to get a better look, before dropping when he spotted the one with the round belly looking right at him. "Shit. Let's go," Travis said, turning.

Not paying attention to where he was going, he stepped into the road, stopping only as a truck horn bellowed and his vision filled with matt green.

31

Bright light flooded Travis's eyes and a low hum of activity filled his ears.

Realising he lay propped up on his back, he flinched when a green truck rushed towards him, but rather than his head flaring with more pain, he found himself on a bed in a small space bounded by a curtain wrapped around on a track fixed to the ceiling.

With his head throbbing, he expected he'd find an egg-shaped bulge protruding from his pounding forehead to match the one Colin had achieved when he'd walked into the Mary May's hidden landing gear.

Attempting to lift his hand to check for the lump, something held his hand back as metal clattered at his side.

Peering down, he found a ring of steel clung to each wrist which, via a black block of plastic in between, connected to another metal bracelet encircling each of the bed's handrails.

Spotting a police officer standing at the edge of the bay, he watched the man look up from his phone, then raise his brow, locking eyes with Travis for a second before disappearing out between the parted curtain.

After glancing at the handcuffs for a second time, Travis looked down at his jeans, but his gaze soon turned to the long rip from the neck of his Skywalker t-shirt to halfway down his chest and the dark marks scuffing the white fabric.

His right sleeve was torn, but despite finding the

jagged line spotted with blood, he felt no other pain besides that in his head.

Scouring the curtained bay as he tried in vain to push himself up the bed, he realised there was no sign of Colin, the space occupied only by a blank monitor high on a stand at his side.

The curtain's movement forced his attention to a tanned older man in blue scrubs with a grey moustache pinned to his upper lip and a stethoscope hanging around his neck. A shorter woman dressed the same followed, her hair in a ponytail.

The policeman stepped in last.

"I don't think two restraints are necessary," said the doctor, his voice rich as he looked back at the police officer. "What's the accusation?" he asked when the cop remained silent.

"I don't know," the officer said, shrugging when the doctor's stare didn't relent.

"Did you kill someone?" the doctor snapped, catching Travis's eye for the first time.

Travis shook his head but closed his eyes as he winced, amplifying the pain in his head.

"Well then," the doctor called out. "Release a wrist so I can examine him properly. Unless you want his death on your hands because you hampered my diagnosis," he added, turning with a nod toward Travis.

Travis watched the cop walk around to the right side of the bed, eyeing him for a long moment before he pulled a key from his stab vest and undid the cuff before stepping away with it.

"Now give this man some privacy," the doctor said, glancing over to make sure the cop did as he was told.

"I'll be just outside," the young man replied, tapping his finger on a small red bottle strapped to his body armour.

Travis relaxed as the doctor worked his fingers around what he thought was the egg shape, but was surprised to feel little more pain when his fingers got closer, only pulling back when he shined a light in each of his eyes.

"You're a lucky man," the doctor finally said. "A few cuts and bruises, and a lovely little lump, but other than that, you got away with it. Next time, use the green cross code." The doctor raised his brow, but when Travis narrowed his eyes, he shook his head. "Never mind. Don't they teach anything of use in schools these days? Anyway, Emma here will do a few more checks and give you something for the pain, then I'm afraid it's time to plead your case to the constabulary. Do you have any questions?"

Travis had many, but not about his health.

"No, thank you," he croaked, his throat dry as the memory of the pain stopped him from shaking his head before the doctor walked between the curtains, leaving the nurse, Emma, to pour water from a see-through jug into a small plastic cup.

"These will make you feel better for a few hours," she said and Travis took the cup, knocking back the pills she gave him, then the water.

"Thank you," Travis said.

"I just need to measure your blood pressure. Do you mind lifting your arm?" she said, taking the empty cup.

Travis nodded with care and felt the woman lift the remains of his sleeve, then he turned his head as he sensed her pause.

"What's wrong?" he said, wondering what the doctor had missed, but found she was shaking her head.

"It's nothing," she eventually said, her tone less than

convincing as she wrapped the cuff around his arm.

Looking away as the cuff tightened with each pump of the balloon in Emma's fist, he felt she was on the edge of speaking.

"Is that a common tattoo?" she soon said as air hissed from the black pump in her hand.

Taking care, Travis looked down at his upper arm and the cartoon version of the Mary May.

"I only know of one other. We both got them together," he replied, his words measured as he watched her brows knit together.

"I hope you don't think me rude," she said, lowering her voice.

"It's fine," he replied, trying not to shake his head.

"Can I ask why the police arrested you?" Emma said, her eyes twitching to where Travis imagined the police officer stood beyond the curtain.

Travis swallowed hard as he looked into her eyes.

"I'm looking for someone," he whispered. "A friend who went missing three months ago," he added just as low. "A woman," he said, watching her brow rise with each word.

"But why are the police involved?" she asked, leaning closer.

"Someone got the wrong idea," he replied, swallowing hard.

The nurse's expression fell, her eyes narrowing.

"Who is this woman to you?" she said, her voice low again.

Travis couldn't help but smile.

"We go back a long way. Ten years, in fact. We're friends," he said, turning to look off into the distance. When his gaze returned to her face, he found her staring back, her cheeks a little bunched.

"I can see how much you care for her," she said, leaning closer still. "There's something about you I don't see in here very often."

"You've seen her, haven't you?" Travis asked, raising himself to his right elbow. "You saw her tattoo. Didn't you?"

"Are you Travis?" she asked, her voice barely heard. His eyes widened as he nodded, not caring about his throbbing head.

"Why?"

"She asked for you in her sleep," the nurse replied.

32

Travis could barely breathe as the nurse kept talking, still absorbed by her previous words.

"She had another tattoo. On the other arm," she continued, and as she pointed to his other side, it took him a moment to realise she'd meant it as a question.

"The Cheshire Cat," he said, remembering its bulging eyes and a smile almost bigger than its face. As the sight of its mouth filled with human teeth rushed into his head, with it came a flood of memories tumbling into his mind as if in that moment they'd breached some invisible barrier, swamping his thoughts with snapshots of their time together. As her laughter filled the space between his ears, rather than bathing him in joy he felt a chasm ripped open in his chest.

"Yes," she said, nodding as she placed her warm hand on his arm and leaned closer. "Are you okay?"

"I'm fine," Travis replied, but not straight away, shaking his head as he tried to lean up on his right elbow. "How was she when she left? Where did she go?"

"There was nothing physically wrong with her that a few day's rest wouldn't sort out. Mentally," she continued, softening her voice further, "only time will tell. I think she went to a woman's refuge. Someone from the centre came to collect her. We get to know them well, I'm afraid."

At the sound of footsteps from the other side of the curtain, she stood up straight, glancing at the hanging blue partition. When it hadn't moved, she leaned close again.

"I just need to find her," he said, his voice a whisper. "Do you know where she is now?"

The nurse smiled back, but the curve of her lips soon fell away.

"I don't know. Have you tried reaching out on social media? I'm sure your story will go viral," she said, her cheeks bunching and eyes bright with optimism. "You'll find her in hours!"

Her sudden excitement buoyed his mood, his eyes widening, but he thought better of asking what she'd meant. Colin would know what to do.

"Someone else was with me when…" Travis said, but interrupted himself. "Is he waiting outside?"

The nurse's expression fell, and she shook her head.

"I don't know, but I can find out," she replied, then giving him one last flash of her smile followed by a pat on the arm, she stepped away and through the curtains.

About to sit up, eager to find Colin and continue the search, Travis turned to his left, remembering the remaining bracelet. With a quick glance around, finding nothing he could use to prize the metal off, and with a tension building in his chest, he blinked as he tried to think past the pain, despite it already easing.

Glancing at the right-hand pocket of his jeans, his heart rate surged when he spotted the slight bulge and reached inside.

Holding the Universal Tool in his right hand, he examined its blank end, which showed none of the detail from when Clutch had turned it into a screwdriver. The end of the surface remained flat as he eyed the square button toward the end. Letting his lids fall closed, he tried to remember their conversation just before he left the ship, but for the life of him, he couldn't recall how to select a tool.

With a glance to the bracelet encircling his wrist, he repositioned his grip around the metal and hovered his thumb over the small button. Reaching across his body, as the pad of his thumb almost touched the outline he heard voices beyond the curtain, just as the metal slipped through his fingers.

Adrenaline surged and his hand darted down, his grip tightening on the edges of the tool before, letting out a slow relief-filled breath, he moved his hand over his stomach in case it fell again.

Taking a moment to let his heart rate settle along with the pounding in his forehead, listening to the silence, he remembered Clutch's words.

It will know.

Concentrating on the bracelet, and certain of his grip this time, he pressed the button and moved the rectangle over to the cuff, pointing the end at the bracelet encircling the bed. As he did, he spotted a point rise from the end to form a tip.

Easing it closer, whilst doing his best to stop his breath from rushing, he envisaged the metal of the bracelet separating. Light poured from the end of the Universal Tool.

He looked away and along the bed. Despite being keen to sense if his wrist was getting hotter, the fear it would draw the copper back was stronger.

When the tension around his wrist eased and he smelt no singed skin for anyone to investigate, he pulled the tool away.

Resting the block on his stomach, he drew a relieved breath when he realised a section of the metal clasp was missing.

Pushing the tool back into his pocket and leaning

over to his left hand, he tapped at the metal. Finding it wasn't hot, he forced the two parts to separate with his thumb and forefinger until the opening was big enough for his wrist.

Letting the cuff down against the bed rail with care, knowing any sound could rouse the man waiting outside, he held himself still and listened.

Apart from the occasional rattle of a trolley, the shuffle of feet or a hushed conversation, the place remained quiet. Taking great care with every move, he swung his feet over the bed's edge. When the bed didn't creak, he lowered his feet to the floor.

Hearing nothing of concern, he stepped to where the curtain met the wall, then leaned up to the curtain before pulling it back and peering out.

Finding another bay on the other side, and the bed empty, he glanced around his own space and spotted the blister pack of tablets the nurse had taken the pills from. After pocketing the remaining pills, he stepped into the neighbouring bay, moving around the bed with soft steps and pulled the curtain's side back.

Relieved to find only space on the other side, and double doors beyond, beaming from ear to ear he stood up tall, striding across the room before pushing through the opening.

As the doors swung in behind him, his sense of satisfaction vanished when he spotted a man in light blue scrubs and a hair net walking towards him from the other direction, pushing a large blue cart on wheels.

Despite hanging his head lower, he knew the man stared right at him.

33

"It's me," a voice Travis recognised hissed.

Lifting his head, he spotted the ginger hair spilling out from underneath the blue net.

"Colin?" Travis replied under his breath, his eyes just as wide as those of the man rushing towards him. Not trusting what he saw, Travis straightened up as they both slowed to a stop. Still gripping the edge of the container, Colin nodded with urgency whilst bouncing on the balls of his feet.

"Let's go," Travis said, reaching out and guiding him to turn, wheeling the cart around as he did. Colin leaned towards him as they walked.

"Are you okay?" he whispered, his gaze catching on the centre of Travis's forehead before their eyes met.

Travis dipped his head with a slow, careful nod. "I got the all clear, and some tablets," Travis said, patting his pocket. "What were you doing?" he asked, taking his first proper look at the blue container Colin continued to push.

"Coming to get..." Colin said with a glance at the white sheets filling much of the bin, but when a high call came from behind, he cut himself short. "Get in," he said, stopping on the spot and delving his arms inside the cart before pulling out a thick bundle of white linen, then nodding down into the space he'd made.

Travis frowned, shooting a glance back the way he'd come, but when a second call followed from behind, he grabbed the plastic sides and climbed inside the cart before crouching as low as he could manage a moment before the sheets fell on top of him.

Squirming for comfort as the rolling wheels sent the floor's every imperfection up through his feet, the few thin layers of material doing nothing to cushion the impacts, he soon settled on his butt with his knees bent in front.

"Sit still," came Colin's muffled voice, barely heard over the race of the hard wheels as Travis peered at the shifting, subtle light and shadows through the thick sides.

The loud trundle of the wheels and the sudden changes of direction took away any sense of where they headed. He imagined rushing through doors at pace as he caught snippets of voices he thought were perhaps from passing nurses, doctors and patients as they went about their business.

When all of a sudden the rattle and rush of the wheels stopped, their echo replaced by silence, he strained his hearing for any sense of what was happening.

"They're coming." Colin's whisper took him by surprise. "We need to hide."

About to complain it was what he was already doing, he felt a sharp change in direction as the wheels rushed back into motion.

"Oh shit," Colin called out, and the container stopped, followed by the hurry of feet and then another pair before all sound decayed to nothing.

Feeling the heat build as moments passed in silence, a bead of sweat rolled down the side of his nose. Travis was about to pull the fabric closer to his face to wipe his brow when a deep, gravely voice stopped him dead.

"What the fuck is this doing here?"

Holding himself still, Travis watched a shadow move around from his right to stand in front of him.

"I bet I'll be the one to get it in the neck if Bates sees this. You're coming with me for a cupper."

Jolted back into motion, Travis heard no other voice before the roll of the hard wheels enveloped everything. It wasn't long before the sound went again.

"Don't mind me," the voice said, and with sweat running down his face, Travis listened to cupboards slamming, leaving him certain the man was talking to himself. Still desperate to press the fabric against his cheeks, he concentrated on the sounds in hope of any sign he could move without being seen.

"We're out of biscuits," the voice said again. "Back in a mo."

Travis listened to the footsteps heading away and, when they were gone altogether, he let go of a long breath.

"How are the wrists?" a plummy deep voice asked, followed by a loud slurp of liquid.

Travis froze.

"They're fine," said another man in a deep Scottish accent Travis recognised.

Holding his breath, Travis forced himself to remain still despite the shock of energy surging through his body as he strained to listen to the voice to make sure he wasn't hallucinating. Ignoring the water streaming down his face, he tried to force himself back to the moment he tied the Scot to the tree, willing the man to speak again so he could search for differences in his tone.

"I've heard the official line, Jock, but what really happened to your team?" the plummy voice asked.

"Sorry, Captain. You know how it is. I'd get into a lot of shit if I spoke out of turn," Jock replied.

It was him. Travis was certain.

"Of course. Yeah. Hush-hush and all that," the

captain said. "I'm not asking."

"You wouldn't believe me if I told you anyway," the Scot said.

"That's not for me to say," the posh man replied, his voice softening. "Someone believed you or they wouldn't have put on this fiasco."

"Yeah. They've bloody poked and prodded me and my team enough for a lifetime," Jock said, his voice a little pained as Travis screwed his eyes together, hoping to stop the sweat stinging his eyes.

"At least you're out of that stupid biohazard suit. Was there any need for that?" the captain asked.

"It felt like I was in a movie. Although I spent most of my time on my back waiting for the barrage of test results to come back."

"But they didn't find anything?" the plummy voice replied.

"Apparently not," the Scot said, as beads of sweat collected on the end of Travis's nose in the silence that followed.

"Can I ask one thing?" the posh man said, leaving Travis thankful for the distraction. "I've been hearing things."

"You can see the medic for that whilst you're here," the Scot replied, and they both chuckled.

"Seriously though, did you really see little green men?"

The Scot laughed, but it soon faded to nothing.

"No," he replied.

"Then why all this?" the captain soon asked. "Look, I know you can't say much, but I have a daughter studying at Magdelan College just down the road." He paused for a long moment. "She's just turned eighteen," he added. "Just tell me one thing. Is she safe?"

Sweat dripped from Travis's nose and he held his breath as the trickle travelled down his skin.

"They looked just like us," the Scot said, his voice almost too low for Travis to hear. He leaned forward as much as he dared.

"Who?" the captain asked, and Travis imagined him leaning closer.

"They had a…" Jock said, but held back. "You should have seen it," he added before stopping again. "It was…" he tried again. "… At least it looked like a spacecraft."

Silence followed and Travis held his breath, desperate not to make a sound.

"A spacecraft?" the captain said after a long moment. "What did it look like?"

"Like a heap of junk," the Scot said, and Travis forced himself not to come to the Mary May's defence.

"Junk?" the captain asked, his voice rising with surprise.

"Well, let's say it looked like it's seen a lot of action," Jock said.

Travis felt himself relax.

"So what happened?" the posh voice said.

"It vanished," Jock replied.

"Vanished? What do you mean?"

"This is the nuts bit," the Scot said. "It wasn't there one minute and then it appeared with some guy stepping down from an opening in the hull."

"What did they look like?" the captain replied, his words getting faster. "Could they have been Russians?"

"They weren't Russians," Jock said. "They looked just like you and me."

Rather than a reply, Travis heard what sounded like a chair scraping back and he imagined one or both of them standing when the dull light through the side of the container changed and a shadow moved across his view. Footsteps paced across the room.

Blinking the sweat from his eyes, a sudden fear came over him as he wondered why the conversation had stopped.

"Don't worry," the Scot said, his voice from somewhere else in the room as another droplet tickled the end of Travis's nose. "Your daughter will be fine."

"But how do you know?" the captain asked.

"The boffs told me they've figured out a way to find them, so if they're still hiding somewhere close, it won't be for long," Jock said.

Travis forced a breath as he felt his heart rate raise even further.

"What if it's flown away?" the captain replied. "I can't believe we're even talking about this. Are you sure of what you saw?"

"I am. My guys saw the same thing," he replied, his voice tailing off.

"So who says this *spaceship*," the captain said, highlighting the last word, "hasn't buggered off already?"

"Apparently it's easy to track in the air. That's why they brought us in a couple of days ago. They thought they were looking for a foreign bogey."

"So the RAF hasn't seen it leave," the captain said. "They can normally only be trusted to find a martini in the hotel bar."

A low rumble of laughter followed, but it soon died to nothing, and not able to stand the itch from the sweat running down his nose any longer, and feeling as if he might sneeze, Travis edged his hand up to his face whilst listening for any sign they'd spotted his movement.

"No. They've cobbled together a radar to search at

ground level. If they find anything that doesn't match up with what the cameras see, then bam," he said, but just as the last word punctuated with a bang on wood, Travis couldn't hold back the sneeze.

"What the?" both voices called in unison, dissolving Travis's hope the blankets had muffled the sound.

Knowing he had no other choice, he burst up to his feet, scattering the sheets across the floor. Red-faced and glistening with sweat, he locked eyes with the Scot dressed in loose blue scrubs and sitting on a chair, before swapping a look with a man stood beside him in the green, black and browns of temperate fatigues, an officer's peaked cap under his arm and a pistol holstered at his side.

34

"Jee Sus, Mary and Joseph. That's the bugger," Jock called, his weighty grey moustache jumping on his lip, knocking his seat back as he stood, his eyes going wide as he steadied himself.

The captain standing opposite frowned back at Travis before lifting his chin with a single raised eyebrow.

"Ty Russkiy?" the captain said, looking Travis in the eye whilst Jock's gaze searched the room.

Travis held the captain's stare for a long moment, holding still despite the sweat dripping down to his chin. Only as the door swung open did Travis jump, not waiting to see who it might be. Lifting his aching legs high in the air, he vaulted over the side of the container before charging toward the door when his feet touched the floor, shoving past the older man holding a bright red packet of round biscuits.

Smearing his hand down his face, Travis ran along the unfamiliar bright corridor to the background of unintelligible calls, some of which weren't in English. The words faded as he pushed through a double set of doors, replaced by unfamiliar voices exclaiming as hospital staff pressed themselves against the walls to get out of the way of the red-faced man running toward them.

People in uniform were everywhere he looked, and many, he guessed, were military by the camouflage pattern or the darkness of their clothes. Each time he spotted someone ahead, he diverted down the next corridor or through another door. Still without glancing back, the rush of footsteps followed, bringing with them the distant calls narrating his every turn.

Spotting the bright day on the other side of a glass doorway, he burst out into the open.

Revelling in the cool, fresh air rushing past his face, he forged onward through a thin crowd gathered around the entrance. They soon rushed out of his way when he didn't slow. Despite the blood pounding in his ears, he heard his name called.

Dropping his pace just enough to twist around, he spotted a hand rising above the crowd. Slowing further still, he checked for those giving chase, but finding no one obvious having rushed through the doors, he stopped to catch his breath as he watched the pale hand waving over.

The throng of people soon parted to reveal a shock of ginger hair and Colin running towards him.

Still trying to recover his breath as a smile filled his face, he gasped when behind Colin he spotted a group of dark uniforms and camouflaged soldiers running at pace toward them.

Beckoning Colin to speed up, Travis grabbed him by the arm as soon as he was within reach and pulled him along. Together they ran, rushing across the main road, dodging cars to an orchestra of horns.

Not looking behind as tyres screeched at their backs, the pair dashed down an alley between two houses. Despite the cover, they continued to speed, rushing between the brick walls to the background of the growing hum of helicopter blades cutting through the air. They twisted their route along roads, cutting down side-streets and taking every change of direction, slowing only when neither of them could keep up the pace.

It must have been a good ten minutes before they came to rest between two houses. Standing with their backs against the cool bricks, facing each other, they fought to gain their breath as their gazes parted to either end of the corridor.

Unable to stop himself, laughter burst from Travis's mouth, stunning Colin until he joined in.

"There's never a dull moment with you around," Colin said as they calmed, then peered up in search of the drumming sound.

"How'd you…?" Travis said, still catching his breath.

"The man running through the crowd was a giveaway," Colin said, stopping to look back at where they'd come from as the helicopter's throb receded.

Nodding, and with measured steps, Travis walked to the edge of the house, where he peered around the corner, pulling back when he spotted a pair of figures slowing from a run as they searched.

Rejoining Colin with his finger at his lips, he nodded toward the other end of the alley before jogging in the same direction.

"We need transport," Travis said, his voice low as he scoured the view opening out into another residential street. "What about these?" he said, pointing at the cars parked on either side of the road.

"I don't know how to steal a car," Colin said, his gaze following Travis's hand as he reached into his pocket and pulled out the Universal Tool.

"I do," he said, as a bright light appeared at the end. "This will get us through any lock."

"It's not just the lock," Colin said, shaking his head as they jogged past the first car before glancing over their shoulders.

"You're a mechanic," Travis replied with a frown

once he made sure the men weren't following.

"I know enough to hot wire an old car, but anything made in the last twenty years will have alarms, immobilisers and steering locks," he said, peering along the occasional car parked at the curb. "But that one," he said, raising his hand and pointing along the curve of the road to a bright-blue Mark Six Mini. "It's perfect. My grandad had one the same colour," Colin called out, before lowering his voice.

After picking up the pace, they soon slowed again when the door of a house on their right opened, a woman in a long yellow summer dress stepping over the threshold, lifting a pushchair. A short boy followed, staring at Travis.

Colin sped up, swapping to Travis's right and putting him in the woman's eye line in case she looked over and saw his dishevelled state.

"We need to get you some clothes," Colin said, his voice low as they slowed to give the woman time to stroll to whichever vehicle was hers. When, after strapping the child in the stroller, she headed back into the house, Travis winked at the kid and they rushed past.

"Stop." A distant call came from behind and they both looked back to find a pair of officers lumbering towards them.

Travis's demeanour changed as they arrived at the driver's door of the compact car. Pulling out the tool and pressing the button with his thumb, he expected the bright light to appear again. Instead, his brow rose when he found a long key protruding from the end.

Swapping a glance with Colin beside him, they held each other's gaze for a second before he shoved the tool in the lock, then twisted and pulled the handle.

Beaming at the open door, he handed the tool to

Colin then ran around to the other side where Colin reached across and unlocked his door. The engine soon spluttered to life as Colin turned the key he'd pushed into the ignition, and they left the kerb whilst Travis folded himself into the cramped space.

"Seatbelt," Colin called out with a glance in the rear-view mirror as the car bounced along the road.

"That thing's amazing," Travis bellowed with delight, nodding to the Universal Tool hanging out of the side of the steering column.

"Where now?" Colin asked, his face fixed with a fat grin as he manhandled the steering around the roads of the housing estate, whilst keeping them in a general direction away from where they'd just come.

"The Mary May?"

Colin looked back, his forehead wrinkled with the same question.

"We have a better chance of coming up with a plan if we're together," Travis said, looking down the road as Colin pulled away from a junction to join the thin traffic.

Colin nodded, lifting his chin as they plodded along the road with the high pitch of the engine in the background.

Feeling the warmth build, Travis followed Colin's example as he wound the lever on the door to lower the windows. With a deep, cool breath, he forced himself to relax into the seat, despite his legs half bent to fit in the footwell. Paying attention to the curves of wood panelling on the dashboard, he spotted three round dials, each set behind the small steering wheel Colin battled with around the corners.

"This is an antique," Travis said, glancing at Colin to find him beaming.

"She's over twenty-five years old," he replied, his

head bobbing up and down with the undulations in the road. His words sent Travis peering back at the detail.

"She's the same age as the Mary May," he replied, his mouth hanging open.

"Oh shit," Colin called out before he could say anything more, his words coming a moment before the air filled with the piercing call of a siren as he stared into the rear-view mirror.

35

Twitching his head around as if impersonating an owl, Travis spotted the police car getting closer, its blue lights bright despite the blazing sun. With the Mini veering to the side, Travis twisted back around in his seat, grabbing the steering wheel to correct their lurching course.

"What should I do?" Colin asked, rushing out the words with his wide-eyed attention focused on Travis as he waited for a response.

"Stay calm," Travis replied, miming for Colin to take a deep breath as he let go of the wheel. "And keep your eyes on the road."

Colin peered ahead, his focus darting across the view as his hands jerked from side to side to move them back from the kerb.

"Relax," Travis said, forcing his voice low, before urging himself to take his own advice despite his white knuckles as he gripped the door handle. Concentrating on Colin, he watched the man's eyes widen even further with each glance into the rearview mirror.

Travis leaned forward to get his own view, and staring into the side mirror, he found the police car straddling both lanes, but pushed himself back into his seat when it came alongside.

"Keep calm," he said, forcing himself not to look across the car to check if the officers stared over.

The sudden sharp rush of its sirens pressed their backs against their seats, but with their hearts pounding in their chests, the car streaked by, overtaking the tall black SUV next in line. The police car's call soon faded away, taking much of their fear with it before the traffic ahead forced Colin to slow.

Feeling the circulation return to his fingers, Travis watched the speedo's needle drop, but it wasn't long before something snapped Colin's attention back to the rearview mirror.

Fearing as if they'd jumped back in time, Travis twisted for another look. Despite finding a police car with its blue lights bright, the red saloon between it and the Mini was enough to tell him it wasn't a temporal blip. As he reassured himself, the police car slowed, taking with them the string of vehicles behind.

Colin soon let the Mini's speed build, following the SUV around the long sweep of a corner before he spoke.

"What are they doing?"

Travis twisted again in his seat and stared at where the police car straddled both lanes as it shrunk in the view.

"They're blocking the road," he replied, before turning back and leaning to the side of the car as he tried to look around the SUV. "Stay on course for the Mary May."

With a nod, Colin swatted at a bead of sweat running down his temple before correcting the steering as he replaced both hands on the wheel.

"We'll be back at the ship soon," Travis said under his breath, his hands tight on their hold.

Colin nodded at the words not meant for him, then jabbed at the brakes as the SUV's red lights came on. Travis lurched forward, pressing his hand against the dashboard before letting out a long breath as the brakes relaxed.

"These things are terrifying," Travis said, shaking his

head as the wheels crept along the road. "I don't know how you can do this every day."

Colin turned in his seat, but Travis raised his hand and pointed through the windscreen.

"Eyes on the road," he snapped, and as Colin's attention returned, he stomped on the brakes when he found the car in front had stopped.

"Sorry. I'm just nervous, that's all," Colin replied, as the suspension's rock pressed them back into their seats. Without a word, the pair looked through the rear window, both of them letting go of a breath when apart from the red car coming to a stop behind them, they found the road empty.

Savouring the calm, Travis stared at the SUV's red lights.

"It's a wonder how people get anywhere in this city," Travis said, leaning out of his window, only to find he still couldn't see around the SUV.

"It's not normally this bad," Colin replied, and Travis looked over, cocking a brow just as the SUV's brake lights darkened and it crawled forward.

"Come to the side of the road," Travis said, beckoning Colin with his curled finger. Turning the wheel, Colin let the car drift to the left as Travis leaned out as far as he could.

"Oh shit," he soon said, his face pale as he drew himself back inside. "There's another roadblock about ten cars up. It looks like they're searching each car."

Colin hit the brakes again, pressing the pair against their seat belts.

"What are we going to do?" he said, as the car stopped a finger width from the SUV's bumper. "That's the way to the Mary May."

"Keep breathing and turn the car around," Travis

replied, until with a glance over his shoulder he realised there was no room to manoeuvre.

"That'll give us away for sure," Colin blurted out.

Travis didn't reply. Instead, he peered out of each front window, taking in the rows of tall three-storey houses set back from either side of the road. With only parked cars between them and the houses on his side, through Colin's window he spotted a second road which ran parallel and was free of traffic, but with a kerb that seemed taller than the Mini's wheels, and a short but sturdy metal fence dividing the two carriageways. Getting there was only a pipe dream.

"We should ditch the car," Travis said, still peering past the metal railing.

"Not here. That's worse than turning around," Colin snapped, his tone high as he shook his head. "If we can make it to the city centre, we'd stand a better chance."

"How far's that?" Travis asked, his gaze locking with Colin.

"A mile or so," Colin said, but Travis shook his head.

"How far's that?"

"Ten minutes, if we ran," Colin replied after a moment's pause as he stared at Travis.

"That's too far," Travis said, shaking his head as the SUV's lights went out again. "Don't move," he added, raising his hand. They lurched forward before Colin jabbed the brakes, leaving a gap to the car ahead.

Travis closed his eyes and pressed the palms of his hands against his face.

"Shit," Colin spat, sending Travis's hand grabbing at the handle, his head darting from side to side.

"What?" he blurted, but found the answer as a tall police officer in a bright-yellow jacket came around the side of the SUV, opening its rear door.

"Look away," Colin said, but Travis couldn't bring himself to avert his gaze. Instead, he watched as the officer's focus lifted and followed along the car's bodywork before jumping the gap and locking eyes with Travis.

They both saw the moment the cop's posture straightened, stiffening with a question a moment before the answer wrote itself across his stern brow and sent his hand rushing under his jacket, where he pulled out a bright yellow gun and pointed it at the car.

"Go," Travis shouted, and the officer's aim flashed to Colin. Despite fearing the ginger-haired man would freeze, the car jumped back, bumping to a stop before it shot forward.

With Colin manhandling the steering, they rushed into the cop's path.

"No," Travis called, lifting his hand to grab the wheel, but held back when the cop jumped out of their way a moment before they roared past.

Whilst rushing the winder around to force his window closed, Travis pointed to their right where, out of the shadow of the SUV, he spotted a small gap in the metal fence.

"There," he called, before glancing to the head of the lined-up cars where he found another officer, his mouth against a raised handset and standing beside his car in the middle of the road.

Less than a second later, Travis tensed, gritting his teeth when their front wheels smashed against the kerb. Fearing they'd knocked the axle clean off its mounts, only the spine-jarring crunch of the rear wheels a split-second later told them their ride had survived.

Already at the gap, and with the throaty roar of the engine seeming to come from all around them, Travis revelled in his newfound respect for their valiant transport.

Wincing as they scraped between the sides of the opening and arriving on the residential road on the other side, Travis glared at the cops running to their car, his neck jarring as one after the other the two pairs of wheels landed on the blacktop.

Despite the discomfort, he smiled, knowing the police car was too wide to follow.

Letting the car slow when they rounded a corner, Colin's focus darted across their view before he spotted the next junction and set the steering for the fastest route.

With his grip tight on the handle and the edge of his seat, Travis gritted his teeth as Colin pushed the car through the turns, weaving to dodge traffic on both sides of the road.

Travis tried his best to force his breath to slow, but each time they veered out of the way of another car or a pedestrian, his grip tightened. When each bump in the road followed with a heavy knocking from underneath, he knew his fear wasn't going anywhere.

"I think she's fucked," Colin shouted, but it wasn't news to Travis.

"Find somewhere quick," he replied, struggling to keep his voice low.

Colin glanced over with a nod, his cheeks flushed bright red.

"How far now?" Travis added, as the buildings on either side of the road went from orange brick houses to towering stone behemoths with flags fluttering high.

Hearing sirens coming from all around, Colin didn't slow as he leaned into a corner, overtaking another car with horns adding to the impromptu orchestra. The smell of petrol joined their list of concerns and another pothole in the road bounced them up high. As the car settled, a rending crack split the air as it came to rest with their new sharp angle punctuated by the roaring scrape of metal.

With the seat springs doing little to cushion every jarring contour of the road, Travis glared across the sharp angle of the bonnet before raising his aching hand and pointing to a left turn and a line of metal bollards blocking their path.

"There," he called out, shaking his finger as he stared at the crowd of shoppers beyond.

With barely a nod, Colin leaned all his weight against the steering wheel to force the turn as they slowed.

"Ready?" Colin shouted over the roar of the engine and chassis scouring across the road, but Travis didn't reply, already holding onto the door handle and bracing himself against the dashboard with his other hand.

Despite the wing mirror's new angle and the glass filled only with flaring sparks, he knew they'd have to run, if not from the police, then the impending fireball.

Lurching to rest against the nearest bollard and not waiting to marvel at the new peace, Travis pushed open the door and hefted himself out of the awkward angle. Then with a glance to make sure Colin was out, he didn't look behind before rushing toward the sea of people, many of which were glaring over.

Instinct pulled Travis to an extensive building nestled between shops. The row of blue flags flying outside announced the covered market just as they ran toward it.

The crowd's glares and hands held to their mouths dissipated as they hurried between them, soon joining the steady stream of people heading in and out of the space, which opened out to the high, glass-roofed market potted with small open-fronted units. A heady mix of aromas rushed in as he breathed, overtaking his senses and dragging him back to the time when Mac could cook.

Shaking away the call of his stomach, and ignoring the shouts and yelps as he pushed by shoppers, Travis forced his focus ahead, barely glancing at the butcher's display, or tea towels embroidered with the Oxford crest, or the chairs and tables of people tucking into all sorts of food.

Instead, he sought out the gaps in the crowd, and a way out.

Turning back from checking Colin was still at his heel, he stared towards the far end of the hall and set his course on the streaming daylight, squinting as the fresh air hit him.

Leaving the continuing shrieks and shouts behind, his stomach mourning the vanished promise of food and despite betting they were still being followed, the pair settled down to a fast walk to blend in with the shoppers.

A call from behind soon forced him to look back to a group of five men in dark uniforms running towards them.

36

With no other choice, Travis darted from amongst the group, knowing only by the heavy steps at his side that Colin ran with him between a pair of stone buildings towering high as golden crests hung above dark, ornate wooden doors.

Rushing away from the high street, they passed those posing for photos before the space opened out into a wide area dominated by a huge domed building in the centre. Guessing it was some ancient observatory, people sat on benches around its walls and they looked up from their lunch at the calls booming out from the alley.

Glancing behind, Travis spotted two cops breaking away from the chasing pack. He couldn't help but marvel at how fast they could run laden down with the gear adorning every space of their heavy stab vests. Already wishing they hadn't ruined the car, Travis changed direction, grabbing Colin by the arm to ensure he followed as he rushed through an archway in the stone to burst out into an enclosed courtyard.

His hopes dashed as he continued to charge forward, despite his sudden fear they'd be easy to corner in the space, but his spirit lifted when he spotted many doors, the first of which opened as he shoved it with his shoulder.

Inside, their footsteps deadened against a stone floor, but finding no one else in the short corridor, he rushed up a set of stairs.

The carpeted stone steps made no noise as they

climbed at speed, soon rising to the third and highest floor. With a glance to make sure Colin followed, and finding him only a level behind and puffing like his lungs could give out at any moment, Travis slowed and leaned up to the window as close as he dared.

Peering down, he didn't linger when he saw the five officers starburst across the lawn, each heading off in different directions.

Choosing a slow saunter in case they came across someone further inside, he opened the door at the top of the landing as Colin joined, puffing at his back. The burgundy thick-pile continued under his feet and along a hallway running both left and right, its walls panelled with dark wood he guessed was older than many of the Mars colonies. In his world, at least.

The dry boards creaked with each of their steps as if tracing their path between the walls and past the many other doors, behind which he heard the low background of voices. Arriving at the end of the corridor, Travis reached out to press the bar across the door, but Colin batted away his hand and without a word pointed to a yellow sign with a black bell and curved lines radiating out.

Travis nodded his relief, then froze when the volume and number of voices increased, followed by the creak of wood all around them.

Locking eyes with Colin, they both turned, glaring as each of the six doors lining the right side of the corridor opened, their hinges squealing with scores of young people streaming out with bags over their shoulders or pinning folders and notepads under their arms.

Thankful when no one gave the pair a second look, Travis turned to the closest door, the only one not to have opened.

He grabbed at the handle. When it didn't move, and after swapping a look with Colin who nodded his ascent at the unvoiced question, Travis pulled out the Universal Tool.

Barely noticing the contents of the small cupboard lined with shelves, or the stale, dust-laden air, he locked the door behind them before stepping between boxes piled on the floor and peering down through the wide window flooding light into the room. The floorboard's creak amplified in the closed space, no matter how softly he tried to step.

Travis was about to speak when Colin raised his finger to his mouth as the sound of the students leaving subsided.

Wincing as the floor seemed to serve better than any intruder alarm, Travis peered out of the window, pulling back when he saw more officers dispersing into each of the openings. With dust motes gliding in the air caught by the bright sun, Travis opened his mouth.

"Let's get to the roof," he said, his voice louder than he'd expected.

"Why?" Colin asked with a frown, shuffling his feet until stopped by the sharp crack from underneath.

"If we could signal the Mary May," Travis said, biting his lip as he rubbed his jaw. "Princess should be able to get her to us."

"You don't sound that confident," Colin replied to Travis's wince.

"She knows the basics, but I just hope Sapphire can guide her through the trickier manoeuvres," Travis replied.

"Anyway, how are we going to signal the Mary May?" Colin said, shaking his head with his low brow.

Travis bunched his lips and looked around the small

room, spotting stacks of plastic-wrapped notepads and boxes of marker pens along with various other stationary scattered on the shelves.

"And we'd blow her cover before we'd found Astra," he added, moving his head to meet Travis's eye.

Finding nothing of use on the shelves, Travis turned his attention back to Colin, who glared back.

"Imagine what would happen if everyone saw the Mary May," Colin said.

Travis was about to speak, but the loud crack of wood under his foot, followed by low voices in the corridor, stopped him in his tracks.

"Searching the top floor east now," came a muffled, deep voice. "Yes. We're checking everywhere," the voice replied a moment later to some unheard question.

The creak of footsteps intensified with several squeaking hinges adding to the complaints.

Colin pressed his hand over his mouth, his face blushing bright red and his eyes going wide as their door handle rattled.

"It's locked."

Colin's face purpled at the man's voice.

"They wouldn't have a key," came another, more distant reply. "Leave it."

"Anyway," the first voice said from the other side of the door, "even if they're hiding, they won't get through the cordon."

"Or out of the city. They can't stay hidden forever," the other man replied.

Colin and Travis stared into each other's eyes as the creak of floorboards tracked the men's movements until they were gone.

Barely letting themselves breathe, Travis focused on Colin until he couldn't bear the silence any longer.

"We can't stay here all day," he said, gritting his teeth and twisting around to the window, wincing with every complaint of the floor beneath him.

Impatient, he chose speed rather than care, and using the Universal Tool he unlocked the door before peering out through a crack and into the empty corridor.

Not turning back, he stepped out. Standing as close to the wall as he could, he nodded when the floor seemed quieter as he travelled to the far end.

"Travis," Colin whispered harshly from the door to the stairwell.

With a raise of his hand, Travis dismissed the man's concern before looking out of the lone window to the grey stone of the neighbouring building.

Bunching his lips, he peered across the gap three times his height but found the wall featureless, only raising his brow when he spotted another courtyard, but much smaller than the one they'd arrived through. Finding no one standing around the grass, or looking up from the windows across the way, he stepped back before lifting the catch to open the thin-framed window.

After leaning out for a better look, he pulled his head back in and glanced over his shoulder, his face bright with delight as he beckoned Colin over. Not waiting for a response, he lifted himself up and placed a foot on the frame.

"What the...?" Colin exclaimed, cutting himself off when he found Travis already out of the window and standing on the other side by the time he'd rushed over.

Beaming through the opening, Travis ignored the shake of Colin's head before sidling along a thin ledge and grabbing at a black metal downpipe at the window's side. Finding it stayed in place as he tugged, he shimmied down the single storey before landing on a low, shallow-pitched roof of another building below.

Grinning up like the cat that got the cream, he motioned up to Colin.

"Look," Travis called out, his loud voice sending Colin's eyes wide, the blood already drained from his face.

"Sssh," Colin hissed with his finger at his lips, before glancing over his shoulder then leaning out to follow Travis's finger, pointing at a rack of upturned canoes.

Not looking up to catch Colin's reaction, and giving him no time for questions, Travis slipped down the tiled roof on his butt. As his feet slapped onto the grass, he peered between the buildings to the far end, where a concrete jetty delved into a river rushing past.

"Come on. It's our way out," Travis called, his voice just above a whisper as he examined the chain holding the open canoes tight to the racking.

Hearing Colin's laboured breath, he looked up and over to where he found him clinging to the drainpipe for dear life, his face pale as he peered all around.

"There's no time for sightseeing," Travis called as he pulled the Universal Tool from his pocket, staring with fascination as the metal end liquified and formed a small key.

By the time Travis had unwound the chain, taking care to stop the links from chattering together, Colin held his arms out either side for balance as he stepped gingerly down the roof's shallow angle.

"Are you still having fun?" Travis chuckled.

Colin glared back, but Travis was already lifting one end of the canoe as he waited for the slap of Colin's feet.

"Have you used one of these before?" Colin asked, his voice shaking as they lowered the canoe into the water rushing by.

"No. You?" he replied, and Colin shook his head whilst holding the boat from slipping away. Travis held the side of the canoe and stepped into the middle before sitting on the rear of the two planks spanning its width.

When the boat settled from its wobble, he rested his palm on the jetty, his muscles tensing as he fought with the current. "Get in."

"Woaw," Colin exclaimed as the boat lurched to one side with the press of his weight. "I'm not sure now is a good time to learn," he added, shaking his head as he gripped the sides of the boat for dear life when his butt touched down.

Before Travis replied, he'd let go of the jetty, the current snatching them clean away from the concrete.

"Right. How do you control this thing?" Travis said, tapping Colin on the shoulder as they rushed along the water.

"What? Where are the paddles?" Colin blurted out, leaning back with their speed building.

37

Colin moved to twist around on the plank spread across the open canoe's span, but as he tried to glance at Travis behind, hoping to spot an oar in his hands, he lurched back ahead to correct the boat's lean he feared would spill him overboard.

"Please tell me you're joking," he spluttered, his eyes wide as, gripping the sides, they rushed down the middle of the river.

"I wish," Travis called as he fumbled beyond the fibreglass lip, but finding only space below, he kicked himself for the mistake.

Their building speed didn't let him linger on his failure for long. Instead, his search extended out to both banks, where to his left a haphazard line of overgrown trees hugged the edge with the occasional branch reaching across the high water, but not close enough to grab on to. On the other side, a tangle of overgrown vines and thorny bushes blocked their escape, their slippery tendrils drooping through the rushing surface.

Finding no hope in reach, his thoughts ran to capsizing the boat, but when a vision filled his head with the raging current pushing them under and dashing them against jagged obstacles hidden beneath the surface, he shook his head.

"What are you doing?" Colin called out, not caring who might hear from the bank as Travis leaned, tipping the boat to his right.

Not replying, Travis instead tried to understand why

they weren't changing direction, but he soon gave up the move, righting himself as the hull's sudden wobble filled him with fear he'd upend them any moment.

"Travis," Colin shouted again. "What are we going to do?" he called.

Spotting a bridge just ahead, hope bloomed inside Travis's chest until he noticed the water's high level gave no space for them to fit underneath its span, dashing all thoughts of grabbing onto the brickwork.

"Get down," Travis called at the top of his voice. Taking one last look at the white water twisting and churning from debris beneath the surface, he forced himself to lean forward, pressing his head into Colin's back, certain their speed was still building as the current funnelled them to the left before sweeping into the centre again.

He felt Colin tense as everything went dark, the rush of the water echoing as his hair touched the span until, in a heartbeat, the light came back.

With a heavy breath, Travis peered around Colin, glancing to another bridge in the distance with even less room.

Sitting up straight as the boat wobbled from side to side, they veered to the right in the chaotic water and toward the overgrown bank. With no way to control their course and forced instead by whatever lay beneath them, the details of which Travis didn't want to think about, he leaned out as far as he felt he could, clasping at anything in reach.

Catching a thin branch, it whipped out of his hand as they rushed away, only to draw closer again.

"Lean to the left," Travis called out, and after abandoning an attempt to twist around, Colin did as he'd asked, Travis countering with an opposite lean. After drying his hand on his jeans, he reached out, stretching as far as he dared and grasping a thick vine, only for it to scrape across his palm.

Glancing at the bridge growing closer with each breath, he reached out again, jostling the canoe as Colin did his best to balance his moves. Still, the boat lurched to the right as Travis extended his stretch when he spotted a thick trunk and forced both his hands out to grab on.

It wasn't enough. The scrape of the rough wood lit up his palms with pain, but realising they'd slowed just a little, it buoyed his spirit. Leaning again, and targeting another thick bow, his grip held as his arms strained against the last of their momentum.

Letting out a heavy breath, he peered at the bridge, relieved they were no longer rushing toward it, but he didn't linger for long. Instead, the strain of his biceps sent him searching across the near bank for where they could land.

Spotting a gap a few boat-lengths downstream and not ready to let go, he tried his best to block out the rush of water all around him, knowing that if he got the next part wrong, the current would dash them against the stone.

When the pain in his arms threatened to release his grip, he drew a deep breath, relaxing his arms just a little before he let go with one hand. As they moved with the current and staring at his target, he let go with the other. Adrenaline rushed as their speed built quicker than he'd expected, but with his gaze not moving from the gap, he pushed his hands out and circled his fingers around the next branch, bringing them to a stop.

Keeping the pauses between his new hold short, he did the same a few times more, building a rhythm until

Colin called and pointed to the landing Travis had already picked out.

Glancing at the bridge looming so close, Travis looked back at his hands as he reached for the next branch, but his heart skipped a beat as it slipped through his fingers.

38

The overgrown branches swept out of reach, rushing away as the current pulled their narrow vessel closer to the centre of the river, despite the pair leaning out further than they knew they should for fear of tipping them overboard.

Shaking his head, Travis pulled his hand back as he racked his brains for how they could stop themselves smashing at speed into the bridge, which would send them sprawling out to fight the current, if they remained conscious.

Glaring ahead, he knew he had such little time left, and was about to call to Colin to ditch the boat, when, as he glanced to his right, he spotted a low branch leaning out so much further than the rest.

Without time to think or call out for Colin to prepare, instinct sent his hand reaching out and with his fingers making contact, he clasped the bough. At first it rushed between his palm but squeezing despite the pain, the boat slowed.

Fearing it wouldn't be enough, his grip caught on a knot, jarring them to a halt.

Despite the pain, his clutch held, drawing the branch away from the tree and with it came a new fear it might just rip the wood clean at the joint.

But it held. Not giving himself time to take a breath, Travis pulled hand over hand along the branch, fighting against the pull of the rushing water. Within a moment, they were up against the muddy bank, holding on for dear life to let Colin clamber out.

Letting go of the canoe as Travis crawled on his hands and knees, he glanced back as it rushed away, watching as it sped towards the bridge then hit the brick with a resounding crack before the water dragged it under, pressing it deep and out of sight.

"Where are we?" Travis asked, panting for breath. Despite savouring the solid ground under his feet, he looked around, then peered down at the mud splattering his knees and the remains of his t-shirt.

Screwing up his face, Colin turned in a circle.

"We've travelled quite a way," he added, turning again as if to make sure. "We're on the other side of town. The shops should be behind that building," he said, raising his hand across the river. "They won't be searching for us here for a while," he continued, before peering at Travis. "But looking like this," he said, glancing at his own muddy clothes and lifting his foot for water to run out. "It won't take long for someone to report us."

Travis nodded and they set off over the bridge, Colin's foot squelching as it left behind a wet trail.

It didn't take long to find the thin crowds along the High Street, surprising the pair when no one paid them particular attention. Seeing the first signs of fluorescence ahead, they stepped into a clothes shop.

Taking little time to browse, they chose a bundle of clothes and after ripping off the tags and dressing in the changing rooms, leaving their sodden articles behind and almost forgetting to retrieve the Universal Tool, they presented the tags at the counter.

Travis watched the woman glance at the rectangles of thin cardboard before looking up at each of them. After flashing her a wide grin, she double took when she saw them in the same clothes, then looking back a third time before she realised they were articles they sold.

"Is that everything?" she said, after scanning each of the tags.

"Yes, thank you," Travis said.

When Colin remained silent, he elbowed him in the side, then stepped away as Colin pulled out his plastic card.

Dressed in a plain black tee that fit better than the Skywalker top he'd stolen from the washing line, and in new jeans, socks and boots, the pair looked almost identical as they stepped from the shop with a tentative glance along both directions.

Hearing distant sirens and spotting the pair of police officers in the bright yellow still milling around, they stepped into the next shop and through the narrow building, stopping only as they reached the far end.

"Can I help you?" a young woman beamed as she sauntered over a moment later, swapping a glance between the pair as, for the first time since they'd arrived, they looked away from the entrance.

Travis took in the woman dressed in a short skirt with a bright-yellow blouse, her curly hair flowing down to her shoulders. He guessed she was a good ten years younger than himself as she smiled with a face full of freckles, whilst she raised her brow and waited for a response.

Realising he hadn't yet replied, and neither had Colin, his gaze fell to a headless figure behind her, wearing nothing but thin lace black and red underwear much like they'd seen on the women in the strip club.

Blinking in the moment it took to realise it was some sort of life-sized doll, he looked away, holding his breath as his gaze fell on a wall filled with more women's underwear hanging on hooks.

"Um," Travis said, stopping himself short, then turning to his other side he stepped back when he spotted row after row of erect penises in a rainbow of colours and hues, each ranging in size from what would fit in your palm to those he imagined would need a visit to the medic afterwards.

"Are you looking for something for yourself, or a gift?" the woman asked, confidence filling her voice.

Travis swallowed hard, glancing to Colin for support, but he already knew he'd be staring at the woman white-faced.

"Sorry. Wrong shop," Travis blurted out, before pressing his hand against Colin's back and ushering him past the scantily-dressed plastic figures. Not thinking to look either side of the street before they turned, he spotted the pair of police officers heading towards them, but with their attention scanning across the crowds, Travis had time to not make the same mistake again. Thankful the window display was filled with stacks of books, he guided Colin over the threshold.

Moving to the back of the new shop, Travis glanced at every face inside, but relaxed when he found each person engrossed with either reading or scanning the bookshelves.

"What the hell was that place?" Travis whispered to Colin as they came to a stop by one of many stacks of tall shelves.

Colin looked up at him with his mouth agape until he blinked, head twitching as if he'd come out of a trance.

"I had no idea…" he replied, his words fading to nothing as the colour returned to his cheeks.

"Were they instruments of torture?" Travis said, shaking his head. "They were enormous," he added, but held back as the colour drained from Colin's face again. "Now I've seen a few things in my time, but…" he said, cutting himself off when Colin's eyes grew large. "Never mind. Back to looking for Astra."

"Without getting caught," Colin added, peering around with the confidence building back in his tone.

"If only we could find that women's shelter," he said, nodding.

"We're the exact sort of people not meant to find it," Colin replied, raising his brow.

"So we're left with getting back to the Mary May, or signalling them somehow."

"I don't like the thought of what could happen if they saw her hovering in the daylight?" Colin said, leaning closer as he dropped his voice to a whisper.

Travis bit his bottom lip.

"But if it brings Astra's memories flooding back," he replied, taking a second look at the shelf behind Colin when he spotted the spine of a book filled with a spaceship. Pulling the dark book from the shelf, he stared at the cover, the spacecraft reminding him of the Mary May as it rose from a bright planet below.

Recognising Europe's form, he frowned at the bright halo and mixture of greens, browns and blues, which he could only recall ever seeing in history books. Seen from above, the seas and oceans of *his* world were a maelstrom of greys whilst the land resembled a dark brown.

"Oh," Travis blurted out, then covered his mouth with his hand at his volume.

"What is it?" Colin asked, his eyes wide with alarm.

"Social media," Travis exclaimed, staring at Colin, but when his face didn't light up with the words, Travis raised his hands. "The nurse said we'd find Astra if we used social media."

Colin bunched his cheeks as he shook his head.

"I'm the wrong person for that. You probably have a better idea about it than I do," he replied, his eyes tightening with sympathy as he watched Travis's shoulders drop.

They stood in silence for a long moment, each of them glancing over the shelves as if for inspiration.

"What defences has she got?" Colin asked, turning back to Travis and watching as he pushed a book back.

With his face still fixed with a frown, Travis locked eyes with Colin.

"A mean left hook," he replied.

"No," Colin blurted out, before covering his mouth with his hand. "The Mary May."

"Ah. None really," Travis replied, turning back to scour the shelves.

"I thought she had shields?" Colin said, and Travis looked up.

"Only for landing. They wouldn't work against energy or ballistic weapons," he said, sliding out another book before slipping it back home when he spotted a man with greasy, long black hair heading towards their section.

"Astra reads," Travis said, sounding distant as Colin followed him to another series of shelves. "She loves the classics," he added, remembering the books on the desk in the room she shared with Princess.

"Me, too," Colin said, nodding toward the stacks of books and reaching out to finger the smooth spine of Great Expectations.

Travis took a step closer, eyeing the books with interest.

"She's got some of these. I'm sure," he said, not hiding his delight.

"Really?" Colin said, his pitch rising as he looked between Travis and the books. "So we share some history?"

"That's how it works," Travis replied with a raised brow. "This dimension thing. Our worlds were the same until someone's decision sent us on different trajectories."

Colin's eyes narrowed before he turned back to the shelves.

"Have you heard of Charles Dickens?" he said, glancing back as he lifted his brow, his eyes lighting up when Travis nodded. "Edgar Allan Poe?"

"Sure," Travis replied, but with less enthusiasm.

"Arthur Conan Doyle?" he asked, but Travis looked back with a blank expression. "You must have heard of Sherlock Holmes?" Colin added before he held his hand out in front of his face, his fist curled around an imaginary pipe.

"Oh yeah. I've heard of him," Travis replied, nodding.

"Curiouser and curiouser," Colin said, raising a brow, but when Travis looked back through pinched eyes, he let his shoulders slump. "Lewis Carroll?"

"Alice's Adventures in Wonderland is her favourite," Travis said, stepping closer to the shelf before he drew out a thin book. He closed his eyes as he remembered Astra leaning back in the seat next to his with her face buried in a dogeared volume, the rear cover illustrated with a faded version of the Mad Hatter's tea party.

"She must have read it hundreds of times," he said, flicking through the pages. "She convinced me to read it once," he added with a shake of his head. "That guy must have been on some hardcore medication."

Colin let a laugh slip before pressing his hand over

his mouth.

"What about F Scott Fitzgerald?" Colin asked a moment later. "D H Lawrence? Virginia Woolf?" he added, but Travis bunched his lips together, then tore his gaze from the book and pushed it back on to the shelf to peer around the shop once more.

Raising his shoulders, he examined every face, but finding no one even close to Astra's description, he shook his head and peered across at the entrance.

"Travis," Colin said after a long moment.

"Yes?" he replied, turning back to him.

"I'm glad I met you," Colin said, and a smile lit up Travis's face.

"Me too," he replied, slapping Colin on his arm.

"I'm having the best time of my life," Colin replied, and Travis stared at him for a long moment, still smiling.

"It's fun," Travis replied, bunching his cheeks. "But we can't forget why we're doing this."

Colin nodded, and Travis looked back across the shop floor.

"You know, Oxford is pretty famous for authors," Colin said, but when Travis didn't acknowledge him, he looked away. "If Astra can't go to work because she thinks strange men are after her…" he said, but stopped when Travis glared over. "Remember what some people might think it looks like," he added, holding up his palms.

"Go on," Travis said, raising his chin. "What were you going to say?"

"I was just trying to think of what she might do if she can't go to work," Colin replied. "What does Astra do for pleasure, other than reading?"

Travis stared over as he scoured his thoughts.

"She loves to fly," he replied, lifting his chin, but a

frown soon followed. "And nature. We don't get so much of it on our Earth, or in the colonies. I think she'd love the nature here. It's everywhere."

"So she's in a strange place with no friends," Colin said, stepping a little closer and lowering his voice. "It's a beautiful day," he continued, glancing through the doors and to the outside as if to reassure himself the weather hadn't changed.

"Perhaps she goes to the park. There are lots of…" he said, but cut himself off and he held his breath and raised a finger in the air. "There's a Cheshire Cat sculpture in the Oxford Botanic Gardens," he eventually said, and Travis watched him turn around and back to the shelf where he reached out for the copy of Alice's Adventures in Wonderland before leafing through it.

With his stare fixed on the pages, he stopped and turned the book around to Travis, showing him a line drawing of a cat that looked normal in every way apart from its huge eyes and a wide toothy smile filled with human teeth.

Travis drew in a sharp breath and pointed to the page.

"She has that tattooed on her other shoulder." His words echoed as his eyes glistened.

39

"What does that mean?" Colin asked, trying his best to avoid the other customer's glares.

"It means," Travis said, elongating the word whilst lowering his voice, "you could be right and we have somewhere to look. Where are these Botanic Gardens?"

"At the edge of town," Colin said, with Travis already taking him by the shoulder and directing him toward the exit.

"Which way?" Travis asked, looking across the crowds as they stepped from the shop.

Colin frowned, relaxing his expression only as Travis caught his eye, then he stood on tiptoes and peered around before glancing at Travis again and pointing to the left.

Without a word, Travis rushed the way Colin motioned.

"When we find her," Colin said, a little out of breath as he caught up. "And assuming we can convince her to go with you…"

"Of course we'll convince her. Everything will come flooding back as soon as she sees us. Just like it did with the others," Travis cut in. Striding with purpose, he glanced over for the next direction.

"This way," Colin said, motioning down a side street. "As soon as she sees *you*, you mean."

"Of course, yes. Cheer up," Travis replied, spotting Colin's downcast expression and giving him a playful shove, which almost sent him over.

"But once she's remembered, we've still got to get across town and through the roadblocks back to the Mary May. All the while hoping the ship's not spotted by the army's radar system."

"You're a ray of sunshine, aren't you?" Travis said with a raised brow as he shot Colin a glance. "I'm kidding. Of course, you're right," he added after a moment when he saw Colin's head turn down.

Thinking better of giving him another jab in the ribs in hope it would cheer him up, the thought fell away when looking up, Travis spotted a series of signs outside of a small shop, the large boards filled with the bright spray of colour rising into a dark sky.

"That's just what we need," he called, changing course to the entrance.

"Fireworks?" Colin said, frowning as he peered up into the bright blue sky. "It's the middle of the day."

Travis was already in through the entrance.

"I need a big bang?" he blurted out to a middle-aged man combing his thin hair behind the counter.

"You what?" the man replied, narrowing his eyes in a way that made him look like a pig.

"I need a loud bang, maybe lots of them. Have you got anything that will show up in the daylight?" Travis said, rushing out the words as he watched the guy purse his lips.

"Daytime fireworks are a speciality I can't do, but I have something that will shatter windows, it's that loud," the man said, the note of his voice rising as he stepped around the counter.

Travis nodded, rubbing his hands together as he watched the man wind his way around counter tops spread across the room, each displaying different colours, sizes and shapes of rockets beneath transparent shields.

Travis glanced at Colin, not noticing his cocked eyebrow as he looked between him and the whiteboard displaying the prices.

"That sounds perfect," Travis added, his attention fixed on the man who'd stopped in front of a display cabinet showing off a pair of long, stout rockets pinned against the wall, each wider than the man's thick neck.

Nodding and glancing back at Colin with a huge grin, it was all Travis could do to stop himself from bouncing from toe to toe with excitement.

"This here is the Galaxy Splitter 27S," the shopkeeper said, huffing with the effort of lifting it from its mounts. "I'm only supposed to let her go for organised events, but," he said, tilting his head to the side as if examining the pair as he arrived back at the counter. "You look like a responsible pair," he added, before lowering his voice.

Travis leaned in when the man let out a breath as he placed the rocket on the counter. "And if anyone asked where you got it from," he said, tapping the side of his nose with his forefinger.

Travis narrowed his eyes, then looked to Colin, who shook his head.

Standing up tall, Travis dismissed the thought, watching instead as the man punched numbers into the till.

"Cash or card?" he said, showing off his yellow-toothed grin.

Travis motioned over his shoulder to Colin, his attention instead fixed on the bright, colourful chevrons adorning the rocket's paper sides amongst the stark warning labels and writing he tried to make out.

"Ah," Travis said, raising a finger in the air. "What

colour is it?" he asked, but before the guy could answer, a low tone from the card machine sent his eyebrow rising.

"Declined," the shopkeeper said, letting out a sigh.

Travis looked away from the Galaxy Splitter and over at Colin.

"Have you got anything a little cheaper?" Colin said, sucking on his bottom lip.

Travis's eyes widened before he glanced between Colin's apologetic expression and the bulbous firework.

"Now I've got to put it back," the man said, letting out another sigh as he shook his head before heading between the tables. "This one," he said, pulling out a rocket as thick as his fist, "is half the price for half the bang."

Travis shot Colin a hopeful look, but deflated when he saw Colin shaking his head. After replacing the large projectile, the shopkeeper turned around and pulled out a fistful of different coloured rockets, each just a little thicker than Travis's thumb.

"I'll do you a deal for six of these," the man said. "A tenth of the price of the Galaxy," he added, nodding towards the counter.

Travis couldn't bring himself to look over.

"We'll take them," Colin replied.

"Are they loud?" Travis added, watching as the man shrugged.

"They come in lots of colours," he said, the pitch of his voice rising.

"Red and blue," Travis said, as his eyes lit up.

"Why blue and red?" Colin asked as they left the shop, carrying a plastic bag with six wooden sticks reaching out of the open end.

Travis tapped at his short sleeve.

"Those are the colours Astra and I chose for the logo," he said, tapping at his arm. "Princess wanted orange, but neither of us thought that would work," Travis added, looking off into the crowd before falling silent for a while as they traced the pathways between houses, guided by Colin's occasional instructions.

"If we don't find her today, then I'm signalling the Mary May," Travis eventually said, straightening himself tall as they walked, then diving down a side street after spotting a police car crawling along the road only open to buses.

"I don't think we should leave it too long. What if the army find the ship before we signal?" Colin said, looking over at Travis.

"They can handle themselves," Travis said, his voice edged with a hardness. "We're finding Astra."

As the pair reached a junction, Colin stopped. Despite finding no traffic from either direction, he didn't move. Instead, he looked up at Travis.

"What happens when you find her?" Colin said, his eyes narrow with the question.

"If Miles has figured out how to control the EQuaNTS device, then we're headed for home. If not, we'll move the ship where no one can follow to give him time."

Colin peered up into the blue sky.

"Which way?" Travis asked, checking along the road for a second time.

"There's only six bunks," Colin said, his voice quiet as he stepped across the road.

Barely hearing Colin's words, Travis followed in silence, his head twitching this way and that as excitement fizzed through his veins with the hope they could be close to finding Astra. He took no notice of Colin's lacklustre walk or his head turned down to the ground, only looking up to check where they were going.

Arriving at the head of another side street, the pair stopped at the edge of the road, both of them looking at the row of stone buildings opposite and a tall arch in the centre with a small queue of people at its front.

"Are we here?" Travis asked, not looking away, but he didn't prompt for an answer when his gaze fell to a sign clinging to a wrought-iron fence confirming they'd arrived.

"What happens now?" Colin asked, his voice tailing off as a helicopter flew close but out of sight.

Travis peered around for signs of the police, but pleased to find no white cars, black uniforms or fluorescent jackets, he crossed the road. Not looking to see if Colin followed, arriving the other side he headed through the gates and stopped.

Lifting himself on tiptoes to get a better look past the queue of people, he scoured the pathways between the raised flower beds beyond.

"Come on," Travis called when, after joining the back of the short queue, he spotted Colin still standing on the other side of the road.

"What did you say?" Travis asked when Colin eventually arrived, turning towards him when he hadn't already replied.

"I asked what happens if you don't find her?" Colin said.

Travis's expression fell for a moment, but he soon lifted his chin.

"But we will," he replied, his voice low as he nodded slowly. "It's just a matter of time. If it's not today, then I'll come back tomorrow, and the day after."

Taking the plastic bag from Colin, he looked up at the sky. "Once we're sure it's not today, and we still can't get back to the Mary May, then we'll signal her and take her somewhere safe."

"It could take years," Colin said. Despite the wetness in his eyes, his brow lifted.

Travis tensed and gave a curt nod as his jaw set. After a moment, he reached out and slapped Colin on the upper arm.

"I'm not leaving without her, but it won't be a problem," he said, his face brightening. "Because we're going to find her today." As he finished speaking, the pair spotted the empty queue ahead, as a polite cough sounded from behind.

"Next please," a woman called from the booth just beyond the stone arch. "Is that two tickets?" the middle-aged woman asked as the pair arrived.

Travis nodded, his enthusiasm back.

"That'll be nine pounds, please."

Travis glanced at Colin, flashing a smile before he stepped through the arch.

Only just hearing the confirming beep, Travis peered around but ignored the flowers in full bloom and the manicured greenery. Instead, his gaze twitched from side to side to each small group of tourists and couples holding hands as they meandered along the footpaths.

"Any sign?" Colin asked, his voice still flat as he joined at Travis's side.

"No," Travis replied, shaking his head. "Not yet."

"It was a long shot," Colin said, resting his hand on Travis's arm.

"Maybe it was a stupid idea," Travis said, unable to stop himself from looking around. "Of all the places she could be right now, why would she be here?"

"I haven't shown you the statue yet and there's more gardens to the right," Colin said pointing to an opening in the clean manicured line of the hedgerow border.

Within twenty minutes they'd walked the place twice, winding their way at speed between the raised planters, then along the paths between the trees in the forest section. Repeating the journey, they did so at a more causal pace, with Travis peering into every nook and examining every formed hedge and fence for any new avenue they'd missed.

"There's still hope," Colin said, taking a seat on one of a pair of wooden benches perched opposite each other amongst the trees.

Looking around one last time, Travis sat beside him in silence and stared along the path to his right toward the entrance arch.

It must have been over ten minutes before his gaze dropped to the rough ground below his feet, but it wasn't more than a moment later that a bird's chirp pulled his survey into the trees.

"There's always hope," Travis said, cocking a brow as he stared into the eyes of a stone Cheshire Cat, whose wide smile beamed up high in the trees.

Without warning, he stood and looked over at Colin.

"Let's do this," Travis said, lifting the bag and opening it wide with both hands.

"Do what?" Colin asked, not hiding his surprise.

"I can't just sit here," Travis said, glancing back up at the cat. "We'll find high ground and signal the Mary May."

"Are you sure?" Colin said, and Travis closed his eyes as he nodded. "We could take another look around town."

"And have the police catch us?" Travis said. "We'll

never find Astra if we're locked up and who knows what they'd do to us."

"To you," Colin replied. Travis nodded. "Or maybe we try to make it back by ourselves. It'll put the others in less danger."

"You know as well as I do they're already in danger," Travis replied, furrowing his brow. "The police and military are hunting them down as we speak. At least this way, maybe we can scare them off and draw Astra out at the same time."

Colin looked into Travis's eyes, holding there for a long moment just before he stood.

"Okay," Colin said. "There's a tall hill just the other side of the gardens," he added, nodding through the trees. "But we'll have to go out and around to get to it."

Turning towards the main entrance beyond the opening in the green wall, Colin took a step and froze.

After almost bumping into him, Travis frowned then followed his gaze, his eyes narrowing as between the rows of planters he spotted a woman who'd just walked through the stone arch.

With short dark hair, her slim build and height sent his back straight, but as a tall man with broad shoulders and mousey brown hair joined at her side, he felt like he couldn't breathe.

40

Colin turned, looking Travis up and down before peering back towards the entrance and the man who'd arrived with the woman he knew must be Astra.

"Is that you…?" Colin said, tripping over the words as he glanced back at Travis, fixing him with his concern.

Travis didn't reply, unable to look away from the pair.

"He's you from this dimension," Colin said, swapping his glance between the two men.

Travis shook his head.

"He looks just like you," Colin added, narrowing his eyes as he stared at Travis. "You shouldn't meet," he said, "or you'll go mad, or maybe you'll both cancel each other out and stop existing."

"He looks nothing like me," Travis replied, his words barely heard. "But it's her," Travis said, his voice still quiet as he winced when Astra laughed with high, child-like glee.

Taking his gaze off the pair for the first time, his attention fell to his feet, his eyes narrowing with the conflicting emotions racing through his brain until a wave of excitement rushed up from his core to wash the nerves away and made him peer up, afraid they wouldn't be standing there anymore.

The man spoke, but unable to hear his words from where they stood, Travis watched him guide her toward the arch Travis had taken so long to spot when he'd first arrived with Colin.

"Travis?" Colin said once the pair had ambled out of sight. "What is it? I thought you'd be overjoyed."

"I am, but she..." Travis replied, the words tripping on his tongue as he stared at the empty archway. "She looked so happy. I'm not sure I can..."

Colin peered up, narrowing his brow as he cocked his head to the side.

"Not sure if you can what?"

Travis shook his head as he locked eyes with Colin.

"What if she's found something she was missing in our world? Like Miles has," Travis said, dropping the bag of fireworks. With a single step backward, he lowered onto the bench.

"The other man?" Colin said, watching Travis nod his reply. "But don't you see?"

"See what?" Travis replied, tilting his head.

Colin turned back to the entrance.

"Even assuming she has no memory of where she came from, somehow she sought you out," Colin said, turning back to meet Travis's gaze.

Travis frowned.

"But if you're not sure," Colin added, looking down at the dirt ground. "Or you've changed your mind, then let's go fire these rockets off so we can get the hell out of here."

Closing his eyes, Travis didn't speak for a long moment.

"You just want her bunk," he replied with a weak smile as he looked up.

Colin gave a weak laugh.

"Yeah," he said before looking away, then turning back with a new brightness in his eyes. "I mean... I wouldn't mind sharing with Princess." Colin picked up the bag of fireworks, then turned, taking a step away.

Travis let out a belly laugh as he stood, then reached out and slapped Colin on the back.

"Thank you. You're a staunch friend," Travis said, and Colin turned to see Travis's usual bright smile back on his face.

"I am?" Colin replied, his chin lifting as the corner of his lips turned up.

"You are, and you're right, too. I'm just nervous, that's all," Travis replied with a nod and not noticing the colour drain from Colin's face when his shoulder's slumped. "No matter how happy she is now, I know how much she loves being part of our crew," he added, peering around.

"Hang on," Colin said, stepping in to block his view.

"What?" Travis asked, moving for a better look.

"Nothing. I just mean…" Colin said. "…Think about it. Are you ready?"

"Ready for what?" Travis replied, laughter tripping from his mouth. "I can't think about it anymore. I'll get nervous again."

"But have you thought about what this could mean for her?" Colin said, moving to get in his eye line. "You'll rip up all that she knows, and…"

Travis lowered himself from his tip toes and reached over, putting both his palms on Colin's upper arms and looking him in the eye.

"You said yourself, if that guy has some resemblance to me, then I must be what she's looking for. She wants me to bring her memories back. She wants me to take her back to the Mary May," Travis said.

"I did?" Colin said, pressing his palm to his chest.

"Not in so many words, but thank you, Colin. And I know you're worried about what's going to happen when we're back at the Mary May. But trust me, there are better times ahead for all of us. You're a good kid and I don't doubt you'll do good things with your life. I can tell," Travis said, lowering his voice and leaning closer.

"I've had the time of my life with you. I just can't be alone again…" Colin said, his voice low, but stopping himself as Travis looked up and over his shoulder, distracted by a couple walking past.

"Sorry," Travis said, meeting his eye. "What did you say?" he added as Colin's shoulders fell again.

"Nothing," Colin said, closing his eyes and unable to speak when Travis looked at him as if he were a newborn puppy. "Can you wait just a minute whilst I go to the toilet?"

"Of course. Is the moment getting to you?" Travis asked, nodding, but when Colin didn't reply, he dropped his hands from Colin's arms before taking the bag of fireworks and looking back up at the Cheshire Cat, unable to stop himself from mirroring the smile. "I need a few minutes to work out what I'm going to say to her, anyway."

Not watching Colin walk away, he looked across the gathering of trees and took slow, deep breaths as he tried to stop his heart from racing at the thought that soon he would talk to Astra again.

Sooner than he'd expected, and before he'd thought over his words, Colin arrived back, his cheeks flushed and his gaze flitting all over the place.

"Ready?" Travis asked.

"Have you decided what you're going to say?" Colin replied, looking at his feet as he spoke.

"I'll wing it," Travis replied, still smiling.

"Is that a good idea?" Colin said as he twisted around to look towards the main entrance and where he'd arrived from.

"I think so, but first," Travis said, holding back when he noticed Colin looking anywhere but at him. "Colin," he said, then repeated himself until Colin looked over, wetting his lips.

Spotting red rings around Colin's eyes, Travis bunched his cheeks and beckoned him to sit down next to him.

With hesitant steps, Colin took a seat, and the pair gazed off towards the entrance, neither speaking as the distant call of a siren pierced the relative silence. When the call faded to nothing, they both looked away from the stone arch.

"Look," Travis said, but when Colin hadn't turned to meet his gaze, he gave him a nudge with his elbow. "I was going to keep it as a surprise," Travis continued, but paused until Colin looked over, his puffy eyes widening. "You've helped us out more than anyone could have expected," he added, placing his palm across his chest. "And I'm shocked and sorry you're not a member of the crew."

Colin's eyes tightened, and he swallowed hard.

"When we get back to the Mary May, I'm going to talk to the others and see what we can do," Travis continued.

"About?" Colin replied.

"About," Travis said, jabbing him in the arm with a playful punch, "becoming the seventh member of the crew. That's if you want to, of course?"

Colin's breath sped.

"But there's only six bunks," Colin said, his voice quiet but rising in pitch.

Travis nodded.

"We've got plenty of space. I'm sure it won't be a problem to work something out, and if you can cook, that will seal the deal," Travis replied, flashing his brow.

"I wish…" Colin said. "I wish you could have told me five minutes ago."

Travis laughed, grinning wide, but the smile fell when he couldn't see the excitement in Colin's eyes, who instead glared at the entrance.

"It's okay if you don't want to, but I thought…" Travis said.

"I do. I mean, I really do, but we have a new problem," Colin replied, but as he looked up at Travis, he found he was peering over Colin's shoulder.

"It's show time," Travis said, standing as he spotted Astra walking into the clearing, her arm locked with the other man's. For a moment he looked at the guy, then shook his head, but swallowing hard and about to step toward the pair, he heard his name and found Colin reaching across him with his finger pointing to the entrance.

"I'm sorry," Colin said, just as Travis spotted the pair of police officers rushing through the stone arch, their eyes locked through the gap in the hedge as they ran towards them.

"Oh, Colin, what have you done?"

41

"I wanted to save you from disappointment," Colin said, pleading with his wide eyes. "We'd run away again."

"Astra," Travis shouted, already twisting away to shoot her a look, but as he spotted her head twitch his way, he span back around to the cops running through the planters and towards them.

"I'm sorry," Colin whimpered, repeating the words as he shook his head. "You need to run," he blurted out, for the first time looking away from the gap in the green border.

Despite his pleading, Travis didn't move, instead seeking Astra again. As her attention fixed on him, he watched as her eyes narrowed and he hurried his attempt to figure out if calling her name had been enough to pull her memories from their hiding place.

The moment rushed by too fast. Not finding the familiar glint in her eye, she instead ran her hand up through her hair that had grown so much since he'd last seen her, even though it was only a few days ago. For him at least.

"Please remember," he pleaded under his breath, but she looked away as the guy beside moved to block his view.

"What the hell?" the guy called out, his head replacing Astra's in the centre of Travis's vision as he stood in front of her. "It's them," he shouted, tensing his shoulders, his biceps bulging as his fists clenched.

Astra stepped around him and peered back, but still Travis couldn't tell if it was recognition he saw.

As the guy beside her spoke, his words barely heard, any curiosity she might of had fell away, replaced instead with a wide-eyed fear.

"They're just like my sister described. Stay back," the man said, holding his arm out.

"Astra," Travis called. As she stepped closer, her eyes stayed wide, but with the frantic calls of the police, he knew all was lost. He had very little time left.

"Stay back," the man shouted, holding out his palm.

"Travis," Colin called, his voice urgent and full of regret.

"Major Astra Sankowski," Travis shouted, projecting his voice as far as he could. "I'm Travis Baxter, pilot of the Mary May, and you're my number two."

Despite the clamour of footsteps and jangle of kit so close, he didn't take his eyes off her, concentrating on her slight frown, dropping the bag of fireworks a moment before he went flying sideways, taken down with a tackle around his waist that sent the wind from his lungs as he tumbled to the ground.

"Do not resist," two male voices called, but Travis paid them no attention as they grabbed at his right wrist, already slapping the cuff on.

Instead, he used all his might to bring his hand around to his upper arm, where he pulled up his sleeve just before a powerful grip wrestled his arm away, pushing his face into the dirt and clamping his wrists together.

As a pressure on his back relented, he turned his head to the side, watching a cop pull Colin's arms around his back before slapping on the restraints.

"I'm so sorry," Colin's voice cut through as the police officer's calls ebbed, the noise of their efforts turning to breathy reports into their radios.

"Two in custody," said the man holding Colin's cuffs.

Unable to move his head as he sought Astra, Travis closed his eyes, letting a long breath leave his body.

The place fell silent, other than a light breeze through the leaves, but as an image of the Cheshire Cat up high in the trees filled his mind, he couldn't help but smile. The man's voice, more distant than before, broke the silence, but still he couldn't quite make out what he'd said.

Travis held his breath, listening for Astra's reply.

"You do not have to say anything," the cop said close to his ear, his voice still breathy and blocking out what Travis attempted to hear. "But it may harm your defence if you do not mention…"

"Quarantine procedure?" the other cop's voice came from almost as close, its tone rising and stopping the other cop's words mid flow. "You could have said that before we arrested them."

"…When questioned something which you later rely on in court. Anything you do say may be given in evidence. What's that all about?"

"…What's that on your arm?" Astra asked, but Travis couldn't reply, and all he could do was watch Colin with that dumbstruck look he had whenever a woman talked to him.

"It's our home," Travis called out, but the words muffled as pain flared up his back from a pressing weight. "Tell her," was all he could get out before pain clamped his mouth shut.

The silence lingered, and it was all Travis could do to shake his head as hope drained away.

"It's him," Colin said, his voice suddenly clear, the high whine gone from his tone.

Travis opened his eyes, half expecting to find Colin speaking to the cops because the other option was unthinkable. Instead, Colin looked across Travis's view as the cop holding Colin's cuffs frowned at Travis.

Uncertainty racked Travis's thoughts, pushing away what he'd heard as a trick, knowing from what Clutch had said and what he'd witnessed himself, Colin hadn't spoken to a woman his whole adult life.

"Stay back," the cop closest to Travis called, and he felt the heavy press return to his back as he shuffled in vain for a better view.

"Do not resist," came the sharp voice, and Travis forced himself to relax.

You've got this, Colin, he said to himself.

"Is this a trick?" Astra said and Travis held his breath when he heard her voice so much closer.

"It's him," Colin called out, his voice high. "Do you remember? Look at him."

Travis continued to hold his breath, desperate to hear her reply.

"Kelly, stay back," the man she'd arrived with called out, his words drowning out her reply.

"It's Astra," Travis said under his breath and shook his head as best as he could.

"Do what your boyfriend says, miss, and stay back," the cop holding on to Travis called out, sending his body stiff at the thought.

"He's not my boyfriend," Astra replied. The words, already louder, sent a rush of adrenaline sparking through Travis and letting him relax.

"Stay back," the other officer shouted, but the words were half-hearted as if his concentration was elsewhere.

Travis felt the pressure on his back relent.

"You catch that?" the cop on his back called. "State

zero at the old gas works. Shit."

"Who?" the other officer called.

"It's the Mary May," Colin shouted, his voice so clear.

"What?" Travis said, pushing up against the weight of the knee on his back, but as the pressure increased with a jab, he collapsed with his face pressing into the dirt.

"It's where we left the Mary May," Colin replied, the words making Travis's heart sink despite the brush of footsteps in the dirt getting closer. "They've found them."

42

"The Mary May?" Astra said, sending a jolt of hope through Travis's chest.

"Yes," he tried to call out, but with his mouth pushed into the mud, it came out as an indistinguishable mess. Instead, he willed Colin to answer.

"Yes," Colin replied. Although the word was quiet, it still warmed Travis's insides. "The others are there, too," he added, his rising confidence clear every time he spoke.

"What is he saying?" the cop above Travis spat. "Be quiet."

"Mac?" Astra said, sending Travis's head nodding.

"Yes," he called, lifting against the pressure.

"What are you saying? Who are these people?" said the other man's voice.

"Princess. Clutch and Miles, too?" Astra asked, her voice growing in volume.

"Yes," Travis did his best to shout, despite the heavy weight pressing down on his back.

"He's not cooking anymore," Colin replied.

"You're kidding?" Astra said. With the bubble of laughter that followed, Travis couldn't help but smile and he forced his head up where he caught sight of Colin's gaze tracking something.

Before Travis could come up with a plan, a heavy thud came from above, followed by another at his side as the pressure on his back relented.

"Kelly, what the hell are you doing?" the man called.

"Have you gone mad?"

"Get back. I have a Taser," one of the cops added to the chaos of calls.

With the weight gone, Travis rolled to his side, finding Astra striding towards Colin, but before Travis could rise to his feet, she stood rifling in the pockets of the second cop she'd knocked out cold.

"What the hell?" the man who'd arrived with Astra said, his mouth hanging open as Travis, still with his hands pinned at his back, got to his feet. "Who are these people?"

Without hesitation, Astra turned and locked eyes with Travis.

"Family," she said, nodding as she released Colin's cuff, then still with her gaze not leaving Travis, she strode back to Travis and separated his cuffs within a few seconds, replacing them on the pair of cops she'd moved into the recovery position.

Before Travis had finished wiping the dirt from his face, Astra wrapped her arms around him, pulling herself close.

Travis closed his eyes and with the maelstrom of shouts gone, the sound of sirens filled the space left behind.

"You remember," he said, his voice soft and still grasping her tight, until a heartbeat later they pulled apart and looked each other in the eye.

"You should go," Colin said as the pair turned towards him.

Travis raised an eyebrow as a memory fell into place.

"You did it," Travis said, his voice low. Colin's head turned downward. "You spoke to Astra. When it mattered, you did what you needed to. You came through."

Colin looked up, confusion furrowing his brow until he glanced at Astra, his eyes widening as if he'd only just realised what he'd done.

Travis watched as his expression fell again and Colin looked back at the ground, then he noticed for the first time the crowds of people gathered by the entrance, each looking on in surprise.

"Who's this?" Astra said, glancing between Colin and Travis.

The corner of Travis's mouth rose as he rubbed at his wrists.

"A genuine friend," Travis said, nodding. "He's been a great help," he added, but Colin didn't lift his head. "Do you remember enough to know we have to get out of here?" Travis asked, stooping for the plastic bag with the sirens sounding as if they were on top of them.

Still looking him in the eye, Astra grasped her upper arm and nodded.

"What am I supposed to do?" the man Astra had arrived with asked.

The three of them looked over, raising their brows as if they'd forgotten about him.

Astra stepped toward him.

"Thank you for everything you've done, and please thank your sister for me as well," she said, watching as the man couldn't hide the confusion from his frown.

Astra didn't linger and with Travis holding the plastic bag as his side, they jogged between the trees, only slowing as together they turned back to Colin, looking from the clearing.

"Is he going to stand there all day?" Astra asked, glancing between Colin and Travis.

"You're more than welcome," Travis said, lifting his brow and offering his hand out.

"But..." Colin replied before cutting himself off.

"I wouldn't take too long to think about it," Astra said, before she turned and ran.

Travis followed, slowing only as they reached a wall a head higher than himself. Without hesitation, Astra leapt up, vaulting high and grabbing at the top edge as if it wasn't vertical.

Travis knelt.

"I'm sorry for calling the cops," Colin said, appearing through the trees.

"I get why you did it. Now climb," Travis replied, motioning to his offered knee.

A cacophony of sirens filled the air as they each dropped down the other side of the wall, leaving them standing at the base of a tall hill with the high pitch wails joined by the rush of helicopter blades. Shouts from all around added to the cacophony, followed by the barks of what sounded like an entire pack of dogs.

As the three of them ran up the steep grass incline, Astra glanced to her side, catching Travis's eye.

"Don't let them get inside your head," she said, her words soft.

Travis drew a deep breath.

Focusing on the climb with their lungs screaming for flat ground, only as the incline plateaued did Astra and Travis look behind to where Colin rushed in their wake, puffing and panting and red in the face.

Not lingering on him for long, their search instead spotted uniformed men with dogs rushing ahead on long lengths of rope, with more appearing from either side of the Botanic Garden's wall, their focus fixed on the threesome.

As Colin arrived, helped over the last few steps with their outstretched hands, they turned and continued their way with speed to the centre of the level part of the vast high ground, where they could just about see the flash of blue lights coming towards them from the surrounding streets before they disappeared behind the hill's brow.

"Here," Travis called, and the three stopped.

"What's your plan, Trav?" Astra asked, barely out of breath.

With her words glowing warm in his chest, Travis upended the plastic bag.

By her lack of reaction to the thin rockets tumbling across the grass, he guessed she'd already figured out what they were as she glanced up at the sky. "Let's hope they can hear them."

"They'll hear them," Travis said, despite the helicopter buzzing above and the many calls from the sirens getting louder each moment.

Stuffing the empty bag into his pocket, he pressed each of the sticks into the ground before drawing them out just a little one by one, in hope they wouldn't get stuck once ignited.

"They're coming," Colin called.

Travis and Astra looked over, following his outstretched arm as he pointed to a group of men led by dogs pulling at their ropes.

"Come here," Astra said, and Colin glanced over, more than a little wary. "Come here," she repeated, gesturing with only her eyes.

When he saw Travis nod, Colin tentatively moved closer, then held his breath and stilled as she lunged, grabbing his wrist, then pressing something into his grip before she drew his arm around her neck.

"What?" Colin said as she pressed her back against his front.

"Make it look like I'm your hostage," she said, her

voice low.

"Right," Colin replied, and let himself breathe as he felt her warmth against his chest, whilst still gripping the unknown cylinder. "No closer," he shouted.

"That's it," Astra replied, as Travis went back to checking over the line of rockets.

"Shit," he called out, kneeling at the last in the line. "How are we going to…?" he said, but cut himself off as he reached inside his pocket.

"Clutch is going to kill you," Astra said, with the pointed end of the Universal Tool glowing red as Travis touched at the fuse.

As it fizzed, he moved the tool to the next one along. Still, he didn't look up, his mouth moving as he counted a couple of seconds in his head before touching the heat against the next two in quick succession.

"Get back," he called, ushering the pair away then looking around to more heads appearing across the hill. The rest of the bodies soon came into view, as did the weapons they held, each pointed towards them.

"Clutch hoped it would help me find you," Travis said.

Astra sucked in her bottom lip just as the first rocket rushed into the air with a sharp whistle, followed by the second a heartbeat later.

Bang went the first, exploding in a washed-out blue before the second burst with red as the initial echo died. The other rockets soon raced high.

The helicopter's engine tone increased as it took avoiding action, just as the other two exploded into faded colour, one after the other.

"Is that…?" Colin said, his eyes narrowed. "Morse code?"

Astra nodded, despite Colin's loose grip around her

neck.

"M," Travis replied.

"That's brilliant," Colin exclaimed.

"He's not as dumb as he looks," Astra said, doing her best not to laugh.

"Oi," Travis replied, before moving to stand with his back to Colin as they turned around in a circle, eyeing the figures surrounding them.

"It's our colours," Astra said, looking away from the last of the dissipating smoke.

"We have your vessel," a voice projected across the hill. "No one's coming to rescue you. There's no way you can escape, so put the weapon down, let the hostage go, and you won't get hurt."

43

"Don't believe them," Travis called. "They'll be here," he added, turning to scan the horizon whilst trying to ignore the circle of cops edging closer. "Where am I looking?"

Colin turned around, needing no effort to urge Astra to turn with him, his arm still hooked around her neck as he searched to get his bearings.

Travis followed, his gaze tracking Colin's until they all held still and nodded across the horizon.

"There," Colin said, and Travis stepped forward. But peering over the mass of helmets, his shoulders fell when all he saw were a sea of roofs and not the silhouette he'd hoped for.

"Put the weapon down and you'll come to no harm." The deep voice resonated over the loudspeaker again, the projected words punctuated by the chorus of barking dogs and followed by the rush of a jet flying low across where Colin had pointed out.

"They didn't see it," Travis said, his voice low as he turned to Astra and Colin. "They said they'd look out for our signal."

"What if the man's right? What if they have the Mary May?" Colin said, loosening his arm from around Astra's neck.

"They wouldn't let that happen," Astra replied, her voice firm as she reached up and pushed his arm back.

"Lay down on the ground and put your arms behind your back," the man's voice projected once more.

"I'll kill her if you come close," Colin shouted, glaring over his shoulder. "One more step and she's done for."

The crowd paused their slow move, and the helicopter buzzed closer, sending the wind swirling around them.

"I'll do it," Colin shouted, as his hair danced before the helicopter backed away.

"You're good at this," Astra said, pressing herself against him. "Keep it up."

In hope Colin had pointed in the wrong direction, Travis turned on the spot, but when he saw no sign of the ship wherever he looked, his fear grew that the loud voice might have told the truth.

With his spiralling mood, he could no longer keep the dog's bark from the forefront of his mind, and as he stared at the hounds pulling at their restraints, he thought he spotted the glint of metal down a dog's snout, and perhaps a line of steel reinforcing each leg.

He looked away, shaking his head, reminding himself the thoughts were from a different time; a different dimension.

Although from what he'd seen this place was so much less advanced than their world, it was also far less cruel. Still, with every bark drawing out a memory, he couldn't help but feel at any time the membrane between the dimensions might rip and the war dogs from his childhood nightmares could burst through and rend them apart.

"Is that…?" Astra shouted at his back.

When her words won the battle with the chaos of his mind, he span on the spot, locking his stare onto something no bigger than a dot rising on the horizon. He leaned out whilst telling himself it would just be another helicopter.

Only as the speck wobbled from side to side did his eyes light up, devouring the ever-growing detail clarifying with every passing second. The wings projecting from a wide mass in the centre came first, followed a moment later by the wide, yawning engines in the middle of each span.

"It's her," he said, the pounding of his heart in his ears blocking out the snap of the dog's barks. "We need another signal," he quickly added, dropping to his knees in front of the remaining two rockets.

"Step away from the fireworks or we'll release the dogs," the voice rushed over the speaker.

Reaching for his pocket, Travis paused.

"They can't hurt you," Astra said, her voice soft. "That was another place and time. You know that, don't you?"

Travis looked up and into her eyes, and even though he knew what she said wasn't completely true – their teeth were still sharp and could rip flesh right from the bone – they were nothing like the monsters from his childhood.

Returning his focus to her eyes from where they'd drifted to the past, he watched her nod and her expression fortify.

"You can do this," she said, and smiled as he pulled the Universal Tool from his pocket.

Together, they stepped from the fizz of the fuse and Travis leaned against Colin's back as the three turned in a circle. Neither of them flinched as the firework rushed up into the air, sending many of the distant faces following the rocket's path, but others matched the threesome's glares, until, one by one, they looked to the side and the mass on the horizon growing larger with every heartbeat.

"They've seen us," Travis called out, feeding on the excitement rushing through his veins, whilst trying not to think about Princess's hands on the controls as it drifted left, then over-corrected the other way.

"Is Mac flying?" Astra said, her face scrunched up.

"Princess, I hope," Travis replied. "Do you remember…?"

"Yes," Astra said, cutting him off, her face as white as a sheet. "And she's coming in fast," she added, leaning forward.

Colin dropped his arm from around her neck, marvelling when he realised he'd been holding a hairbrush to Astra's throat.

"Slow down, Princess," Travis said under his breath, as the Mary May, with her landing gear still down, loomed large and low, rushing toward them. "She's doing fine," he added, a little louder this time as he imagined Mac shouting for her to slow as the other two gripped their seats, feeling every deflection to the left and right with Princess trying to keep the ship straight.

"She's going to overshoot," Astra called out, but movement in his peripheral vision made Travis glance at the surrounding crowd, where it didn't take him long to spot there were so many more people and the black uniforms of the police had withdrawn, replaced by others in green, brown and black camouflage and pointing long rifles at the rushing craft.

"No," Travis shouted, shaking his head, his eyes going wide as the ship continued to rush. But when she seemed as if she would pass right overhead, she came to an abrupt halt, hovering around twenty car lengths away. She hung in the air for a few beats, her stillness silencing the crowds and leaving only the dogs barking behind them.

Without warning, she dropped through the air, Travis's stomach lurching as the ground shook under their feet when the giant landing gear took the ship's weight.

Before the three of them could react, the ramp opened to reveal Mac holding the long hose of the vacuum cleaner two handed as he swept it across his view.

"Is that...?" Astra asked.

"Run," Mac called before Travis could answer.

But he didn't run. Instead, no longer hearing the barking, he twisted around, glancing over his shoulder to where four dogs pumped their legs hard and raced towards them.

"Run," Travis shouted, even though there was no chance they could get to the ship's safety, despite the dogs having double the distance to cover.

Still, they pumped their legs, leaving the single rocket poking from the ground.

Concentrating on the opening to the Mary May's hull, Travis watched as Mac continued to shout, wielding the nozzle of the cleaner despite it being just for effect.

Miles appeared at the opening and pointed over, his lips moving but saying what, Travis couldn't tell. He stopped the guesses pinging through his mind when Quark rushed out and ran in their direction.

"No," Travis called, knowing there was nothing the dog could do. Perhaps she could have held one beast back, but there were four of them. She had no chance.

But still Quark rushed out, soon running past as a gun fired somewhere close.

Not able to bear a look back, Travis kept running, knowing whatever Quark could do, it wouldn't be enough. Any moment his legs would go, clamped by a canine grip, taking him and the others down.

44

Somehow Travis made it to the ramp, and despite his confusion that his legs were still intact, he pushed down the relief when Mac threw the vacuum's hose into the darkness of the hold as two more pairs of feet clattered up the metal in short order.

"Take the controls from Princess, please," Mac pleaded at his side. "And we need more sick bags when we're next in port," he added, but before Travis could respond, he watched Mac's mouth fall open as he stared at where the three had just run from.

Travis was already twisting around, his thoughts turning to concern at how Quark had stopped the other animals from taking them down. Names bellowed out across the field, each a short, unrecognised single word snapped out as a sharp command.

Completing the turn as Miles added Quark's name to the calls, Travis lifted his brow at what he saw in the centre of the field.

The four dogs milled around where Quark stood, with three sniffing at her butt as the last, a grey Alsatian with a streak of white down its head, mounted her. He thrust, lurching back and forth with a considered rhythm, before jumping off and wandering back towards its red-faced handler.

"You go, girl," Astra said as another took its place. Pressing the tip of her thumb and forefinger into her mouth, she let out a high whistle. "Who's the bad ass bitch?"

"That's Quark," Colin replied.

"Miles fell in love with her. They were this close to starting a commune," Mac said, pressing his fingers together in front of his eye before laughing to himself. "It looks like she's had a change of heart."

Miles called her name again, but the dog took no notice.

"You spoke?" Mac said at Colin's side, his brow quirking up in surprise. "You spoke to Astra. You know she's a woman, don't you?" he asked, his eyes pinched.

"Yes, I did," Colin said, lifting his chin and puffing out his chest.

"As nice as this reunion is, we need to go," Travis said, peering around the circle of surrounding soldiers. Although many of them gawked open-mouthed, looking between the dogs and the ship, more than enough stared through their rifle sights at the crew mates.

"Quark," Travis bellowed, and before the echo died, the dog turned, nipping at the leg of the beast still on her back before racing toward the ship. The remaining two dogs ran after her.

"Girl power," Astra said, stepping back into the hold and stopping only to stroke down Quark's back as the ramp rose.

"Never again," Princess said, jumping from Travis' seat as he arrived on the bridge, her face white as she jogged the few steps to find Astra before wrapping her arms around her.

"Miles," Travis called out.

"He's just with Quark," Colin said, and Travis turned to Princess.

"Has he figured it out yet?"

"No," Princess replied. "He's been banging his head against the wall since you've been gone."

"I guess there's only one option left," Travis said, falling down into his seat.

Not waiting to strap himself in, he paused long enough to glance at Astra as she jumped into the seat next to his, her grin stretching as she marvelled at the controls.

Pulling himself from her wonder, he scanned the array of lights and displays.

Finding everything set as he'd hoped, he grabbed the stick and thruster, his stomach lurching as the ship lifted into the air. He watched the monitor as the soldiers peering up shrank, the view widening to a sea of flashing blue lights until the details merged.

Spotting the long High Street, Travis noticed the river snaking in parallel to the pedestrian precinct, replaying the rush as they let go of the bank before realising they had no way of controlling the canoe. He revelled in the relief that followed when they rescued themselves, but soon the maze of buildings were indistinct as they rose higher still.

"Your signal was just in time," Clutch said.

Travis glanced over, only just noticing the man sat at his station.

"Have you got my UT?" Clutch added, his voice uncertain.

"Of course," Travis replied with a smile, then reached for his pocket, his eyes going wide as he patted.

Clutch sat up straight, drawing a sharp breath until Travis checked the other pocket, and grinning, threw the metal block underarm to Clutch.

"Don't do that to me," Clutch said, letting out a long breath as he caught it and held it tight.

"They had us surrounded," Princess said from her seat next to Clutch. "Goodness knows what they were going to do next."

"You took your time," Mac called out as he arrived on the bridge and scurried up to his seat.

"Finding Astra was a little more complicated than we'd guessed," Travis said, glancing over to Astra, whose cheeks bunched. Then, as he looked over at Colin, they nodded at each other.

"What's going on?" Mac said, his face red as he frowned.

"Oh nothing," Travis replied. "It's just good to be home," he added before pausing. "Sapphire, give me a threat analysis."

"There are four fast moving aircraft on an intercept course," Sapphire replied.

"Not for long," Travis said, pushing the throttle further forward. "I'm taking us up. I don't think those jets can leave the atmosphere."

"You're right," Astra replied, pulling on her restraints and securing them at her front.

They each turned to the bridge door.

"How's Quark?" Travis said as Miles walked in, his face a deep red.

"She's fine," he replied, quirking his head to the side and looking at Travis with narrowed eyes.

"What wrong?" Travis asked, then burst out laughing. "Is she walking with a limp?"

Most of the crew joined in.

"Nah, he's pissed that she only came back when you called," Mac said, grinning at Travis before glancing at the other man. "Don't get jealous."

"You know I'm better with the ladies," Travis replied, winking at Miles as he took his seat.

"I'll take that bet," Princess called out, and laughter erupted across the bridge.

"I suggest everyone straps in. This might get bumpy," Astra said as her seat slid forward.

"What? Is Princess taking the controls?" Mac chipped in before Princess sent a notebook sailing through the air.

"At least we're still in one piece, not like when you tried to kill us all," Princess shouted, renewing the laughter as the pages hit Mac in the head.

"Um," Colin said as each of the crew strapped themselves in or otherwise checked their restraints. "Where should I…?"

"You're talking now?" Princess said, taken aback as she glanced over. "You can sit on my lap if you want," she added with a wink.

A ripple of laughter spread as the colour drained from Colin's face.

"Stand over there," Travis said, motioning in the vague direction of the port side as the windscreen darkened. "I'll take it as easy as I…" He stopped himself as he felt their acceleration falter along with the background hum. "What was that?" he said as it returned to normal.

No one spoke and Travis twisted around in his seat, his smile gone as he sought Clutch.

"Both engine temps are a little higher than I like," Clutch eventually replied. "But otherwise, everything else is looking good. Nothing to worry about."

"Good," Travis said, before leaning forward and tapping a button to cycle the information displayed on the screen in front of him, stopping only when it showed a table of numbers. "We have two minutes until we escape this Earth's gravity and then I'll power down for you to take a look."

"Affirmative," Clutch replied, but just as he did, the

pressure pushing them into their seats relaxed.

"Woah," Colin called out.

Travis glanced over to find Colin's feet lifting off the deck as alarms sounded across the bridge, followed by a sea of flashing indicators.

"Engine one is out," Clutch called.

"Can you give me more power on two? I need enough to get us out of Earth's gravity?" Travis asked, his voice loud but void of any panic as he peered around to Clutch, flicking his finger over his touchscreen and shaking his head.

"No can do. Two is already feeling the pressure. If I give it more, we could lose both."

"Fock," said Princess.

"Give me some options," Travis said, his tone rising in pitch.

"Engine two will give us enough power for a controlled descent. We'll have to find somewhere to lie low and fix engine one," Astra said.

"What about the fighters tracking us below?" Mac said.

"We have multiple additional craft launching across Europe and North America," Princess replied. "I guess they're waiting for us to reappear. Considering the amount of satellites I'm seeing in orbit, I think they'll know exactly where we are. I'm not sure we'll have a chance to disappear to some backwater."

"I need options. Come on, people," Travis called.

"And I don't think they'll give us the benefit of the doubt this time," Mac chipped in.

"Miles," Travis shouted. "Don't be quiet."

"Okay," he said. "I have an idea. But it's not pretty."

"Spit it out, brain box," Mac rushed out.

"We plug the EQuaNTS back in and make a jump,"

Miles said.

"And jump to where? I didn't think you'd figured out the route home yet," Travis said, his words firm.

"I haven't. I don't know where we'll appear. But it won't be here," he replied.

Other than the still-chiming alarms, the bridge fell silent.

Travis shared a look with Astra.

"No," he replied after a moment. "I don't think anyone's willing to do that again."

"Agreed," Clutch said, his word sharp.

"Anyway," Travis said. "We can't wait forty-five hours to jump. It'll all be over by then."

"I've cut the lead-in time," Miles rushed to say. "That won't be a problem."

"What other choices are there?" Colin asked, his voice strained with his fingers clinging onto the edge of the dashboard to stop himself from floating across the bridge.

No one replied, despite knowing from their stomachs they had little time to decide.

"Doing nothing will just get us killed," Astra said.

"Does anyone else feel like this has happened before?" Travis replied, looking around at Astra.

She nodded.

"Do it, Miles. We have no other choice," he said, then pulled back on the thruster, sending Colin falling the short distance to clatter back onto the deck.

Miles jumped from his seat, all eyes turning to follow as he rushed through the door. No one spoke as light poured through the windscreen and everyone soon turned to the far corner where digits flashed onto the monitor.

Within a blink of an eye, a minute was already

counting down. Ten seconds had passed by the time Miles arrived back.

Punching his restraints to release, Travis leapt from his seat and opened his arms.

"Get up everyone. Get up," he snapped, beckoning them over with his arms wide as if he wanted to give them a group hug. "Come here. The closer we are, then the less likely we are to separate if we scatter," he blurted out.

Everyone but Mac and Colin jumped to their feet, rushing over and pressing their bodies as close to Travis as they could.

Travis looked out of the side of the group, catching Colin's squint as he rubbed at his neck.

"Colin," Travis said, his voice even. "Are you any good with a microwave?"

Colin's eyes narrowed further as he nodded.

"Then you're on the team. Get in," Travis said, beckoning him over. "We'll get an extra seat for the bridge, and sort you out a bunk. Miles can bed down with Quark."

A muffled laugh came from somewhere in their hold.

"Come on, Mac," Travis shouted as Colin joined the huddle.

Mac let out a huff of air and slowly unclipped his harness before jumping down from the seat.

With ten seconds remaining, Travis felt the push of each of the bodies. As Astra's warmth pressed in at his side, he couldn't help but smile.

"You remember," Mac said, "if we scatter, we'll materialise like this but stark naked."

Travis cocked a brow as he felt bodies twitch, but glancing over at the monitor, with only a second left, it clicked down to nothing.

He closed his eyes as a bright light rushed through his lids.

FATE'S AMBITION

GJ STEVENS

James can convince anyone of just about anything, but he's seen nothing but trouble come of it, and he just wants to live a quiet, normal life. So when he and his friends are out, camping and climbing Mount Snowdon, everything seems perfect.

Then Susie, one of his friends, goes missing, and James is caught up in the ineffective police investigation that ensues. Distraught at the slow progress, he's able to convince a higher authority to help him find Susie, but his attempt to rescue his friend soon becomes the very thing a shadowy government agency needs to hunt him down in order to harness his skills.

With an international ring of white slavers fighting their every move, James must team up with his hunter, Agent Carrie Harris, if they ever hope to save Susie and the other women who are disappearing before it's too late. But can James put his guilt and past behind him, knowing that every time he uses his ability, someone else might end up hurt…or even dead?

Fate's Ambition is a high-stakes, action-packed adventure as our reluctant hero is forced out of the shadows to fight for his friend. If you like adventure with a paranormal twist, then you'll love GJ Stevens' compelling novel.

https://mybook.to/FatesAmbition

or search

'Fates Ambition'

to grab your copy.

www.gjstevens.com

All my books are available from Amazon on Kindle, paperback & most on audio.

Search 'GJ Stevens'

Printed in Great Britain
by Amazon